Intrigue in the Night

They were two shadows standing close together, but they were not lovers. They spoke in whispers; by some trick of the space she heard every word, though she could not have named those who spoke, save that they were both men.

"Where is the king this time? As far as we can tell, he's been gone for a fortnight."

"You know where he is."

"Do I?"

"He's where he always is when he disappears with one of his armies: out conquering the world."

"I thought he'd grown bored with that after he set his hooks in Quitaine."

"The king is never bored. If he's not stalking and killing something, you can be sure he's plotting his next hunt."

"What is it this time, then? Gotha? Moresca? Holy Romagna?"

"Why would he trouble? He's hunting larger prey. He brought down the Rose; now he's mounting a fleet to bring down the Isle."

"That's mad."

"You think so? No one's ever attacked the Ladies. No one's even tried."

"For good reason. They have magic enough to hold off the world."

"Maybe once they did. The Rose withered in a night. The Isle won't be so easy, but he'll win it. None of these mages of the Making and the Book can stand against the power he's won for himself."

Tor Books by Kathleen Bryan

The Serpent and the Rose
The Golden Rose

The Golden Rose

KATHLEEN
BRYAN

TOR®
fantasy

A TOM DOHERTY ASSOCIATES BOOK
NEW YORK

This is a work of fiction. All of the characters, organizations, and events portrayed in this novel are products of the author's imagination or are used fictitiously.

THE GOLDEN ROSE

Copyright © 2008 by Judith Tarr

All rights reserved.

Map by Jackie Aher

A Tor Book
Published by Tom Doherty Associates, LLC
175 Fifth Avenue
New York, NY 10010

www.tor-forge.com

Tor® is a registered trademark of Tom Doherty Associates, LLC.

ISBN-13: 978-0-7653-5175-3
ISBN-10: 0-7653-5175-7

First Edition: March 2008
First Mass Market Edition: March 2009

Printed in the United States of America

0 9 8 7 6 5 4 3 2 1

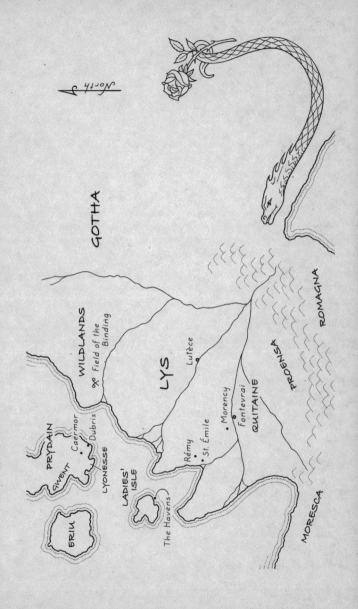

The Golden Rose

1

I T'S TIME."

Gereint raised his head. He had been kneeling all night on the stone floor, half dreaming and half praying, but there was no sleep in him. He felt light, empty, exalted.

Slowly his eyes focused and his mind came back from far and magical places. The chapel was full of shadows and whispers. Its jeweled windows were dark, its banks of candles burning low as the night wore its way toward dawn.

The man who had spoken moved into what light there was. His face was somber but his dark eyes were smiling. "They're waiting for you," he said.

"Already?" Gereint bit his tongue. His self-control was still imperfect, though he had labored long and hard to master it. "I don't think I'm ready. Maybe I should wait. Maybe—"

"You are ready," said Riquier. "Come with me."

Gereint was bound to obey. Riquier was a Squire and his teacher, and far outranked him.

He rose stiffly, resisting the urge to crouch and stoop. No matter what he did, he would loom over most men of his nation.

Riquier led him out of the chapel and through the cloister into the court of the testing, where he would either become a Novice of the Rose or die trying. He did not share his teacher's confidence, but it was too late to turn back. The only way out of this was through the test.

They were waiting: all of the order that had escaped alive from the kingdom of Lys, and a good number of the Knights and Squires and Novices of the Rose on this island of Prydain. Gereint slowed and almost stumbled. He had not expected so many.

Riquier tugged him onward until he stood in the center of the circle. The sky was just beginning to brighten with dawn, but the courtyard was full of light: clear and shadowless, born of magic and the combined will of the Knights. They were all gathered to watch their most troublesome Postulant attempt to become an initiate of the order.

Gereint drew himself up. Maybe they wanted him to fail. If they did, he would put on a brave show.

Riquier nodded as if he could read Gereint's thoughts. "Remember," he said: "from the mind to the heart and the heart to the hand—that is the secret of all that we are."

He left Gereint in the middle of the sandy circle. Novices came out in his place, bringing the weapon with which Gereint would be tested: a two-handed greatsword. They had practice armor, too, and a light helmet, both of which fit him surprisingly well.

Gereint rolled his shoulders under the padded leather, trying to work out the tension. He had been hoping, like a fool, for a different test.

Books, now—he had been studying diligently all year long, and could recite whole pages in three languages, almost four. Or magic. He could control it now, mostly. He had mastered all of the simple spells; he could make an almost clear rod of glass, though shaping it was still giving him trouble, and binding magic into it was more than any Postulant was trusted to do.

Weapons were his worst weakness. If they had brought out pitchfork and mattock or asked him to plow a straight furrow, he would have done well enough; but they were not farmers here. They were Knights. And he, a farmer's son, had the temerity to want to be one of them.

Of course he could only rise to Novice through a bout of armed combat. If he had been asked to test a candidate with his particular weaknesses, he would have done the same. A Knight who could not fight was a dishonor to the order.

His fingers closed around the hilt of the sword. He weighed it in his hands, drawing deep breaths and trying not to think too hard. Thinking was deadly. A good swordsman simply had to be.

The man who came out to face him was a stranger. He wore leather armor like Gereint's, and he was a big man, tall and broad. He was even bigger than Gereint.

All of Gereint's practice had been with smaller men. It was almost a relief to meet his match for size and strength—and, he was sure, by far his superior in skill. It would be no humiliation to lose this match.

He took his stance and raised the long, heavy blade, saluting with a flourish. His opponent grinned and returned the salute.

Gereint frowned. Something about the man was odd. His edges seemed to shimmer; Gereint could see through him to the sand of the circle and the ranks of Knights in the stands. But when Gereint peered closer, the man was as solid as he should be, and the strangeness was no more than the first light of morning on his polished armor.

Gereint drew a long breath. His fear had melted away. He would do the best he could; that was all anyone could ask.

He waited for the other man to move. He was light on his feet for once, and the sword was well balanced. He opened himself to whatever might come.

The other waited, too, making it a test of patience. Gereint resisted the urge to break and lunge. That was a trap. If they stood here from sunrise to midnight, so they would.

The long sword flicked, almost too fast to see. Gereint's blade was there, blocking it. The force of the blow rattled his teeth. He beat it back and struck—not too hard: just enough to drop the man back a step.

Gereint returned to guard position and waited again. That was unexpected: his opponent reeled against an attack that did not come.

Again the grin flashed, and a dip of the chin: a swift salute.

Then the attack came in earnest: a whirling wall of steel. Gereint's lungs burned; his shoulders went swiftly beyond pain. He could feel where the next blow would be, could be there to parry and strike again; but his body was merely mortal.

Was it?

There was earth underfoot. The sun was coming up. Earth and fire were his elements: they gave him strength.

Pain faded away. Exhaustion shrank to a memory. This was a dance and he was the dancer.

The blows came faster, faster, faster. No matter how strong he was, the other was stronger.

One of them had to end it. There was a pattern to the dance, circles within circles—the great strength and weakness of the Knights of the Rose.

Gereint broke the circles. He sighted along the sword's

blade, direct to the body behind the wall of steel. He struck the big man down and set his foot on the broad chest.

The other's sword flew wide. Gereint's swordpoint came to rest on the hollow of the throat.

"Cut off my head," the big man said.

Gereint's teeth clicked together.

"Do it," said his erstwhile opponent.

Five hundred king's men had died in the heat of Gereint's magic. The guilt of that would haunt him until he died. But he had never killed a man with his hands. To do it now, in front of the massed ranks of the Rose . . .

A Knight was sworn to obedience. That was his first vow and his last.

"Cut off my head," the man said again.

Tides of magic eddied around them. The sand was searing hot—a burning glass. The air was singing.

The sword sang descant, sweeping up and round and down. Gereint braced for the shock of steel cleaving bone, but the blade passed through that seemingly solid neck as if it had been air, and lodged in the sand.

Where Gereint's opponent had been was a shape of molten glass. It twisted and shimmered; the heat of it blistered his feet and legs. The sword's blade melted and flowed and dissipated into air.

Gereint let the hilt fall. Instinct screamed at him to fling himself away. He bent instead and with his gloved hands lifted the work of living magic that had worn the shape of a man.

There was heat in it still. He blew coolness on it, drawn from the depths of earth and shaped from a cloud that had come to chase the sun. The molten thing turned solid in his hands, a branched shape like a wind-worn tree, but glassy-smooth and pale as ice.

Magic sang in it. Without thinking, Gereint damped the power. The clear high note faded into silence.

Gently he set the tree of glass back on the sand. As he straightened, he realized that the silence was complete. No one seemed to breathe.

They were staring at him with such intensity that he began to wonder if he should run for it while he still could. He had killed—something. Not a man. But there would be a price to pay.

At long last, just before he would have turned and bolted, someone moved. It was the Knight Mauritius, by whose command Gereint was in this place on this day. He leaned toward a somewhat older man who happened to be the father general of the Knights in Prydain and said, "There. Did I not tell you?"

"You did indeed," said Father Owein. He leaned back in his chair with an air of carefully cultivated ease. "Have your way, then."

Mauritius bowed. "My thanks, messire," he said.

Gereint hesitated, torn between bafflement and curiosity. By the time he thought to move, the path to escape was blocked. The Novices who had armed him were coming back, with more behind them carrying buckets and basins and a silver cauldron inlaid with a dizzying pattern of crystal and enamel, and the Squire Riquier carrying a long bundle wrapped in dark wool.

They stripped him in front of everyone, down to the skin, and let him stand naked and resisting the urge to blush and crouch and cover as much of himself as he could, while they filled the cauldron with steaming water. When they urged him into it, he found it hot enough but hardly boiling. They scrubbed him until he stung all over, rubbed him with fistfuls of herbs that foamed and tingled and gave off a sharp pleasant scent, then half-drowned him with bucketsful of cold water.

When they were done with him, he was cleaner than he had ever been in his life. They dressed him in fresh new linen and finely woven hose and a cotte the color of the sky at dusk, embroidered over the heart with a golden rose.

He snapped out of his half-trance of astonishment and joy and tried to push the cotte away. "That's not the right one," he said. "It's supposed to be green. I'm not supposed to—"

"You are," said Riquier. His face was expressionless, but Gereint could tell he was laughing. His own cotte was the same deep blue, though the rose had four blood-red thorns rather than one.

"I'm supposed to be a Novice," Gereint said stubbornly. "You're dressing me like a Squire."

"Yes," said Riquier. "Stop wriggling and let them finish."

"But I can't be—"

Riquier unfolded the remains of his bundle, shaking out a deep blue mantle with a golden clasp, and a long sword in a blue sheath bound with gold. He knelt to belt the sword around Gereint's middle, which stopped the babbling though not the flood of protest.

When he rose, Gereint's mouth was clamped shut. Riquier's lips curved ever so slightly. He swept a bow to the assembly and said in a clear and carrying voice, "Messires, I bring you the Squire Gereint, who has proved through the test of mind and heart, heart and hand, that he has the arts and powers proper to his rank."

"But I *don't*," Gereint started to say—but Riquier's hand gripped his wrist, grinding the bones together. The sudden pain drove the words out of his head.

By the time he found them again, the court had erupted in a torrent of shouts and cheers. He did his best to look worthy of it—no matter what he might be thinking. They had given him a great and unprecedented honor.

He would be happy when the panic stopped. He had been prepared to lose and either die or be sent away. He had been ready to be a Novice, with a Novice's duties and instruction. No one had said a word of making him a Squire. That should have been years away, if it was going to happen at all.

A wave of deep blue overwhelmed him: all the Squires in the chapter house, slapping him on the back and roaring with delight. They lifted him up, sword and mantle and tree of glass and all, and carried him off to celebrate this unexpected elevation.

2

WHILE THE REST of the Squires roistered themselves into a rare stupor, Gereint caught Riquier slipping out the back of the dining hall. They were both giddy with wine and celebration, but Gereint had to know. He could not rest until he did.

The Squire smiled wryly as Gereint blocked his escape. "You have to tell me why," Gereint said.

Riquier had never lost patience in all the time he had been contending with Gereint's oddities. He kept hold of it now with apparent ease. His eye slanted toward the tree of glass, which held pride of place on the high table, gleaming in the lamplight. "That's why," he said.

"How can it be? You were ready long before that ever happened. Mauritius and Father Owein—"

Riquier sighed and arched a brow. Gereint moved aside without thinking, but stayed with him as he passed the door and stepped out into the cloister.

The moon was up, turning the sand to silver. There were no marks on it of this morning's combat. It was raked smooth.

Riquier sat on one of the benches along the edge of the cloister. Gereint was too restless to do the same. The wine he had drunk was bubbling in him, making him at once dizzy and painfully clear-headed. "I have to know," he said, "to understand."

"So you do," Riquier said. "There was a difference of opinion among the Knights, as you saw. A few would have sent you away untested for all the usual reasons: you're not a nobleman, you're godborn, your magic is at least half wild and at best half trained. Mauritius argued that you would astonish us all. He convinced the rest to have you tested as a Squire."

"But—wasn't that—"

"Postulants who would be Novices are tested in weapons, horsemanship, and magic of the Book—word for word by rote, just as you studied. They don't do magic. They're tested by the Master of Novices and certain of the oldest Novices."

"I knew that," said Gereint, "but I thought—"

"Novices who would be Squires," said Riquier as if he had not spoken, "are tested differently—and that test is different for each man. The Knights work the magic, but that magic chooses how it will show itself. From that, they draw their conclusions as to the worth of the candidate.

"You fought yourself, messire, as you would be if you were a Knight. That's high magic, Knights' magic; and what you did with it, many Knights could not have managed. That pretty thing in there is the first great working you will make for the order. It convinced even Father Owein—and he was inclined to dismiss you out of hand."

"I think," said Gereint after a slight but significant pause, "I would like to strangle Mauritius. You know what would have happened if the magic had taken control of me."

"But it did not," said Riquier. "We gambled on that and won. You're not the deadly child who ran away from his mother's farm before he destroyed it and himself. You won't be blasting Knights or shattering great workings after this— until you choose to. You've come far, messire."

"But have I come far enough?"

Riquier frowned up at him. "Doubt is as dangerous as lack of control. Remember that. You have to trust yourself."

"Even if there's good reason not to?"

Riquier sprang up without warning. Gereint saw the blow coming, a blast of magic as potent as a bolt of lightning. He turned it aside as a knight turns a blow with his shield, and aimed it toward the moon. It dissipated into the aether, harming nothing, even the flock of wildfolk that danced in the moonlight above the chapter house.

"You see," Riquier said.

"I have a long way to go before I understand what I just did."

Riquier laughed—which startled Gereint. "You think I'm any different? I've read a few more books and learned a few more words, but when the power rises, all the words in the world shrink to nothing. All that's left is instinct."

"I think that's heresy," said Gereint.

"It's true." Riquier kicked the knees out from under him and dropped him onto the bench. "There. No more looming over me. No more underestimating yourself, either. Learn to vaunt a little. You've leaped from Postulant to Squire in a day. Let yourself be proud of it."

Pride was not the difficulty. But Gereint kept the words inside.

He smoothed the sleeve of his new cotte. It was a fine thing, he had to admit. As for what he would do with it, he had ample guidance. No initiate of the Rose was ever alone.

Still . . .

Riquier's hands came to rest on his shoulders. "Come. It's time we both slept. Do you even remember the last time you did that?"

Gereint shook his head. He was not tired. Really. Which must be why, when he tried to stand up, nothing happened.

Riquier pulled him up and braced him until he had his feet under him. They went on arm in arm.

NOVICES, LIKE POSTULANTS, shared a dormitory. Squires had rooms—two by two, with room for armor and weapons and books and lesser works of magic.

Gereint was asleep on his feet before he came to the room he would be living in. He had no memory of undressing or falling into bed.

It was not morning light that woke him. Nor was it exactly a dream. He was aware if not precisely awake, and the moon was westering.

He stood on a tower above a sleeping city. Its streets and alleys were engraved in his heart; the earth beneath was a part of him. Magic had made it so, and a year away from it had done nothing to change it.

He yawned and stretched, opening his arms to the sky. Wildfolk swirled around him. They were everywhere, dancing on the wind, glimmering in the gardens, crouching on the battlements beside their images carved in stone.

"They all come out at night," said a voice behind him. "In the day they're shy still."

Gereint turned. It always amazed him to see how beautiful she was. She was a little taller than the last time he had seen her, and her face was a little thinner, but the rest of her had not followed suit.

He realized where his eyes were resting and looked away quickly. If she noticed, she let it pass. She had much more self-control than he did.

Averil came to stand beside him, not quite close enough to

touch. He could feel the warmth of her body. She seemed oblivious to the heat of his. "I'm leaving tomorrow," she said.

Gereint's heart contracted. "Already?"

"It's been a year," she said. "I made a promise. I have to keep it."

"I know," Gereint said. "I was hoping you wouldn't have to."

She shrugged. The movement did interesting things to her breasts under the gown, what with the wind and the moonlight and the sheer linen. Gereint told himself his glance was drawn to the pendant that hung on a silver chain between her breasts, the intricate enamelwork that glowed strangely in this light, but he never had been a good liar, even to himself. He fixed his eyes sternly on the roofs and towers of the city.

Down inside at least, he was calm—or tried to be. Where she was, heart of his heart, was coolness and peace. The magic that was part of them both seemed unperturbed by the storms that racked his foolish body.

"Nothing has changed," she said. "I swore to consider the suitors my uncle finds for me, not to marry any of them. I'll go to Lutèce, show my face at court, and do my duty exactly as I promised."

"And then? What happens after that?"

"God will guide me," she said. She paused as if to gather her thoughts. Then: "Something is in the wind. It's been too quiet. The king hasn't made any new conquests since I turned him out of Quitaine. He's up to something—and I mean to find out what it is."

"You know what he's up to. He's captured two of the Mysteries of the Rose. He's hunting for the third. He wants to free the Serpent and loose disorder on the world."

Averil shuddered, a frisson of fear that spread to Gereint. Neither of them was superstitious about naming the vast thing asleep somewhere in a prison that the Knights guarded: a secret they had kept for two thousand years. Simply speaking of it would not set it free. But when they thought of what it was and what it would do, that the king of Lys was doing his utmost to bring about, they had to fight back a surge of pure visceral panic.

Averil shut her eyes tightly as if to force herself to focus, then opened them again and drew a deep breath. "Yes, I do know what he means to do in the end. But it's a long road and full of obstacles. The Rose was one of the greatest. I'd like to know which of them he'll topple next."

Gereint's heart tried to stop. "For God's sake, be careful. You know how dangerous he is. He's corrupted half the mages and priests in Lys, and far too many lords and their armies. You know he'll try to corrupt you."

"He won't succeed," she said. Her hand went to her breast where the pendant hung on its silver chain.

Gereint felt its warmth over his own heart. He had worn it before he gave it to her, since an ancient Knight gave it to him as a gift; more often than not he felt as if he still had it. What it was or what it did, he never had discovered, but he kept hoping it could protect Averil somehow.

She was going to need it. While she was in her own duchy of Quitaine she was as safe as anyone could be under the traitor king. But she was going to the king's own palace in his own city, straight into the dragon's lair. And there was nothing Gereint could do to stop her.

He did try. "Can't you stay here in Fontevrai? Make him send his pack of stud dogs to you. Then when you toss them out again, you'll have your own army to fight for you and the wildfolk to feed your magic. You know they won't be able to survive in Lutèce."

She shook her head. "I can't do any more from here. I have to see what the king is plotting. There isn't anyone else who can do it. He knows I'm no friend of his—but I'm still his blood kin. And," she said, "since he has no heir and seems unlikely to get one, he's as likely as not to keep me alive and able to breed."

"That didn't seem to have occurred to him last year," Gereint said, "when your servant died wearing your face. What's changed since?"

"A great deal," she said. "My father is dead. I've made a bargain. Who knows? He might think I can be corrupted. I'm alone, after all, and vulnerable—poor orphan child that I am, raised to be a sacred sorceress and not a courtier. Bind me to the right man, seduce me properly, and I'll be his perfect little shadow."

Gereint's gorge rose. That was one thought he had not known enough to think. He was a farmer's son; duchies and dynasties were as alien to him as the mountains of the moon.

The moon was Averil's native element. She was duchess of Quitaine; her blood was royal and her ancestry both ancient and illustrious. Gereint was hardly worthy to labor in her stable, let alone stand on a tower of her palace and tell her what he thought of her.

That never had mattered between them. They were bound, soul to soul and magic to magic. The fact a Knight could not marry at all and a duchess could not marry a commoner lay always between them—but magic cared nothing for mortal laws.

Averil took Gereint's hands in her own and deliberately kissed each one. Gereint shuddered so hard he almost fell out of the dream. "Listen to me," she said. "Whatever my royal uncle might think, I'm not alone—not here, not in Lutèce, not anywhere. If I need you, I will call on you—and all of the Rose with you. I promise."

The Rose was in Prydain, across the sea. So was Gereint, though he felt real and solid beside her. His body slept in the chapter house in Caermor while his spirit stood on the tower in Fontevrai. If anything happened to her, he would have to pray that his magic was strong enough to defend her, because the rest of him was unreachably far away.

"I'm coming back to Lys," he said. "I'll find you in Lutèce."

"No," said Averil firmly. "We can't risk it. I have to let the king think he's isolated me from all my old allies. If he believes I'm vulnerable, he's more likely to betray himself. Stay where you are, safe in my heart. I need you there."

As much as Gereint hated to admit it, she was right—if she insisted on doing this at all. She was still holding his hands. He pulled her to him—because after all this was not real; they were only in each other's dreams—and kissed her hard.

Lightnings crackled above them. The Wildfolk spun like a whirlwind. For a breathtaking instant she opened to him, matching passion with passion.

They pulled apart. They were both breathing hard. Gereint would not have blamed her if she had laid him flat, but she looked as stunned as he felt.

He let the dream spin him away. It was cowardly and unbecoming of a Knight, but it was the only sensible thing to do.

3

I T WAS ONLY a dream.

Averil kept telling herself that. In daylight as she rode with her escort—but not her Wildfolk—from Fontevrai to Lutèce, she could distract herself with a multitude of things, but at night when she lay alone in a succession of unfamiliar beds, the memory came back to haunt her. The taste of his lips, the breadth of his shoulders, the strength of his hands engulfing hers, and above all the way her body went molten at his touch, filled her mind and her dreams and left her limp and exhausted in the morning.

They were only dreams. She was mage enough to know the difference. He had not come back in the nights that followed, nor did she want him to. He was the last man in the world she should be dreaming such dreams of.

It was almost a relief to come within sight of Lutèce. The country she had ridden through was much quieter than she had thought it would be, and the people seemed ordinary enough.

The things she had seen when she fled with the remnants of the Rose were not in evidence here. She had searched the face of everyone she passed on the road, but none of them seemed other than human. Their souls were firmly in place. Whatever spells were on them had nothing to do with the king, as far as she could see.

Only once had she seen a company of soldiers with the empty eyes and soulless faces of the king's sorcery. Even before she saw the eyes she knew what they were: they marched in perfect unison and in perfect silence, without a drumbeat to set the pace.

They were marching on a road that led away from Quitaine. Wherever they were going, for whatever purpose, it could mean nothing good. But Quitaine was safe, for the moment.

Averil had done all she could to make sure of that. The Lord Protector ruled in her stead; he was the last Knight of the Rose left alive in Lys, and both his magic and his generalship were strong. Where his power and the strength of his soldiers did not defend it, the Wildfolk waged their own war against any power that might threaten earth or air or water. If there was an attack on Quitaine while its duchess was absent, Bernardin and his forces would drive it back.

She paused on a hill above Lutèce, where the road curved down toward the river. Twelve bridges spanned it, the largest of which united this road and the processional way that ran straight through the heart of the city.

Lutèce was an island shaped like the hull of a vast ship. Its prow was the cathedral church of the Holy Mother, and where a deck would be was the king's palace. A warren of streets and alleys surrounded these two great edifices, spilling across the bridges and running up the hills on either side.

There was strong magic in this place, born of the river and the stone isle and the cathedral with its windows of enchanted glass. Averil was surprised to see them intact. She would have thought the king would break them as he had done to so many elsewhere, but it seemed that he had left his capital alone.

That would not last. As lovely as the magic was with its strong clear strains of ancient power, something else stirred beneath. Averil knew too well that sense of vastness, with the hiss and slide of enormous scales.

The Serpent slept: the living embodiment of chaos and old Night. But the king was doing all he could to wake it.

Part of Averil wanted to wheel her mare around and bolt back to the safety of Quitaine. The rest drew a long breath. She had been right: there was something stirring here.

Her escort was growing impatient. So were the wagons and the mounted parties behind her who had had to wait while she dallied on the hill. People on foot were streaming around her, muttering about nobles and their arrogance.

The grey mare squealed and kicked at a pilgrim who came too close. Averil rebuked her sharply and eased her back into the stream of travelers.

Once the mare was in motion, she settled to her work. Averil did her best to do the same. This was a battle she was riding to, and she had to be strong and clear and focused.

It was difficult. For all the months she had devoted to preparation and study, readying herself for the intricacies of the royal court, one thing she had not reckoned on. She had never been in a city so great. Beside this, Fontevrai was a provincial town and the Ladies' Isle a remote hermitage. The streams of magic that flowed here were so powerful and so varied that they threatened to overwhelm her.

She began to regret leaving her Lord Protector in Fontevrai. The captain of her guard was a capable man and unshakably loyal, but he was not a master mage. She had no mages with her except her maid Jennet; that had been deliberate, but now she wondered if she had gone too far in resisting Bernardin's advice.

"You'll want a counselor," he had said, "a guide through the shoals and reefs of the court, for as admirable a woman as Madame Jennet may be, a courtier she is not. Nor, lady, are you."

"I'll manage," Averil had said, as firm as a door shutting.

Bernardin had persisted, but she had closed her ears and mind to him. When she left, none of the courtly advisors he had suggested was with her, and Bernardin perforce had to stay behind. However much Averil might need him in Lutèce, Quitaine needed him more.

It was too late to turn back. The city surrounded her; King Clodovec's palace was directly ahead. People cheered as she rode by. They did love to see youth and beauty in high places.

She resisted the temptation to see the palace as a beast crouched to spring. It was enormous and very old; the heart of it had been built for some long-gone provincial governor from Romagna. Generations of governors and tribal chieftains and kings had raised new walls and torn down old ones until the whole seemed to have grown out of the earth like a forest of trees.

Clodovec's serpent magic barely touched the surface of this ancient place. That reassured Averil somewhat, but it disturbed her, too. No wonder the king had been able to get as far as he had; most of what he did was lost in the complexity of the magic here.

Averil willed herself to be calm and focused and quiet within. For the whole of a year she had prepared for this. Whatever courtly skills she lacked, her powers were honed to a fine edge. Even her dreams of Gereint could help her. When she faced temptation, she had only to remember him.

She rode through the gate with her head high. The guards bowed before the banner of Quitaine, the silver swan on its

deep blue field. A lofty and exquisitely arrogant majordomo
waited inside with an army of servants at his command,
ready to sweep Averil into their net.

AVERIL TURNED SLOWLY in the suite of rooms that would be
hers while she was in Lutèce. They were large and richly
appointed—royally so, for a fact. When there was a queen,
the chief of the servants told her, she lived here.

"We've had them redone for you, your grace," the woman
said. "We hope they're to your liking."

They were much too elaborate for Averil's taste, and the fur-
nishings were heavy and oppressively ornate, but she bowed
and smiled and murmured thanks. Dame Meraude seemed
content with that. She left Averil to the care of her maid and
the flock of lesser servants whom the king had given her.

That at least some of them were spies for the king, Averil
had no doubt whatever—and the rest were in the pay of various powers in the court. Jennet seemed to be of the same
mind: she was tight-lipped and expressionless, marshaling
the maids like a troop of soldiers and setting them to work
transforming her travel-stained and relentlessly unpreten-
tious charge into a proper duchess.

It was like putting on armor—though no knight had ever
shown so much breast and throat or so little leg. Her chemise
was of finest linen, her undergown of pale golden silk. The
overgown was of cloth of gold brocaded with the swans of
Quitaine swimming in a field of golden roses. From hip to
breast she was sheathed as if in steel; skirts and extravagant
sleeves flowed together into a shimmering train.

Her breasts were all but bare, her neck clasped with a collar
of gold and pearls; her face was painted with artful subtlety
and her hair wound into intricate plaits and crowned with a

golden coronet. The servants sheathed her feet in golden slippers and belted her gown with gold.

The only oddity was the silver chain and the bright enamel that she would not put aside. But Jennet had long since found a remedy for her mistress' foolishness: she tucked the pendant into Averil's bodice, where it rested warm and familiar between her breasts.

Jennet stood back, satisfied. "There now," she said. "Hold your head high and remember: no woman there is nobler than you."

Averil might debate the philosophy of that, but as a literal fact, it happened to be true. She ranked higher than anyone but the king.

That was her advantage. She intended to exploit it.

As she moved toward the door, Jennet's hand on her arm made her pause. "You're sure, lady? You won't rest today and go out fresh tomorrow?"

"I'm sure," Averil said. The sooner she faced the king, the sooner the battle would be done.

Jennet shook her head, but she knew Averil too well to argue. She took her place beside her lady. The rest of the maids formed in ranks behind. They marched on the great hall as if they had been a bejeweled army.

"AVERIL MARGUERITE EMERAUDE Melusine de Gahmuret," said the herald at the door of the hall, "duchess of Quitaine."

The murmur of music and laughter paused. Every eye had turned toward the one who stood framed in the door.

Averil made no effort to transform the blur of light and color into faces and bodies. She looked out over the hall as she had upon the city, seeing the shape and the substance of it.

It was remarkably like a rose window in a cathedral: circles within circles transcribing patterns of shimmering light. Little by little she made sense of those patterns. There were lords in cottes with sleeves that trailed the floor, and ladies in gowns cut so low and so tight that Averil felt almost dowdy beside them, with brows plucked to the thinnest of lines and lips painted as red as blood, and hair more brightly gold than nature had ever intended.

Averil, with the brows and lips she had been born with and hair of a rather unfashionable shade between red and gold, suffered a moment of panic. But she mastered it.

She was what she was. Either fashion would follow her or it would not. She never had elected to follow it; she was not about to begin now.

She took a deep breath. The court began to move again. She swept down the long stair into the thick of it.

She had made no effort to find the king among so many glittering creatures, but he did not suffer from the same insufficiency of character. He was waiting for her in the center of the hall, the only man there who was surrounded by a circle of clear space.

The last time she had seen him, he had been riding out of Fontevrai, pursued by the voices of angels. He looked less harried now but still rather preposterous in his antique robes with his long curled hair and flowing beard. If Averil was out of fashion, he was so far beyond it that there was no touching him.

What she felt for him was beyond words. Hate was too small for it. Disgust was too insignificant.

He was destroying the heart of his own kingdom, stripping the souls out of its young men and corrupting its priests and mages. He had crushed the Knights of the Rose and pulled down every house of that order in Lys. He was the worst enemy this kingdom had ever had—and he was its anointed king.

She bowed to the rank if never to the man. It was a point of honor and one of respect, however undeserving of either he might be.

He raised her with studied grace. His hands were dry and cool; his touch did not linger, and that was merciful. "My lady," he said.

"Majesty," she responded.

"You are most welcome here," he said. "Your rooms—are they adequate? Are the servants to your satisfaction?"

"I'm well looked after," she said, "and I thank you."

He bowed, smiling. If she could have forgotten all that he had done and all that she feared he would do, she might have found him charming. He played this game of princes very well.

She could do worse than to follow his lead. The irony of that made her smile. He smiled back, seeming a perfect innocent with his fair hair and his wide blue eyes.

"Come, lady," he said, taking her arm and turning her softly but irresistibly about. "Walk with me. So many of the court have been eager to meet the beautiful young duchess—shall we oblige them?"

A great number of them, Averil was sure, were eager to marry the richest heiress in Lys. If she also happened to be young and presentable, so much the better.

The king was subtle. Not every name and face he presented to her was male or looking for a wife. Of those who were, he pressed none on her. He let her do as she pleased.

He was an excellent host, watchful and considerate. When they had made the full round of the hall, he left her seated in comfort with a tray of delicacies to nibble on and a cup of iced wine to sip. The courtiers who danced attendance seemed to be taking turns at it, so that there were never more than half a dozen at any one moment.

He had separated her smoothly and irresistibly from her maids, even the determined and fiercely protective Jennet. Averil could not find them anywhere. They must have been ushered out of the hall and ordered to stay away until called for.

Her mind was spinning with names and faces. When she escaped from here, she would set them all in order in her head and remember each one clearly, but that needed quiet. There was no such thing to be had in the court.

None of the young and would-be young men seemed to mind that she lacked the art of light conversation and easy laughter. They had each other to spar with, and they did so with relish, casting barbs of wit that now and then drew blood.

She began to reckon the distance to the door and wonder if there was another and nearer route of escape. Even as little wine as she had sipped had gone to her head: she was tired and her stomach was empty, and sweets and tiny dainties did little to fill it. A good, solid bowl of stew and a brown loaf and then a full night's sleep would work wonders—if she could achieve them.

"Ah, lady," said a smooth accented voice. "I see we bore you."

She blinked and frowned, peering at a face she did not recall from the king's many introductions. It was a keenly foreign face, darker and narrower than one tended to see in Lys, with blue-black hair brushed back straight from a high forehead, and eyes as darkly liquid as a doe's. But there was nothing timid about their expression, and little that was gentle, either.

She shivered lightly. He made her think of a sword's blade, shimmering and deadly, and yet she was not afraid of him. He was smiling; his eyes were as warm as she imagined they could be.

"Messire," she said, "boredom is not a thing I know much of. But I have traveled far, and the day began well before dawn. I don't suppose there's a graceful way to retire, with so many still waiting their turn."

"They can wait until tomorrow," the dark man said. He held out his hand. She hesitated a moment, then took it.

His smile was remarkably sweet. "Ah: trust. Lady, I'm honored."

"The honor would be mine," she said, "if I knew your name."

He grinned, a flash of white teeth in the closely trimmed black beard. "Now that's a fair stroke! My name is as long and elaborate as you would expect, but when I am with friends I am Esteban de Cordoba. My brother is a king in Moresca; my sisters are married to princes. I suffer from the curse of superfluity—but I have some use as an ambassador."

"Or as a consort for a duchess in Lys?"

"That could be," he said, "though it's rare for one of your blood to look past the borders of your own country."

"Maybe it's time we did," she said, more to be contrary than because she meant it. But once she had said the words, she had no desire to unsay them.

She let him draw her to her feet. She was interested to see that she came just to his chin. She was tall for a woman in Lys, but he was a tall man, slender but not slight, and light on his feet like a dancer or a swordsman.

He was also a mage. It was not obvious: he was warded with spells so subtle they were almost invisible. That bespoke strong power and great skill.

She wondered if the king knew. He must. This was a remarkably appealing man, and his presence here was exquisitely well calculated.

She had to marry; that was not in question. Could she marry this man? It was not impossible. She had to know him well first, and be sure that she could trust him.

There would be time for that. Today she needed to rest and eat, and he was the first of them all who had seen it. She was not going to soften simply because he had eyes in his head, but it did dispose her favorably toward him.

PRINCE ESTEBAN LEFT Averil at the door of her chambers. He did not try to thrust his way in, nor did he offer any insolence. When he kissed her hand, it was but a brush of the lips, a gesture of exquisite and careful respect.

He had driven Gereint clean out of her head. Her sleep that night was heavy and dreamless, but she woke to the memory of Esteban's touch. Only after that did she remember that other, much more disturbing one.

It might be a spell. Or it might be her own body telling her it was time; she was ready to do what the law required of her.

She would consider every man who was presented. That had been her promise, and she would keep it.

4

THE FLOCK OF messengers and idlers and suitors had begun to congregate at dawn. By the time Averil was up and dressed and ready to face the day, they filled the passage outside her door. Her guards were sorely taxed to keep them out.

Averil set her flock of maids to work winnowing messengers from idlers and collecting messages, love-notes, nosegays, and scraps of poetry written on vellum and bound with a jewel or a ring or a string of pearls. It was an impressive array, well beyond anything she had expected.

"I would say, lady, that you've made an impression," Jennet said dryly.

"They're calling me the Golden Rose of Quitaine," Averil said. "Do you think even one of them appreciates the irony?"

"Maybe one or two," said Jennet. "I've never seen so many yellow roses."

"Or so much bad poetry." Averil shook her head over the one that had come with the pearls. The poet had clearly written it to another lady whose hair was as bright as buttercups—and scored out the flower and written over it "a new copper penny."

Better a penny than a carrot, she thought. The pearls were lovely; she hung them around the neck of her youngest maid, whose skin had nearly the same shimmering pallor. Then she judged it wise to share other gifts with the rest, until each had a new trinket.

Not all of them were as grateful as they might be, but she had not made enemies this morning. There was still the court to face and a myriad invitations to ponder: to a hunt, a soiree, a ball.

The hunt was tempting. So was the offer to hear a scholars' debate in the university. But it would be impolite to accept any invitation too quickly. A lady should consider each with due care, then respond as she judged best.

Averil had studied diligently, but she had not been raised to it as these courtiers were. She could work magic and rule a duchy; she could even master a court, if that court was her own. But this life was stranger than she had reckoned on.

She would manage. She had to. But first she had decisions to make.

She should admit certain of the mob to a private audience; that was expected. But which of them and for how long were matters for great tact and diplomacy.

She turned to Jennet. "Madame," she said, "I am your pupil."

Jennet sniffed audibly and shook her head, but Averil could tell she was pleased. That was uncommon enough to be worth noting.

In very short order, Jennet had Averil seated in the solar surrounded by a judicious selection of gifts and flowers, most of the mob disposed of, and the rest brought in for what she had made clear would be an hour's diversion.

Generals should study such strategy. Averil could see that it would be a long and exacting apprenticeship.

For today her task was to be polite and, if possible, charming. She had learned already that silence and the hint of a smile invited courtiers to be witty and entertaining; then they thought the same of her, though she had done nothing to earn the accolade.

While they exercised themselves to charm her and one another, she watched them behind the shield of her smile. She marked who was a mage and who was not; whose smile was genuine and whose was as false as Averil's own. Jennet had chosen the highest in rank but also the most likely to be useful: rulers of court and council, and princes and high lords in search of wives.

She was interested to see that none of them suffered from the indisposition that had been so prevalent in the year before: the loss of will and spirit to the king's sorcery. The south and west of Lys, all around Quitaine, was rife with it. But these lords of the east and north still had their wits about them.

It seemed the king was keeping the heart of his realm untainted. That would not last, surely. It was both a puzzlement and a possible advantage.

Jennet gave them precisely an hour. When it was time to turn the glass, she herded them out—all but one quiet person who had been standing near the door, watching and waiting.

There was nothing distinctive about him. He was a mage; but so were many others. He was sensibly rather than ostentatiously dressed as courtiers went, and he looked like a man who knew the use of a sword.

After so many flowers of the nobility, this was a breath of more familiar air. His bow was graceful but not extravagant, and the rose he presented to Averil was the color of blood.

Averil's brows rose. He bowed over her hand. "Dylan Fawr of Caer Usk in Prydain," he named himself. "I bring you the goodwill of my queen and all those who defend our island in her name."

The rose was just swelling into bloom; its scent was heavenly sweet. Inside the blossom, just visible as Averil turned it in her fingers, was a clear jewel—a crystal. It slipped into her hand and so into her bodice, where it lay cool and hard and humming with magic.

"I am glad," she said, "to make your acquaintance. Will you visit me again?"

"If my lady wishes," said Dylan Fawr.

"My lady does wish," she said.

"Then I shall," he said. "Are you fond of roses, lady? The gardens here are famous; they've gone somewhat to seed in recent years, but they're still lovely."

"I should like to see them," she said. "It's somewhat of a miracle they've survived, is it not?"

"There are some who still tend them," he replied, "though the wind blows cold and men's hearts are turned to stone."

"But not here," she said.

"Here more than anywhere," said Dylan Fawr.

Averil shot him a keen look but did not ask what he meant. There could not be Knights of the Rose left in Lutèce of all places. But allies and friends—that, she could believe, as she believed that this man was one of them.

She gave him her hand to kiss and saw him on his way. "We'll meet again, lady," he said.

"I do hope so," said Averil.

AFTER HE WAS gone, Averil had a moment of actual solitude. Jennet sent the maids to prepare the lady's bath and then her gown for the day's court. That left Averil to herself, though the interlude would be brief.

She slipped Dylan Fawr's gift from her bodice. It was no larger than the nail of her smallest finger, but as she cradled it in her hand, she looked down into infinite space.

That space was full of stars: a firmament of jewels bound by the thinnest of silver threads.

She caught her breath. Dylan Fawr had given her a gift beyond price: the web that bound the Knights of the Rose. Through it each man could speak to any other, and if he wished, see what he did and how and with whom.

They were aware of her, with welcome and a distinct sense of relief. After so long, to know that the Rose was with her again was a most peculiar sensation, half joy and half fear. Here of all places, if she betrayed the slightest sign of what she had in her hand, she could undo the order in Prydain as it had been undone in Lys.

This was a trust almost too great to bear. She closed her fingers over the crystal.

The web was still inside her. Please God, she would not lose both it and herself to whatever sorceries the king meant to practice on her.

She could give it back. Most probably she should. But as terrifying as it was, it was also a comfort. She was not alone in this alien place.

Her bath was ready and her maids were waiting. She drew herself upright with the crystal still in her hand.

A thought struck her. It was wild and maybe mad, and yet it filled her until she could not help but act on it.

The crystal was cold on her tongue, with a strangely sweet taste. She swallowed it.

She had dreaded that its edges would bring her pain, but it melted in her throat, filling her with cool sweetness. The web of the Rose was truly part of her now, and she encompassed the whole of it. Her body tingled; her ears hummed.

For a moment she could see the matrix of magic that bound the world. It was more intricate than any mage's working, and vast beyond comprehension.

It was more than her mind could hold. Mortal sight fell over her again, clouding that supernal clarity. But the memory of it stayed with her.

It was beautiful and deadly—as she needed to be if she was to survive. She had done something that could not be undone; it might turn on her and destroy her, or it might save them all. Only time and the good God would tell.

5

THAT NIGHT THERE was a masque in the court, such a frivolity as Averil had heard of but never seen. Jennet insisted that she continue as she had begun and dress in gold ornamented with roses. Apparently monotony was not a sin when it set a fashion.

By now Averil was prepared for glitter and extravagance. She had not expected to find among those masks and strange costumes a striking similarity to the flocks of wildfolk that had begun to fill Quitaine. Here as there, she saw an excess of fangs and horns and wings and eyes, whirling in a dizzy dance to the music of drums and pipes.

Did they know how ancient that music was, or to what they paid homage? She suspected they did not. They were caught up in their web of intrigue, much of it so vastly trivial that she could only marvel.

Prince Esteban did not seem to hunt her down, and yet when she descended into the hall during a lull in the dance, he was there at her side, bowing over her hand. He was dressed like a prince of the Fey in black and silver, with a mask shaped like an extravagantly jeweled and winged and antennaed silver moth.

"No flattery," she warned him. "No pretty words. Will you teach me this dance?"

"Gladly, lady," he said.

She did not know why she had asked him that. The air made her dizzy; it was thick with wine and musk and mingled perfumes. Almost she felt as if these truly were wildfolk, and somehow she had fallen through the veils of the world into their eerie country.

There must be a spell on this place. She looked for the king but did not find him. Either he had chosen not to attend or he was watching from a hidden gallery. She would have wagered on the latter.

The web within her caught the spell and drowned it in silver brightness. The wonder of it made her pause. She nearly stumbled, but caught herself before she fell out of the dance.

Prince Esteban's hand was warm and firm on hers, guiding her through the steps. His magic was clearer to her now, either because hers had grown so much or because he chose to let her see it.

It had a fine clarity and a clear structure, but something about it was odd. Not odd like Averil's, which concealed a deep core of wild and forbidden magic, but it was not the usual sort of ordered magecraft, either. It was freer, she thought; it went its own way, taking paths that she had not seen before.

Again she caught herself before she succumbed to the spell. She had to see and study but not become a part of it. That was why she had come here. At the very least, she could last a full day before she lost the war.

The dance was unexpectedly complicated. As it went on, the music quickened until the mind could not follow it and the body had to dance by instinct and ingrained memory.

Averil whirled out of it as the music rose to a crescendo and abruptly stopped. She was flushed, damp and breathing hard.

Prince Esteban seemed as cool as ever, although his eyes were glinting. She had a moment's piercing awareness of her own sweaty mortality before he tucked her hand under his arm and said, "Come. There's better than this to be seen tonight."

Suspicion ran like cold fingers down her spine. She resisted the urge to turn and run.

She had come to discover what the king was doing. He had something to do with this: it had a certain indefinable smell of him. Which meant that if she followed this man, she was probably walking into a trap; but if she did not, she might lose her chance.

She was as well protected as any mage could be. She had her wards and her magic and the pendant that in its way bound her to Gereint, warm as ever between her breasts. She was ready for this war—in whatever form it might come.

Prince Esteban escorted her smoothly through the hall to a colonnade that concealed a row of doors. He chose one with the ease of long custom. It had no lock or bar that the eye could see; magic bound it, glimmering along its edges.

At the touch of his hand, the wards flared briefly and then faded. The door opened on starlight and moonlight and the sweet scents of a garden.

Autumn had begun in the world without; it was harvest time, and the night air promised frost before too long. But in this garden it was still the height of summer. Even at night the heat was heavy, the air thick with moisture, distilling dew on blossoms richer and sweeter-scented than any Averil had known.

This was a garden of paradise, but such a paradise as would haunt a fever dream. Its paths were made of moonlight and mist, winding under branches heavy with blossoms and

strange glimmering fruit. There was no straight line anywhere, no direct path; intricate convolutions led in time to a
sward of grass under the moon.

The dancers there had little regard for fashion, or for
clothing at all. Their garments, when they were there, were as
light as spider-silk, clinging to bodies that dipped and spun to
a wilder rhythm than Averil had heard in the outer court.

The part of her that had been learning for a year to be a
proper lady of Lys was appalled. The rest, which had studied
for fifteen years among the Ladies of the Isle, was both fascinated and intensely wary.

The magic here was stronger than that without, but it was
of the same kind. She saw none of the darkness that had
haunted the Field of the Binding and transformed free men
into soulless slaves. It was not wild magic, either, although
there was wildness enough in it. If she would call it anything,
she would say that it was magic of the flesh, of bodies freed
from the constraints of modesty and churchly doctrine.

"Before the Serpent fell," said the man beside her, "before
bright magic was bound with leaden law, this was the dance
that mortals danced."

Averil's brows rose. She wanted to ask what this dance had
to do with stealing souls, but that would not have been wise.
These dancers seemed whole enough, though their eyes were
bright with wine or worse.

For all her protections and her careful resistance, her body
was not immune to the lure of the dance. Her skin prickled
beneath its armor of linen and silk; a slower, deeper heat was
rising from the meeting of her legs up toward her breasts.
The fabric of her chemise seemed suddenly harsh; her bodice
was so tight she could hardly breathe.

Of all the magics that mingled in her, the one she reached

for was the deepest. It was also the most dangerous for the state she was in, because it was the bond she would never for her life's sake let the king see: the twinned power that she shared with Gereint. Even more than the arts and skills she had learned from the Ladies, even stronger than the web of the Knights, and even stranger than the wild magic that she still had not learned to accept, it was the closest to her heart.

So was he, and that could not be a thought she let herself think here. Nor could she think of him, either his body or his spirit, because if she did, she would lose what control she had.

And yet their magic was stronger than anything else she knew. It was armor and a shield, and a potent defense against the spells that lay thick on this place.

Prince Esteban had his own armor: he was as cool as she wanted to be. He watched the dance with a dispassionate eye, apparently unmoved by the flashes of bare skin, buttocks ripely rounded or boldly flat, and long hair lashing arched backs and swelling breasts. What they all were moving toward came abruptly clear.

Averil looked away from bodies coiled with bodies. The dance's rhythm had shifted to one her own body knew too well, though it had never danced that particular dance. Every body was born knowing it.

She turned her back on the dance and began to walk down the path that had brought them here. She more than half expected Prince Esteban to bar her way, but he followed without speaking.

It was a long way to the door. The path was more convoluted than she remembered; it reminded her rather too vividly of a snake's coils.

At length she saw the door ahead, glimmering with wards.

She stopped then and faced Esteban. "Whomever I marry," she said, "will be faithful to me. Whatever gods he worships and whatever rites he celebrates, he will remember that."

"The old ways have room in them for fidelity, lady," said Esteban.

"I would hope so," Averil said.

She saw how he smiled just as she turned away. He had hopes of this; and why should he not? He was everything she was meant to choose, for beauty and breeding. No doubt his magic was equally suitable.

These things that he had shown her were anything but suitable. She wished she could believe that he meant to shock her into fleeing to safety. But there had been nothing of that. He wanted her to see what he saw: the beauty, not the sin.

She did see it. It was more than she was ready for.

Esteban seemed to understand. He did not try to stop her from passing through the door and returning to her rooms. He followed until she reached her guards, then let her be.

She was half relieved, but rather to her dismay, she regretted it, too. He was a surprisingly pleasant presence, for all her suspicions as to his allegiances.

THAT NIGHT, FOR the first time in Lutèce, Averil dreamed of Gereint. He was dressed in black like the Knight he would not be for years yet. His arms were tightly folded and his face was set hard.

She had never seen him look so stern. His face as she remembered it was still unfinished, a boy's face, neither handsome nor ugly—it was simply itself. Usually there was some hint of confusion in it: a line between the brows as he tried to make sense of this cipher that was the world.

Now she saw the man he would be. If she wanted a rock to

lean on, that big body would offer as much and more. If she needed a will that matched hers, he had it, and it was turned against her.

In the dream, as usual when they dreamed of one another, they were in a high place: as near as she could tell, one of the towers of the king's palace. Beyond Gereint's head she could see the shadow of the Holy Mother's cathedral, black against the stars. He looked down through a window set in the floor, an oblong of glass that cast golden light on his face.

There was a room below, a chamber like many in this palace: neither small nor large, closed in with tapestries, with carpets on the floor and brocaded hangings half-concealing a high, carved bed. The man who lay in it was naked, and he was not alone.

Averil hardly noticed the woman. The man's face she knew all too well. It was as cool as ever, with its wide-set dark eyes and neat black beard.

She took in the rest of him with deliberate thoroughness. He was as lean as a fine racehorse, with long smooth-muscled arms and legs and broad shoulders tapering to narrow hips. His skin was fine-grained, its color like dark cream, dusted with soft black hair. He was, she could not help but notice, well able to satisfy a woman.

She glanced at Gereint. He might seem blocky and coarse: a peasant's fatherless son, gifted with neither beauty nor refinement. And yet the most valued creature in any kingdom was the heavy destrier that carried a knight to battle; he was more highly prized than a stableful of slender-boned racers.

Gereint scowled down at the man on the bed. "I don't like him," he said. "I don't trust him, either. Maybe he's not the king's man, but he belongs to the Serpent. It's written all over him."

"Would you like any man who might become my husband?"

She had thought to prick his temper, but his glance was merely impatient. "Of course I wouldn't. But that has nothing to do with this. Don't you see what he is?"

"Clearly," she said.

"Would you still marry him? Knowing what he worships?"

"I have to marry," she said.

It was not what she had meant to say. It slipped out ahead of anything more sensible; then it was too late to change it.

"But do you have to marry *him?*"

"No," she said, "but I might. He doesn't set my teeth on edge, in spite of what I know he is."

"Spells," Gereint said with a growl at the bottom of it. "Sorceries."

"Maybe," said Averil. "And maybe if I pretend to be besotted, he or my uncle will let slip what we need to know."

"What, only pretend?"

"When I'm too strongly tempted," she said, "I'll think of you."

That made him flush, then scowl; which made her laugh. In laughter then the dream spun away.

6

AVERIL WOKE IN a most peculiar state of mind. Prince Esteban and the Serpent's dance mingled strangely with her dream of Gereint. Her wits were heavy and slow; it was all she could do to rise, bathe, stare balefully at yet another elaborate golden gown, and steel herself to face the court.

They were most careful of mirrors here, of windowpanes and bits of crystal and random glass, because magic could live in any of it. Still, a lady should have a mirror, and Jennet had brought Averil's from Fontevrai: a roundel of polished silver, perfectly plain and unadorned.

As Averil's eye glanced past it, the surface of the silver rippled and shimmered. The maids seemed oblivious, absorbed in acres of golden silk, nor did even Jennet appear to notice that magic had come to lodge within the mirror.

Averil's back tightened with wariness, but she was oddly unafraid. Whatever came to her had no air of threat about it, nor could it have passed the protections on this place if it had meant her harm. It was, in fact, familiar: it carried the scent of the Isle.

Damp earth and apple blossoms, new-baked bread and the salt of the sea. For a moment she could barely breathe, struck with such homesickness as she had never allowed herself to feel in the year and more since she left that blessed place.

The mirror's shimmer steadied. Averil looked for the green bowl of the Isle, or the face of one of the Ladies whom she knew. But the eyes that met hers belonged to a stranger.

It was a woman, true enough, and a lady of rank from the look of her: fine-drawn with age but still beautiful. She had the air about her of a Lady, and yet, not quite. The magic in her was different, if subtly so.

She had come from the Isle as Averil had. She was kin as much in the spirit as in the blood.

Already Averil was so poisoned by this place that she looked for the marks of deceit in that face or the magic that had brought it. She found none.

This was the royal court of Lys. She should in no way be reassured. Of all traps she might have stumbled into, this was the easiest and the most obvious.

And yet . . .

It was a summons, but exquisitely polite. It asked rather than compelled. She could comply, or she could refuse. Refusal would bear no consequences.

Except of course that in this world of whispers and intrigue, every decision had its consequence, for good or ill. Averil firmed her mind and heart and let the substance of the summons wash over and through her. Then, in a cool, soft voice that she barely recognized as her own, she said, "Not that gown today, ladies, if you please. I'll be riding out; Jennet will attend me. The rest of you, do as you will."

Averil noted the flicker of glances in a pattern that she was not schooled enough to understand. But she would be.

That was a new sensation, that feeling of calm conviction. She committed the pattern to memory, for study later, then stared down the two who looked ready to object, and willed the lot of them to withdraw.

She was somewhat startled when they did. They would spy on her, of course; one or two might try to follow. But they had given way to her will, and that was oddly gratifying. She was not entirely enslaved to these unwelcome servants.

Jennet was carefully saying nothing. Her arms were full of fabric that was not, the good God be thanked, golden. Averil turned gratefully toward plain and honest leather and simple brown wool, boots rather than soft slippers, and belt and baldric meant for use and not merely for ornament.

There was another way out of these elaborate chambers than past the mob of suitors and petitioners. Like servants' passages everywhere that Averil had known, it was narrow, not especially well lit, and as plain as her boots. Servants who passed appeared not to recognize her or the maid and the lone guardsman who walked behind her, or else observed the courtesy of pretending they did not know who she was.

She had not far to go. The cathedral of the Mother was some little distance from the palace if one traveled on the common streets, but her guide had shown her another way. It seemed an odd bit of ruined cloister on the edge of an over-grown garden, but it shared a wall with the cathedral. A gate there led into a cloister garth with rigid rectangles of flowers and herbs, and strictly disciplined apple and pear and fig trees.

The wild magic in Averil shuddered at the relentless air of order in that place. And yet it had its purpose: serpent magic could not dwell in comfort, either, where every line was perfectly straight.

In a sunlit corner of the cloister, beneath a jeweled window that cast flecks of many-colored light on the pale golden stones of the paving, sat the lady who had summoned Averil. Two younger ladies stood behind her. They shared with her the air of the Isle; Averil recognized the youngest of the three, though vaguely: she had been a novice when Averil was a child.

"Mathilde," Averil said.

That lady smiled and inclined her smooth dark head. "Ah, so you remember me."

"A little," said Averil. "I was very small."

"Small and bright-eyed and always asking questions," Mathilde said.

"I'm still full of questions," Averil said.

The ladies smiled. They might have been three faces of the same woman, young and middle-aged and old. Averil had no doubt they were kin—as she was herself. They were all children of Paladins.

Mathilde was not so very much older than she. Next in age was Darienne, and eldest of them all was Richildis. Each was the wife of a high lord, a duke or a count, and high in the king's court.

Averil vaguely remembered their faces. They had done nothing to draw her attention, but clearly they had been watching her.

The Duchess Richildis held out a hand as smooth and pale as ivory. "Come, lady," she said. "Sit by me."

There was room beside her on the stone bench, not too uncomfortably close but familiar enough. Averil sat stiffly upright and folded her hands in her lap as she had done so often before the Lady of the Isle.

This lady recognized the posture: her brows rose slightly, and the corner of her mouth curved upward. "We're all equals here," she said. "All well schooled, none initiate, brought home to marry as the law decrees."

That was true, but Averil doubted it was the whole of the

truth. There was too much power here, so quiet it might have seemed nothing at all, but her bones felt the force of it.

This place, she realized with a shiver down the spine, was perfectly warded. The shape and color of each bed of flowers mirrored exactly one of the panels of the roundel above Richildis' head. Any magic that entered here would be perfectly contained.

The Serpent's prison could be such a place. All that twisted magic would coil on itself within such rigid order and be altogether powerless.

Magic of the orders belonged here. The three ladies bloomed like the roses trained in perfect lines and corners upon the lattice of a trellis.

Averil should have been as much at home as they. She caught herself wishing for a mob of wildfolk, no two of them alike, leaping and tumbling through the too-clear air.

She was corrupted. She looked into those clear eyes and those exquisitely well-bred faces. They were so like her own, and yet, within, so profoundly different.

Or were they different? What did she know of her own kind, after all? The Isle had been home all her life. This world she had been forced into was stranger with every breath she drew. She had been raised to work magic, not to be a courtier.

So too with these. It was not Mathilde in whom she found that answer. It was the one neither young nor old: Darienne. She had neither Mathilde's native warmth nor Richildis' wisdom, but something in her called to Averil.

Averil met eyes that at first seemed dark but in truth were deepest blue. She was not moved to smile, but her heart had eased.

"Tell me," she said out of that newborn quiet. "Why have you brought me here?"

"You brought yourself," said Richildis. "We merely offered the possibility."

"Why?"

"Because," Mathilde said, "every one of us has come to this place as you have, lost and ill prepared, while the wolves close in and the huntsmen watch and wait. We all found husbands, some sooner than others, and so will you. But more important than that, we found friendship."

"The three of you?" asked Averil.

"And more," said Richildis.

Averil nodded. That was logical. Courtiers, children of warriors that they were, liked to send outriders ahead of the army. Why should these be any different?

"If you would like," Mathilde said, "there is a gathering this morning. It's nothing dangerous, no meeting of conspirators: only a coming together of friends. Will you come?"

Neither of Averil's guardians appeared to object. It would not have mattered to her if they had, but she found it interesting. It was all interesting, and slightly disconcerting.

"I'll come," she said after not too significant a pause.

ONCE AVERIL HAD agreed to the adventure, Richildis rose and walked through the wall. Averil knew an instant's astonishment before the pattern of light flowed around her. It was cool, like a breath of wind; there was a faint singing in it.

The singing faded. Averil stepped out of the jeweled light into a sunlit hall. It was high and airy, with a breathless swoop of vaulting; the windows that marched around the circle of it were alive with many-colored magic.

It put her in mind of the Ladies' Chapel on the Isle, but this was much younger and brighter and more exuberant. It was like laughter given shape, or the taste of wine raised up in glass and stone.

Averil was gawping like a yokel at a fair. She lowered her eyes from the splendor of the vaulting to the human faces that watched her with interest and, here and there, a glimmer of mistrust.

They were all women, all ages, but all alike: they had the air of the Isle. Averil had never expected to see so many. There must have been a score of them, sitting on chairs or benches or standing at ease while a young woman played on a lute and a somewhat older one sang a sweet, sad song.

It could have been any lady's solar in this kingdom, though grander than most—except for the magic that shimmered all about it. Something, some taste of the air, told her that she was still in Lutèce and still in the cathedral: in the chapter house, perhaps, or what would be the chapter house when the ladies had no need of it. For the moment, no one could come here who was not shown the way.

Every woman here was a mage, and trained in the way of the Isle. Their presence together was power, strong enough to set Averil's bones humming.

Averil's guides found places in the circle, drawing her with them as the song wound slowly into silence. When it was done, Averil tensed, ready for the interrogation that she was sure would come. But after those first glances, whether curious or suspicious, they seemed to have forgotten her.

The singer withdrew into the circle. The player on the lute went on, weaving an intricate melody.

The circle flowed apart into smaller circles. A soft murmur of voices rose to the vaulting. Such snatches as Averil caught seemed harmless enough: bits of gossip, inquiries after husbands and children, daily commonplaces that seemed peculiarly exotic in this wonder of a hall.

Averil's guides had left her to her own devices. She indulged in a moment's resentment, but she was too well trained after all: she saw what she had to do. She gathered her wits and her charm and such courtly arts as she had, and began the dance she had been brought here to perform.

7

I T WAS NOT so difficult to be a courtier here. Averil was being shown how to move, how to speak, what to say. It was not obvious, but her senses were heightened, her awareness honed to a keen edge.

As she moved from circle to circle, she followed the signs: the lift of a brow, the tilt of a head, the slant of a word. Each face had a name, and each name belonged to a great lord of the realm, as did the lady who held it.

These were not chattel. There was power here, and not all of it was magic. While the men met in the king's council, their ladies met with much less fanfare.

"If there were a queen," Averil said, "she would be here. Wouldn't she?"

She was between circles just then. She had paused, struck to stillness as understanding dawned. When she spoke, it was to Darienne, the quiet one, who had yet to say a word.

Now she did speak, soft and clear. "The queen is here."

"I am not the queen," Averil said.

Darienne's shoulder lifted, as eloquent as words.

Averil shook her head. "My uncle could still marry. He's eluded the law for as long as I could hope to, but even he must have taken some thought for what will happen if I inherit."

"Perhaps," said Darienne. "Perhaps he thinks to live forever, and never need an heir at all."

"No man lives forever."

"Some would say he's not a man."

Averil shuddered. That roused visions she would have preferred not to see. "He's still a man. Maybe not for much longer, but he's not immortal yet."

"Yet," said Darienne.

Averil went still inside. "Are you saying someone should do something about it?"

"Do you think so?"

"I've done more than most," said Averil.

"But not enough."

"Can anything be enough?"

"We are here," said Darienne, "to answer that. Not today, probably not tomorrow, but whatever we can do, in ourselves or through our kin, we will."

Averil paused. She could say what she was thinking, or she could keep it inside until it festered—but if she did that, she would keep herself safe in this gathering of strangers.

Had she ever done anything that was truly safe? "Where were you, then," she asked, "when demesne after demesne lost its lord? Where were you when the Rose withered and died in Lys? What have you done to save the mothers' sons of the realm from loss of will and soul? What use have you been, lady, in the world your king has made?"

The circles had drawn in, and every eye turned toward her. The quiet words that she had meant for Darienne had echoed round the hall.

She refused to flinch. From childhood on the Isle she had learned that if words were worth speaking, they were worth speaking to the world.

No one here seemed willing to answer. Just as she was about to turn away in disgust, Richildis said, "We were blind.

The court is like a bubble of glass; we believe we see the world, but we see only our own faces."

"There were hints and warnings," said a lady from Proensa. "We looked for enemies beyond the kingdom; we searched the tides of magic. As did the Rose until it fell, we found nothing. We never looked into the heart of our own kingdom, at our own most sacred king."

"Of course not," said Averil. Some of the edge had worn off her anger. A year ago, no one had known the truth. Those who guessed it had died or been soul-bound. Then the Rose fell, destroyed in a night, and with it the strongest defenses the kingdom had.

"When the Rose fell," Darienne said like an echo of Averil's thoughts, "those of us who had been living in a dream found ourselves all too wide awake. Some had lost husbands or sons; we had all lost kin. But we were still blind."

"Maybe you should have left the court," said Averil, "and seen the world as it truly was."

"So should we," Mathilde said, "but it was no longer safe to leave the kingdom's heart."

"You are trapped, aren't you?" Averil said.

"No," said Darienne. "Not any longer. We've taught ourselves to see."

"Have you taught your husbands? Your sons?"

"Those who can be taught, yes. The rest will learn, or not. It doesn't matter."

"It's war, you see," Mathilde said. Her gentle voice made the words seem all the more implacable. "We've waited for you, lady. We've watched and listened and understood as much as we've been able. This king will not endure—and when he dies, you will be queen. Then the world will be set right again."

"As easy as that?" said Averil. "If you believe it can be so simple, you've merely traded one breed of blindness for another."

"Tell us what to see," Mathilde said.

Averil shook her head. "If you can't see for yourself, there's nothing I can show you. You're no better than any other courtier, believing every word your liege lord speaks, and turning your back on any hint of the truth."

"You speak harshly," said a lady who had not spoken before. Averil was growing more skilled in this game of courts: she remembered the name, Jehanne, and the lord to whom she belonged, a Comte from the Marais, downriver from the city.

"Lady," Averil said to her, "the time for speaking softly is long past. If you or your menfolk had been awake to what was happening around you, we would never have come to this. But that's done; there's no changing it. The best we can do now is try to keep the worst from happening. Do any of you know where the king is, or what he does when he goes away?"

Most faces were blank, staring at her. A few shook their heads. "He wraps himself in glamour," said Darienne. "As often as not, what presides over the court is an image and not the man himself. We've taught ourselves to see, but he's clever; just as we pierce the spell, he changes it. We haven't found him yet, or discovered what he does—though we can all too easily guess. Whatever glass we scry in, whatever art of magic we try, we see only darkness."

"You haven't tried serpent magic," Averil said, "or wild magic. With those you could see him."

The air in the hall went strangely cold. Averil faced it with fierce heat. "Don't close your minds to me! You know you're blind—that's a beginning. But familiar ways have failed. We all have to change, or we'll die or worse."

"If that were true," said Jehanne, "would we not be dead already? Why are we still alive and safe, if we're meant to be destroyed?"

"The Serpent only devours live prey," Averil said.

She had horrified most of them quite properly. A few, her three guides among them, seemed less appalled and more—gratified?

So, she thought: not all of them were as blind as they professed to be. To them she said, "You may not be wise to trust me."

"Maybe not," Richildis said, "but from all we know of you, you're unlikely to turn to the king's way of thinking."

"But will I turn to yours?"

"Have you not already?"

"That depends," said Averil, "on what you believe I am."

"The Isle raised you," said Mathilde, "as it did the rest of us. Your father was the old king's dear friend, but was never beloved of the new one. You held him off as none other has, and have kept your duchy free of him through a bargain that has become, dare I say it, a bit of a legend."

"I did what I had to do," Averil said.

"So we ask you," Darienne said, "will you lead us?"

"You ask so soon?"

"We've had a year and more to ponder it," said Richildis. "That this kingdom suffers vastly from misrule, we all agree. We've let it go on too long, been too weak, seen too little—of that there is no doubt. But that time is past."

"What, then?" said Averil. "Would you have me slip poison in his wine? Cast a death spell?"

"That has been tried and failed." Richildis' gaze was level. "He's too well defended."

"You have another plan?"

"Light," said Darienne. "Knowledge. Understanding. Magic alone won't save us, but if we know what he's doing, if we can forestall it, at least we'll slow the inevitable."

"You think there's no hope," Averil said.

"I think we've let it go on so long, in such willful ignorance, that there's no simple solution left. Therefore," said Darienne, "we look for hope wherever else we can find it."

"An uprising? A pretender queen?"

"Would there be any pretense?"

"He is the anointed king," Averil said.

"He is a destroyer of souls, a sorcerer of the blackest order, a monster such as this world has seldom seen since the Young God bound the Serpent."

That was all true. "But," Averil said, "he's the king by blood and breeding, bound to the land and the kingdom by the good God and all his hallows."

"All that is forfeit," said Richildis, "for what he has done."

"What office do you hold, that you have the right to judge him?"

"I am duchess of Careol," said Richildis, "daughter of the Isle, descendant of Paladins. None of us is less than that, and you are more. Who better to judge this king who has betrayed every oath he swore to court and kin and kingdom?"

Averil turned slowly about. The circle had closed. Each woman in it held a fragment of the magic. Whatever they said within the circle was safe; nothing and no one could pass those wards.

This was a most complete conspiracy. "You hardly need me," Averil said. "Any one of you could claim the throne by right of blood and magic."

"None more than you," Darienne said. "We've looked in the glass and reckoned the omens. It's all in your hands, lady. We'll stand behind you in whatever you choose to do."

"And if I do nothing?"

"That is not in you," said Darienne.

"I'll not take anyone down with me," said Averil. "What I do—what I intend to do—could be more than deadly. You have husbands, children. Would you endanger them?"

"All of us are in danger," Richildis said, "and more with every day that passes. Better to die fighting, our men would say, than to wither away in body and soul."

"I'll think on it," said Averil. "That's all I can promise you."

Richildis nodded. The rest of the circle sighed slightly: disappointed, maybe. But Averil could give them no more than that.

Maybe she was too cautious. If she could trust anyone, it would be the folk of the Isle. Still, this was a momentous thing, and she dared not move in haste. A day's thought and a night's pondering would do no harm.

Darienne guided her away from the hall; the rest remained behind. Jennet and the guardsman waited in the cloister garth, lost in a glamour.

While they wandered in whatever pleasant dream the ladies had given them, Averil paused. "Everyone wants to own me," she said, "either to control or destroy me."

"Or to follow you," Darienne said.

"To control me," Averil repeated. "The ruler serves those whom she rules."

"Even Clodovec?"

"Maybe." Averil paused. A thought was rising, but it was too fragile yet to grasp. "Maybe even Clodovec."

Darienne did not press her to explain. That was a small thing, but it told Averil much.

When Jennet and the guard woke from their enchanted dream, Darienne walked with them back to the palace. No one spoke. It was a remarkably companionable silence, with such ease in it that Averil was almost alarmed. Should she be feeling such a thing now, here of all places?

It was what was. Sometimes, even the wariest courtier had to learn to trust.

8

ONCE AVERIL WAS away from the gathering of ladies, she realized how much they had given her. It was not so much what they had said as how they had said it, and when and where. Somehow, by some art or power she did not quite understand, they had shown her a way through this world of courts and intrigue.

The patterns of it, the swirl of factions, had begun to come clear. It was a kind of magic. She could almost see it in colors like enchanted glass, innumerable fragments flowing together or breaking sharply apart.

The ladies were the matrix. Their kinsmen fell into a shifting pattern of camps: for the king, against the king, for the Church, against the Church, for the army, for various of the magical orders, for this lord or that. And every one had something it wanted of Averil.

She had known she would be sought after for her wealth, for the power her father had had and she might be imagined to keep, for her beauty and lineage. It had not struck her truly how much it mattered that she was the king's niece. She was his nearest kin, yes, but in the old way, the way a surprising number yearned to return to, she was more than that. It was a sacred bond, that of sister-daughter.

They were all looking backward in this court, and the king

more than any—all the way back to the Serpent and the world it had made.

One or more of the ladies was always near Averil like a talisman, Darienne more than any: she was a duchess, too, and could reasonably be expected to befriend the newcomer. She guided by nod and glance, by hint and suggestion.

But neither she nor any of her sister conspirators was there the third morning after Averil came to the ladies' hall. Nor were the usual crowd of petitioners and suitors. One lone dark figure sat in the anteroom, tonsured head bent and long pale hands folded as if in prayer.

"Father Gamelin," Averil said. Her voice was no warmer than her heart.

He took his time in deigning to notice her. As he let the pause stretch to breaking, his hands unfolded. Something gleamed in the cupped palms: a sliver of glass, sharper than a spearpoint and even more deadly.

Averil went still, within and without. There was magic in that thing, and poison, and slow death. Just such a dart had come near to killing her father; strong magic and fierce vigilance had saved him for a later and less painful passing.

She met that flat dark stare. "Is that a threat?"

"A warning, rather," said Gamelin. "This was waiting for you when I came here. She who would have wielded it has been disposed of."

Averil's brows rose. "One of yours, I presume?"

"No," he said.

"I don't believe you."

She had never seen that false priest smile, nor did he so weaken now. But his eyes glinted with a cold light. "Of course you would not. It was a bitter war we fought, a year and more ago."

"We're still fighting it," she said.

"Are we?" He rose. The shard of glass melted in his hands, withered and vanished. "You'll not keep your bargain, then?"

"I will keep it," she said. "I'm here, am I not? I'm doing as I promised."

"So you are," said Gamelin. "His majesty is pleased. He will be even more pleased when you choose from among the suitors he has assembled."

Averil drew a slow breath. She had been expecting this— not so soon, but she was prepared for it. "So many suitors," she said. "So many splendid choices. I'll need time to consider them all."

"Indeed," he said. "His majesty has summoned them to dine with you on the feast of blessed Longinus. There you will choose, and there you will wed, and the kingdom will rejoice."

For too long a moment Averil's mind was empty. Longinus? The Paladin who was her ancestor? His feast? But that was—

"That's within the month," Averil said.

"Four and twenty days," Gamelin said. "Time enough for your quick wits, lady. You've had a year to ponder it, after all. Surely you took thought for the prospects."

"I have considered all my choices," Averil said levelly. "I decline the invitation. I will keep my bargain, but in my own time. I'll not be forced into unseemly haste."

"You will do as your king commands," said Gamelin. "In four and twenty days, lady, you will marry. Take careful thought for the man you choose. You'll be bound to him for as long as you both shall live."

That might not be long, Averil thought, still and cold. She had always had that gift or curse, to go quiet inside when anyone else would be thrashing in panic.

The king needed an heir. He was not willing or perhaps not able to fill the lack himself. His nearest kinswoman, his sister-daughter, was young and strong and presumably fertile. There would be spells made and magic raised, Averil had no doubt. Then when the vessel had served its purpose, he would discard it, and keep the child to raise as his own.

She saw it all in the false priest's eyes, a plan so simple, so perfect, it could not fail. That was a gift, too, to see patterns that fell together, and to read a man's heart though it was as cold as a snake's and hardly more human.

She had thought to dupe the king, to feign a choice and a betrothal and escape to the safety of her own duchy, then delay the wedding for so long that either the bridegroom or the king would grow weary of waiting. She could have held them off for years if Clodovec, or his counselor, not been at least as clever as she was.

Four and twenty days. So little time to save herself, her duchy, maybe even her world.

"I will take careful thought," she said to the king's man, who might be his master—who knew?

"You grow into wisdom, lady," said Gamelin.

"One would hope so," Averil said.

HE LEFT THEN, thank the old gods and the new. Averil sank to the stool that was nearest. For a long while she could barely breathe.

So soon, so soon. She drew herself up, drinking air in long gulps. What time she had would have to be long enough. She would discover what the king was doing while the court danced and feasted and dallied from day into dark. She would settle on a man she could stomach, or failing that, one she could be rid of in as short order as possible. She would make her way through the factions that swirled around her, and maybe—maybe—find either help or salvation there. She would do it all in four and twenty days.

She would do it because she must. That was the only choice she had.

She called for her maids and her bath and her finery. One maid was missing, and no one spoke of her; the gap had filled as if she had never been there at all.

Averil put on her most courtly face, smooth as a mask. The skin of her back prickled, but no new dart flew out of shadows to destroy her. If there was to be another attack, it would not come this day.

She would be ready when, or if, it came. She had laid the thread of a spell around herself, an invisible and impalpable barrier. If any weapon or any magic tried to pierce it, she would know.

Above all, she needed time to think, but that was the one thing she could not have. She had to do her thinking on her feet, in the crowds of the court, where she was both safe and in deadly danger.

She marched as into battle, with the army of her maids behind her. Loyal or false, they would still follow her—to help or destroy her. At the moment, it little mattered which.

THE ROSE COULD not help her. Gereint was the last person who needed to know how short a rein the king had given her. Here in Lutèce, it seemed she had allies—but what could any of them do?

She danced, she feasted. She reckoned the numbers and the mettle of the men who eyed her with marriage in mind. They were no fewer and no better than they had been yesterday or the day before. Prince Esteban was not among them, she happened to notice. She might find that significant; she might not.

There was always a lady or two or three within sight, familiar faces that took care not to intrude. They were watching her, as was every other courtier, whether openly or in secret.

Because her whole heart yearned to run and hide, she stayed late and reveled long. If she only feigned to sip from each of the many goblets that were given her, maybe no one happened to notice. Her mind was fiercely, painfully clear.

When the last of her suitors toppled over, stupefied with wine, she withdrew at last and put an end to that brutally long day. Her maids were asleep on their feet; she dismissed them summarily and undressed herself, welcoming the tedium of unfastening each lace and garter.

In a clean shift, with her hair combed out and braided, she lay awake, staring at the carved and gilded ceiling. Three and twenty days now. Unless she found a way out of the trap.

Did she want to? Should she? The law bound her to it, after all. If she could find a man whom that law allowed, who was loyal to the old ways and not to the king, that would serve.

These were cold thoughts, but it was a cold world. Her own duchy, full of wild magic and free folk, seemed as distant as the moon. The Rose was farther still. And Gereint—him she dared not think of at all.

She sat up. The web of the Rose inside her was quiet. Sparks of thought and will ran along it, but there was nothing urgent. Without knowing quite how she did it, she diverted a thread of it into Lutèce, unfurling it toward a glimmer of familiarity in the manifold levels of awareness that were the minds and hearts of mages in the city.

Darienne was not asleep, either. She sat alone in a mage's workshop, transforming a rod of heated glass into an intricate work of the mage's art.

The shape of it put Averil in mind of the web through which she had come, though Averil doubted it served the same purpose. Rather it looked as if was meant to draw and contain magic. Light glanced upon it and then sank within it, binding the power that wrought it.

It was a great working: Averil had seen its like on the Isle. Even there it would have won respect.

She waited while Darienne completed the last binding, weaving threads of glass and light. When she was done, she sat for a long moment, perfectly still. Then she said without looking up, "You have great skill, lady, to pass the wards of this place."

"Yours is greater," Averil said, "to make such a working."

"That may be," said Darienne. "It's little enough, but it has its uses."

"It captures magic," Averil said. "Can it capture a soul, too?"

"It might," said Darienne. "Or it might offer refuge to one that had been stolen, to restore to its body."

Averil paused. Behind that serene face she sensed a deep and terrible pain. "Your son?"

"Two sons," said Darienne. "My youngest, God be thanked, died of a fever before he could be taken. The good God has him safe."

There were no words to console such grief. Averil could only say, "Now I understand."

"Do you, lady?"

"I've seen his soldiers," Averil said. "I've seen how he takes them and makes him his slaves. He's raising armies against the day when the Serpent comes again—to fight for it; to feed it. To conquer everything that isn't already his."

Darienne bowed her head. "Yes. Yes, we've seen it, too. We've all lost kinsmen, servants, vassals. Some have lost whole towns and villages: every man taken and every woman left to fend for herself."

"And you've done nothing to stop him."

"He can't be stopped," said Darienne with banked heat. "No magic touches him. We have tried; oh, by the good God, we have tried! This little thing that seems so great to us, to him is a child's toy. Nothing that we do even begins to sway him."

"He's working a different magic," Averil said: "Serpent magic. You have to learn to see differently; to think sidewise. To break out of the bonds of glass and fly through the formless air."

"So," Darienne said after a pause. "It is true. You've abandoned the orders. You've submitted yourself to . . . other magics."

"Wild magic," said Averil. All too well she felt Darienne's tightly contained horror. She had shared it; she still shrank from thinking too closely of what she did or what she was. To the orders of mages, wild magic was a terrible thing, unbridled, dangerous. Those who gave way to it were reckoned mad.

Serpent magic was worse. "Our teaching hobbles us," Averil said. "It blinds us. The king knows that; he uses it ruthlessly. We have to learn to see beyond our tight constraints, our rigid rules and strictures. We have to let in other magics. There's no other way to stand against him."

Darienne shuddered. Yet she laughed—painfully, but honestly enough. "I feel as if I'm facing the Serpent itself, and yielding to temptation. We'll all lose our souls, in our fashion. Won't we?"

"I hope not," Averil said. "I hope we'll find them again, stronger than before."

"That would be a marvel," said Darienne.

"I'll hope for it," Averil said. "I'll pray it be soon. The king has given me my sentence. Three and twenty days until I choose a man and marry him."

"Ah," said Darienne, then was silent for long enough that Averil wondered if she had heard a word. At length she said, "He wants to be sure of you."

"And I? Can I be sure of anything? Is there a man in Lys who has no wife yet, whom we can trust?"

"None that I know of," Darienne said with evident regret.

"Not even among the foreign embassies?"

"Least of all among those," said Darienne.

She knew about Prince Esteban. She could hardly fail to have seen it. But she seemed quite sure of her judgment.

So, when it came to it, was Averil. She did not know what she felt. Relief? Regret? The Morescan was a lovely creature, but so was a snake: smooth and supple.

She withdrew along the web, followed for a little while by Darienne's wonder at the way of it. The warmth of her body was welcome, the beating heart, the soul safe within. She found sleep there, and rest, and for once, no dream that she remembered.

9

AFTER THAT FIRST masque, Prince Esteban had withdrawn to a judicious distance. Maybe he wanted Averil to fret over his neglect. More likely he was leaving her to ponder what he had shown her; then when he reckoned the time ripe, he would come to tempt her again.

It was a pity that she could not trust him. It would have been convenient. Pleasant, too, as such things went.

There was one man from over the sea whom she could trust, whatever Darienne and the ladies might have to say. She reckoned Dylan Fawr a friend and an honest ally.

He was not a suitor, though his age and rank and unmarried state were all acceptable. His eye was drawn in the same direction as Averil's; he was discreet, but in her watchfulness she could not mistake it. Maybe if she was desperate she could beg him to save her from a worse fate, but she was loath to set that strain on their newborn friendship while there might still be hope elsewhere.

He was with her ten days after the king had set a limit to Averil's freedom. Every morning when she woke, she counted off the days and prayed that that day would bring a means to escape. But none of them did.

There was a fortnight left. A cold rain was falling, which had quashed any hope of riding in the royal park where the beeches had all turned to gold. Most of the court had withdrawn to the hall. In light and warmth they amused themselves with dicing and dancing and a little casual swordplay.

Averil would not have minded crossing blades with an opponent or two herself, but that would have been a scandal. A lady was not allowed to gamble with dice, either—only with suitors' hearts. That left dancing or trading gossip, if sitting to be admired proved unduly tedious.

Dylan Fawr was an agile and tireless partner in the dance. As her breath began to come fast and the music skirled toward the edge of hearing, he spun Averil out of it into sudden quiet.

The colonnades along the edge of the court were made for trysts. Averil might have expected it of a suitor, but this man was anything but that. She opened her mouth to ask what he was doing.

His hand stopped the words before they began. His eye directed hers down the colonnade.

They were two shadows standing close together, but they were not lovers. They spoke in whispers; by some trick of the space she heard every word, though she could not have named those who spoke, save that they were both men.

"Where is the king this time? As far as we can tell, he's been gone for a fortnight."

"You know where he is."

"Do I?"

"He's where he always is when he disappears with one of his armies: out conquering the world."

"I thought he'd grown bored with that after he set his hooks in Quitaine."

"The king is never bored. If he's not stalking and killing something, you can be sure he's plotting his next hunt."

"What is it this time, then? Gotha? Moresca? Holy Romagna?"

"Why would he trouble? He's hunting larger prey. He brought down the Rose; now he's mounting a fleet to bring down the Isle."

"That's mad."

"You think so? No one's ever attacked the Ladies. No one's even tried."

"For good reason. They have magic enough to hold off the world."

"Maybe once they did. The Rose withered in a night. The Isle won't be so easy, but he'll win it. None of these mages of the Making and the Book can stand against the power he's won for himself."

"It's true the orders aren't much use against him. Half of them are his by now, and the rest are too weak to fight. But—"

"Everyone's afraid of the Ladies. That's what they lay their wagers on. But he's afraid of nothing."

"Even death?"

"He believes he can't die. The One he worships will give him the power to live forever."

"Ah. Well. That's even madder than the rest."

"Is it madness if it's the truth?"

The music had ended while the men spoke. When it struck up again, it drowned out whatever else they might have said.

AVERIL HAD HEARD all she needed to hear. She turned to Dylan Fawr. He nodded slightly, just before he pulled her to him and stooped over her as if to kiss.

She stiffened, but before she mustered wits to fight back, her ears caught the rustle of skirts and the titter of a lady tumbling into the colonnade with an extravagantly jeweled and velveted lord. As they passed in a waft of perfume, their eyes slid over the two who seemed to have the same intention. His hand was already up her skirt, and hers was on his codpiece.

Somehow Averil found that more shocking than the naked dance that Esteban had shown her in the garden. That had been altogether free of pretense. This was as false as the painted mask of the lady's face.

Averil was glad to let Dylan Fawr draw her back out into the hall, but gladder to retreat to such sanctuary as she could find in her own rooms. He left her there with Jennet and her sharp-eyed maids, but as he bowed to take his leave, he said for her ears alone, "Later, as you need me—only ask."

She inclined her head, which could be taken for graciousness as well as assent. Once he had withdrawn, she pleaded a headache and a general indisposition that required her to be undressed, fed a posset, and left alone in a darkened room.

The headache was not feigned. She lay in the dim light, listening to the rattle of sleet on the shutters. What she had heard should have been no shock. The Knights had long been expecting it; the Ladies been shoring up the magic of the Isle to defend against it. All power that was in the world to fight the king's sorcery was gathered there, waiting for him to strike.

And yet the two lords had seen the great flaw in their planning. The orders had suppressed older magics so completely that they were now forgotten. However bravely the Ladies might try to fight, they could not know what would strike them or how—and it might be a working against which they had no defenses.

The heart of Averil's magic lived outside of the orders. Gereint's was even more distant: he had spent most of his life in ignorance of them. He had not even known to be suspicious of wild magic, which every mage in the civilized world was taught to hate and fear.

She turned to the silver shimmer within, the net of stars that bound the Knights. Although he was not in charity with her at the moment, Gereint was there, too, woven through the whole of her, so that there was no telling which magic was hers and which belonged to him.

Whatever irritation he felt toward her, his magic surrounded her like warm, strong arms. It guided her through the net of stars to one that glimmered a little brighter than the rest. When she touched it, it bloomed into a windy headland and a dash of rain and a cottage tucked under the hill. Beside the cottage was a foundry where a Knight and a Novice labored over a furnace, transforming sand and seaweed and lime into glass.

On a table against the wall stood a mirror. The Knight nodded toward Averil's unseen presence, bowing low enough that she wondered what tales had been told of her. She moved toward the mirror, which had been recently uncovered: a square of black silk lay folded beneath it.

The mirror was larger than the usual run of scrying glasses, and its quality was remarkable. Even on the Isle, such a thing would have been a rarity. Averil bowed to the mastery of the man who had made it, shaped a prayer for all pure hearts, and looked into the mirror.

AT FIRST SHE thought she looked on the face of the pendant she wore always, tendrils of red and green and gold and silver and blue twining around and through one another across the surface of the mirror. Then the shapes resolved into serpents coiling in convoluted patterns, the mouth of each biting the tail of the next. Part of her was cold with horror, but the rest found only beauty in those sinuous shapes and glistening scales.

Without warning they broke apart, slithering into the depths of the mirror. She looked down from a great height on a deep bay and a sheltered harbor, and in the harbor a fleet of ships. There were hundreds of them, and more on the strand, receiving the final strokes of the shipwright's hammer.

They were black ships with black sails, and each prow was painted with yellow serpent-eyes. The spells that were woven into the timbers had the too-familiar hiss of scales; the men who labored on the decks and in the shipyards had the blank eyes and empty faces of those whose souls were gone.

She had seen whole armies, and priests and clerks and mages, too, whose lives and spirits had been taken away. Yet somehow this relative few struck a greater chill in her heart.

They were like ants swarming over the ships. Each one by himself had neither mind nor will, but together they moved with terrible purpose.

Averil had been living in a bubble of glass, surrounded by the illusion of the court. Here was the reality that the king had made. Nothing was safe from him or from the power he served.

She felt the slither of his presence in the low square castle that sat atop the headland. It was very old; its walls were worn smooth with the passage of years, but the rooms within were new. He sat in the hall in a high gilded chair, chin propped on fist, scowling at the man in priestly black who read to him from a crumbling scroll.

Averil knew the language of the scroll. It was ancient and all but forgotten outside of the Isle and the Rose. The words that

Gamelin read were obscure and nearly incomprehensible, but seemed to speak of a shroud and a spear and a glass cage.

Her nape prickled. Those were the Mysteries of the Rose: the shroud in which the Young God was buried after he died casting down the Serpent; the spear with which he had done it; and the prison in which the Serpent had been bound.

On a table in front of the king lay two things: a bundle of cloth tied up with a yellowed cord, and a spear with a broken shaft. Of the third she saw no sign. Then the king said, "You are sure? It doesn't say where the other is?"

"Not here," said Gamelin, "not anywhere. That knowledge must never have been written down. If it had, my spell would have found it."

"One of the Knights knows," the king said. "The order is destroyed in Lys, but they still infest the rest of the world. Surely there is a spell that can find the one who carries the secret."

"They were always masters of defensive spells," Gamelin said, "and this they defend above all else."

"Find it, Gamelin," the king said. "Find it soon. The last ship will be ready by the dark of the moon. We must sail then or risk the winter seas."

"We might wait until spring," Gamelin said, "majesty."

"No," said the king.

Gamelin opened his mouth as if to object further, but clearly thought better of it. He bowed and rolled up the scroll, sliding it into a case that looked as old as the parchment.

The king already seemed to have forgotten him. His gaze had returned to the spear and the bundle that must be the shroud, and his scowl had deepened even further. "Useless," he said as if to himself. "Worthless. They're nothing but a scrap of rusted iron and a rag wrapped in silk. If Its prison is not on the Isle . . ."

"We will find it," Gamelin said. "Somewhere a word or a thought or even a glance points to it. And then, my lord, we have it."

"No more words," the king said. "No more promises. Go, cast your spells. Don't come back until you've found it."

Gamelin bowed low. The obeisance concealed his face, but there was no mistaking the heat of anger that radiated from him.

As the false priest retreated from the hall, Averil withdrew from the mirror. There was a dizzying moment in which she existed in three places at once; then she lay in her room in Lutèce once more, and her head ached worse than ever.

Her heart was hammering hard. She had what she needed—many times over. But what she would do with it, she was not yet certain.

The Isle had to know what was coming toward it. So must the Knights; after all, she had used their web and their mirror to discover it. She could leave that war to them while she waged her own in Lutèce.

And yet . . .

The thought had no form or coherent sense. It was a foreboding, no more; a feeling under her breastbone. She was missing something. Some small but very important thing that had to do with the third Mystery and the priest's spell-casting and even the king's petulance.

The dark of the moon was nearly a month away: the moon was just waxing. At the full, the king would force her to make her choice; then he would go on with the rest of his plotting.

Tonight she should try to sleep, to rid herself of her headache and bring her mind back to some semblance of clarity. Tomorrow at last, somehow, she would decide what to do about all of her dilemmas.

10

PRINCE ESTEBAN WAS waiting at Averil's door in the morning. She would hardly call him the answer to her prayer, but he was all too welcome a distraction.

He was alone; no one else waited with him. "I sent them away," he said.

"How enterprising of you," said Averil.

He bowed to her irony. "There is a hunt," he said, "in the Golden Wood, now that the rain has blown away."

That caught her interest, but it would not be wise to let him see that. "A hunt? Indeed? Would that be the whole court or a judicious fraction thereof?"

"That would be for my lady to judge," said Esteban. "Will you ride with us?"

Averil swallowed a yawn. She had roused before the sun, little enough refreshed after a night of sleeping like the dead. As the morning brightened, so had she, but she still felt heavy and slow.

A hunt would get her blood flowing. It might gratify her curiosity, too, as to what had driven Esteban to play the messenger.

"What do we hunt, then?" she asked. "Birds? Deer? Boar?"

"Lady," he answered, "in the Golden Wood, we hunt our heart's desire."

Averil stared at him until he caught his breath and looked

away. He knew better than to play courtiers' games with her. She left him to wait while she dressed and armed herself for a hunt.

IN THE PLAINEST riding skirts that her maids would allow, with a bow fit for hunting deer—or men—and a quiver full of gold-fletched arrows, Averil rode out with Jennet and half a dozen guards and the prince from Moresca. The hunt was still gathering in the great court of the palace, a milling mob of huntsmen and courtiers, servants and hangers-on, with hounds baying and falcons screeching and a pair of stallions clashing in battle.

It was a fine fair morning, washed clean by the rain. A good portion of the court seemed to have decided that it would be a splendid day for a hunt. Any beast or bird that hung about to be chased by such a crowd deserved to find itself in a cookpot.

A handful of young men in more sensible hunting garb than the rest came to greet Esteban and bow to Averil. Most of them had Morescan faces and accents; one or two spoke with the lilt of Proensa.

"Shall we?" one of them asked as the mob showed no sign of departing before the morning was past.

Esteban slanted a glance at Averil. "My lady?"

All of these men but Esteban were strangers; but she had her guards and her maid. When she glanced at Jennet, the dark woman frowned, but she shrugged. She was not going to speak against it.

Averil inclined her head in assent. Esteban's quick smile rewarded her.

They left the rest of the court to do as it pleased, claimed their horses and mounted and rode out of the court. The gate

Esteban chose led through a maze of gardens to another, slightly larger gate and the bank of the river.

Esteban had a talent for finding hidden or little-used but convenient paths of escape. This one opened on a wide and well-kept but deserted road that ran beneath the palace walls to one of the twelve bridges of Lutèce: one for each of the twelve Paladins. The bridge they crossed was called Longinus for the First Paladin, which was rather apt. Averil was his descendant.

Past Longinus' bridge they rode through fields stripped of the harvest, then turned toward a distant shimmer. The Golden Wood had lost some of its glory in the storm; its floor was strewn with gold but its canopy was still pale golden, with the silver trunks of the beeches holding up the roof.

In these glades and along these forest tracks, only the king and his favorites were permitted to go. A commoner caught poaching the deer here not only lost his life but saw his wife and children hanged as well.

That was the king's right; the land was his, and whatever he chose to do with it, he could do. But Averil had been raised in another philosophy. She had not thought past preventing the king from rousing the Serpent; but if that could be done and Lys still survived, she could change the laws. She would make this world in a different image.

Those were dangerous thoughts in the world as it was, with serpent magic winding through it in unexpected places. She made herself focus on the slant of sunlight through the golden halls, and the turn of the track as they rode deeper into the Wood.

One of Esteban's allies proved to be a huntsman of some skill. He found the spoor of a deer: a stag of no mean size, he said.

If Averil slanted her gaze just so, she could see where the beast had gone. The memory of his passing was written in the air as much as in the mould of leaves that rustled underfoot. The spread of his antlers was broad: branches were broken and trunks of trees scarred where he had polished the tines of his weaponry.

The men were keen to hunt him down. Averil lagged somewhat. The morning was glorious, cool and clear. She breathed deep of the sweet clean air and let her horse choose its own pace.

Her guards and her maid hung back with her. Esteban's allies pounded off on the track of the stag. Averil was not surprised that he forbore to follow. He had not struck her as a man who lived for that kind of chase.

She had never ridden in the Wood before, but she knew where she was. It was a peculiar sensation, as if these tracks were as much a part of her as the whorls of her fingertips.

The last time she had felt this sense of the land had been in her own Quitaine. There was no wild magic here, no wildfolk flitting in and out of shadows or peering at her from the branches. Magic of the orders was too strong in this place for those airy spirits.

And yet the land remembered them. This grove had stood before the orders came, even before the Serpent fell. None of the trees that she saw was so ancient, but the heart of the Wood had been beating since the world was new.

Averil had hardly expected to find such a place in the very center of Lys. But then the Serpent's magic should have been long gone and buried deep, yet the king had not only found it, he had learned how to wield it. This country had more secrets than the orders of mages had been willing to acknowledge.

The hunting of the stag had slipped from Averil's mind. What she hunted now was deeper and stranger. She was looking for the heart of the Wood—which might be the heart of Lys.

THE GOLDEN WOOD stretched far over the rolling hills to the west of Lutèce, down along the river and up toward the low spine of a ridge that Averil had heard called the Dragon's Back. She suspected that it had had another name once: the Serpent.

There was no spawn of old Night asleep under those tree-clad slopes. The earth's bones were prominent here. One might have expected to find a castle perched on a jut of crag as castles were wont to do, but these hills had been cleansed of human habitation.

The royal hunting lodge lay deep in the Wood, sheltered in a valley beside a glassy jewel of a lake. It reminded Averil somewhat too keenly of the Ladies' Isle: steep slopes all around it, the green bowl and the clear lake and the stone manor beside it.

The king had not built this. It was generations old, and the latest part of it had been raised in his father's day: an airy confection of a tower with windows of colorless glass. They were deliberately not magical; the glass was so clear that nothing could catch or be held in it. All that came through it was light.

There were servants in the manor, discreet persons who welcomed the unexpected guests with grace and offered them food, drink, and rest. Averil was glad to accept. This was not quite the heart of the Wood, but close enough.

It was almost like being in Quitaine: the quiet; the peace. The absence of spies and whispers and intrigue. No one here wished her ill, or indeed cared who she was at all.

She dared not grow complacent in this sanctuary. Esteban was here with her, and he was not a comfortable presence.

He had brought her here for reasons of his own. She would do well not to trust them. As peaceful as the manor was and as benign as the Wood seemed to be, they still belonged to the king. And the king wanted nothing less than to overturn the world.

When she had eaten and drunk and rested, she found that her guards seemed to have melted away and Jennet nodded to sleep where she sat. The spell was subtle and masterfully wrought. She arched a brow at Esteban.

He stared blandly back. Even yet she felt no danger from him. "Messire," she said, "if you think you have me in your power, I may beg to differ."

"I wouldn't dream of it," he said. "There is something here that you might wish to see. May I escort you?"

"Another naked dance? Thank you, but no."

"This may scandalize you less," he said, "or shock you out of all sense. But I can promise that you won't find it dull."

Curiosity had always been Averil's weakness. She rose, with a glance at Jennet. The maid was sound asleep, upright in her chair, snoring gently.

She would not wake soon. Averil caught herself wondering if she would wake at all.

Of course she would. Such spells were made to seem unbreakable until their casters broke them. Averil left Jennet sleeping and followed Esteban into the depths of the house.

11

T HE MANOR WAS even older and larger than Averil had thought. That part that stood above the ground was only the uppermost reaches of a great and ancient edifice. There was no telling how far down it went; there were caves beneath the cellars, and far below, on the edge of perception, a deep cold river that ran into the lake.

They did not go down so far. Esteban descended a surprisingly wide and open stair beneath the wine cellar. Lamps of crystal glimmered there, enspelled to burn whenever they sensed the passage of magic.

The walls of the upper reaches were plain stone as befit a cellar. As Averil descended in Esteban's wake, hints of color began to appear: fragments of paintings long since flaked and faded, and lower still, the jeweled tesserae of mosaics in the style of old Romagna. The mosaics grew cruder and then vanished, replaced by paintings again—but such paintings. Averil had never seen their like.

They seemed harmless enough: images of forests full of trees, with beasts and birds; herds of humpbacked cattle and stocky dun horses and stags with antlers that spread from wall to wall. Odd sticklike figures hunted them with spears and arrows.

There was beauty here, though not in a style she had seen before. She followed it down still farther, leaving Esteban behind.

The stair ended at last in a vast and shimmering hall. It was a cavern as wide and high as a cathedral; its walls and pillars seemed made of gold and pearl, malachite and jasper and ultramarine.

There was no work of human hands here, and yet the walls were full of images. Sinuous shapes coiled among the pillars, up and down the walls and across the floor. They were not all serpents; some were winged and some unsheathed glittering claws.

Averil looked within herself for repulsion, but only found a kind of peace. It was like being inside the pendant that Gereint had given her.

One twining shape drew her across the hall. It looked like a great tree, a world-tree, with a serpent in its branches. The serpent was red and blue, gold and green. Its eyes were clear gold.

A deep shudder shook her. She had seen those eyes once before in a place far less probable than this one: in the Chapel Perilous of the Isle, before she came across the sea to claim her inheritance.

Now as then, all her teaching commanded her to be rent with horror, but her heart found nothing that it could call evil. There was beauty in those jeweled scales and golden eyes; there was ancient wisdom and godlike calm. The Serpent regarded her with profound understanding.

It recognized her. She was the descendant of Paladins, but her magic was older by far than that. The Mother of gods had blessed her, and the wild magic had acknowledged her for one of its own.

In the Ladies' chapel she had shrunk from a truth she was not ready to face. She still was not ready, but she had seen and done more since then than she had ever expected. Some of what she had seen . . .

"Slavery," she said. "Sorcery. Souls taken out of living bodies and consumed until nothing is left, not even memory. How does this turn into that?"

"How does anything turn from good to evil?"

Esteban stood behind her. He did not presume to touch her, which was wise of him.

"Do you reckon that the king is evil?" she asked.

"I do believe he follows a form of worship that was not intended by those who first began it."

"A left-hand path?"

"Indeed."

"I prefer my left hand to my right," said Averil.

"Do you prefer the king's way to the one you see here?"

"What do I see?"

"Truth," said Esteban.

She turned to face him. His eyes were dark, and yet they reminded her of the Serpent's: clear and wise, with a glint of wickedness. "What is the truth?" she demanded of him. "I've seen what my uncle would make of our world. Every evil that we were taught to shun, he would do; he'll make us slaves and destroy our souls."

"He was taught as you were," said Esteban. "Are you surprised that he turns against it?"

"No," Averil said. "But isn't that how it was? The Young God saved us all and set us free."

"So the priests would have us believe." Esteban traced with his finger the curve of the Serpent's tail. That was more than Averil would have dared, but nothing seemed to come of it. "Did the Young God free us or bind us to a different slavery? Our orders of magic are rigid in what they will permit; anything that defies their strictures is crushed without mercy. Our nobles are compelled to marry one another; if they dare to love outside the princely houses, their love is condemned as a sin and their offspring are forbidden any inheritance. Whatever the orders and the noble houses fail to bind in chains, the Church crushes under its heel. The whole of our world is imprisoned in glass, and yet none of us can muster the will to escape."

Averil set her lips together. His words were seductive, and for the most part they were true. She had heard the same in the Wildlands from creatures who had suffered far more from the world's order than any human thing.

"Even if that is so," she said, "no mage or priest would do what the king and his servants have done. Whatever laws may constrict us, we keep our souls intact."

"Do we?"

"I do."

"Lady, you are sublimely fortunate—and you have yet to choose a husband as the law compels you to do."

Averil's heart contracted. He must know what was to come a fortnight hence—he knew everything, that one. She looked him in the face. "Are you warning me that if I choose you, you will make me your slave?"

His lips twitched. "Only if you are a slave of love, lady— and only if you do the same to me."

That was courtier's talk, but before she rebuked him for it, she searched his face with care. She found no falsehood there.

Serpents lied. So she had been taught. They were devious, cold-hearted, and deeply evil.

Devious, she could believe—but so were most human folk. This man's heart was not cold. Coolly restrained, yes, and carefully controlled, but there was passion beneath.

Evil? No. He was not what she would call a good man, but

he was not a bad one, either. He was interesting. He made her want to know more of him.

"You are apostate," she said, "and bound to powers that have long been banned from the world. My soul may be damned if I trust you at all."

"It may," he said. "Or it may be saved."

"Suppose I believe you," she said. "Suppose further that we enter an alliance. I am the king's enemy, now and always. I will not suffer him to transform the world according to his vision. Can you stand with me against him? Will you?"

"I would see the world set free," he said, "unbound by false teachings, whether of Church or mages or traitor king."

Averil's breath came quick and shallow. She came within an instant of telling him what she truly was: what magics lived in her and who was the other half of her.

She would be mad to trust him as far as that. For her own sake she might not care, but Gereint and the Rose were inextricably bound in this. For them she kept silent.

Esteban touched her cheek. She shivered, though his hand was warm. "Would you be free, lady? Free to choose your lover? Free to work whatever magic truly belongs to you?"

"What would be the price for that? Marriage to you?"

"If you choose," he said.

"And you? What would you choose—if you were free? Would I be so alluring if I were not the duchess of Quitaine?"

"You would be beautiful if you were born a slave," he said.

"But would you want me for your wife?"

A slow smile warmed his face. "I would be tempted," he said.

"Only tempted?"

He raised her hand to his lips and kissed it. She felt it through her whole body. In spite of herself she saw him as he had been in her dream: sprawled naked in a tumbled bed. The woman beside him had a mane of red-gold hair and a body shaped altogether too much like her own.

She was not given to blushing, however fair her skin might be, but she could feel the heat in her cheeks. The thoughts she was having were nothing to do with her. They must be born of this place.

He drew her away from the wall. She had no will to resist, even when he led her farther into the cavern, down toward the source of the shimmering light.

It was a pool, deep and perfectly clear. A low wall of stone rimmed it: the only work of human hands in the cavern. Averil paused to look down into the water.

Something was coiled there, sleeping. It was hard to tell through the lens of the pool, but her bones told her it was very deep and very large. Its colors were familiar: red and blue, green and gold. Its golden eye could not close, but it was blank with sleep.

The pendant between her breasts was suddenly heavy, dragging her down. When she pressed her hand to it, a flash of sudden heat made her breath catch.

As soon as the strangeness began, it was gone. Probably she had imagined it. This was an odd place and she was in a most peculiar mood.

She drew back carefully and turned to Esteban. "Is that? . . ."

He shook his head. "An image only. But a true image. The spell reflects the Great One, wherever it is."

Averil drew a deep breath and made herself move forward again, back toward the wall. Of course this was not the Serpent's prison. If it had been, the king would have taken possession of it long ago and roused the sleeper.

She looked down at the shimmering coils. It was a beautiful thing. Its scales seemed made of jeweled glass; its eye was golden amber, the pupil a sliver of jet.

Deep calm and supernal peace surrounded it. There was none of the trapped rage that she had been taught to expect. It seemed to Averil that it had chosen its imprisonment, as if it was part of some vast plan that mortals were too feeble to understand.

All her life she had believed that the Serpent was the utmost evil and its downfall had been the salvation of the world. If that was not true, then how much of the rest was a lie? Had even the Mother of gods snared her in falsehood?

Averil's head throbbed. She had thought herself tormented enough when she came to understand how much of the magic in her was wild magic, which also was condemned as a great ill thing. If the Serpent itself was altogether different than she had been taught, the world had no foundations. She was adrift in nothingness, with no surety to offer an anchor.

Esteban was watching her. He was silent, but his eyes were keen. He had brought her to this place to shake her out of all she had thought she knew.

It would be easy to hate him, but Averil never had been fond of either ease or comfort. Still, this was more than she knew how to face.

She had conducted herself badly before the wild magic: spurned it, then defied it, and finally and with poor grace given in to it. She did not want to do the same here. She found in herself enough strength—just—to say, "I don't know that I can worship this."

"It never asked for worship," said Esteban. "That is a human fallacy, and one that led to such excesses as you see in your king."

"What did it want, then? Besides souls to feed on?"

"It only wanted to be," he said. "Mortals have always feared what they do not understand. Sometimes fear turns to worship, sometimes to hatred. But those whose minds could encompass what the Great One taught were freer of heart and spirit than men have ever been—so free that the gods became afraid. And when gods know fear, worlds can fall."

"What were the gods afraid of?"

"Clarity," said Esteban. "If mortals understood what the gods truly are, they might cease to worship; then they would cease to believe."

"And gods feed on belief." Averil's back and shoulders were tight to the point of pain. "I know what the gods are—yes, even the good God and his son. I've seen what came before them and before this thing you . . . admire, is it? Since you don't worship it?"

For the first time she saw him off balance. Had he not known of the Mother?

He recovered soon enough, adroit courtier that he was. "Then you know, lady, what it offers us. It frees us from the gods. It teaches us to scale the heights of heaven. Magic is no longer constrained, and love is not a matter for compulsion. We can all be whole and not shattered into fragments."

His words tugged at Averil's heart. She whose magic had so many facets, most of them outside the reach of the orders, knew better than most how constricted her world could be. If she could be truly free, if she could choose where she would love and how she would work her magic, none of this dance would be necessary. She would be on the wing to Prydain, into Gereint's arms—with never a thought for this lovely and seductive prince.

She met his stare. He flinched. Yes, she had him off guard.

He had not expected to find her so strong. "What do you want of me?" she asked him.

"Your power," he said, "and if you wish, your hand. Clodovec is a danger to us all. I will help you destroy him, then make you queen in Lys."

"Queen under this?" Her head tilted toward the pool. "Will you wake it, too?"

"If it will bring down the orders," he said, "yes."

"First you have to find it."

"The king will do that for us."

"Plot and counterplot," she said. "How serpentine."

He smiled. "And appropriate, yes?"

"You have allies?"

"A few," he said, "here and there."

"The king has more than a few." And Averil had a few of her own; but she was not about to tell this man that.

"That may be," said Esteban, "but most of the king's allies are slaves or zealots. Mine—ours if you will—are men of wit and skill. Their minds are their own, and their souls are secure in their bodies."

"I should have to meet and speak to them," Averil said, "and assure myself that this is true."

He bowed. "Of course, lady."

"They're waiting for us," she said, "up above. Aren't they?"

His smile escaped again. "Indeed."

"Let's not keep them waiting any longer," she said.

12

THERE WERE NOT as many in this conspiracy as in the gathering of ladies in Lutèce: only nine sat in the solar behind the hall, and they were all men; no women. They were dressed for the hunt, though Averil recognized only two of them. The rest looked as if they had ridden far and fast: mud on their boots, stains of travel on their mantles.

She took note that they were all mages, but none wore the badge of an order. They were not all from Moresca or the realm of Lys; two big broad-shouldered men spoke in the accent of Gotha, and one appeared to hail from Romagna.

None of them came from Prydain. Averil wondered if she should see significance in that. There was none from the spice countries, either, or from over the sea, or the far lands of the south.

They bowed to her as if she had already been crowned queen. She bent her head in return. Protest would only waste time.

She was carefully feeling nothing. Her mind was focused on the moment, on the faces in the circle and the eyes that watched her: some curious, some speculative, some openly greedy. If she were to guess, she would presume that all of these men were unencumbered with wives.

Even in the world they yearned to make, a woman's body

was chattel. She had no doubt that she was free to choose—if she chose as they wished her to do. They were no different from the king, when it came down to it. How much time would they give her? she wondered. More? Less? None at all?

She kept her thoughts to herself. There was a chair for her, and wine and cakes and all the trappings of courtly manners.

Esteban named each man for her. She tucked those names away in memory, but for the moment she let them be what she saw: the tall Gothan, the fat Gothan, the wiry little Romagnan with his nervous hands, the elderly Morescan, the excessively pretty lordling from Tenchebrai in Lys, and so on around the circle. Most did not speak. Apart from Esteban, the tall Gothan—Erdrich, his name was—seemed delegated to say what they all were thinking.

It was he who said, "Lady, we are most glad to see you here. Now that you have discovered the secret of this place, we hope you will become one of us."

"I shall consider it," Averil said. And she would—though what she would decide was no one's affair but her own.

Erdrich did not know her well enough to understand what she had said. His broad face brightened. "Good! Very good, lady. Will you also consider the plan we propose?"

She raised a brow, inviting him to continue.

He did, at length. She let the words roll over her, listening for the grains of wheat amid the chaff.

It was a simple enough plan, and rather elegant. Averil would continue to play her part in the king's court. She would even, if necessary, submit to the king's will; any one of them, they made clear, would be delighted to call himself her husband. The conspirators meanwhile would set themselves close to the king—some in fact had already done so, and more of them would follow.

When they were all in place, they would move to denounce and destroy the king, undo his slaves with a great working, and raise Averil as queen.

"Will this happen," she asked, "before or after he destroys the Isle and rouses the Serpent?"

That gave them pause. They glanced at one another. After a moment the Gothan said, "We would hope for it sooner rather than later—but it would serve us well if he had found the Serpent's prison. If that is on the Isle—"

"It is not," Averil said.

"You are sure of that, lady?" asked Esteban.

She should not have been, but in her heart she was. She nodded. "Where it is, is nowhere so obvious."

She braced for a storm of objections, but they all nodded, agreeing with her logic. "It does serve us if the Isle falls," the Gothan said. "With the orders and the Rose broken, there is no greater power in the world than theirs, and no worse threat to our cause."

"What of the Church?" said Averil. "What of the magi in the east? Do they have nothing to say to this?"

"The Church is the king's," Esteban said, "or else it is too feeble to move—like the orders of mages. The east is more with us than against us. The magi have always believed that the orders were poorly conceived and their rule oppressive."

"The king has paved the way for us," the Gothan said. "It would serve us if he continued for yet a while. Once the Isle is taken, then we may make our move."

"We might even let the king escape," said the lord from Tenchebrai, "and let him lead us to the Great One."

"That might be our undoing," said Esteban, "but it will be decided when the time comes." He turned to Averil. "Lady, you have heard us. What do you say to it?"

Averil had been dreading that question. "I say," she said slowly, "that I need time to think. May I be given that?"

"Of course," said Esteban without evidence of disappointment. "Of course, lady. This is a great thing and in all ways a terrible one. You do well not to choose in haste."

"I won't take long," she said, "but I must ponder everything I've heard and seen. You are asking me to turn against all that I ever was and become a thing I never thought to be. I was not raised to be queen."

"All the more reason to believe that you are admirably suited to it," Esteban said.

Averil had considerable doubts of that, but she refrained from expressing them. She acknowledged their bows and sat still as they withdrew.

Esteban might have stayed, but she did nothing to encourage him. He left last and with many backward glances.

THE ALLIES' DEPARTURE did nothing to lift the burden on her spirit. They retreated only as far as the hall, where they hovered, waiting with varying degrees of patience.

If she had had any hope of delaying them for days or weeks, that died quickly. Days she might manage. Weeks, months—not likely.

Nor would she escape intact if she refused; not after all she had seen and heard. At best she would be seized and married by force: if Esteban was not capable of it, one of the others surely was. At worst she would suffer a tragic and regrettable accident, and another one of the royal kin would be found to take her place.

She pushed herself to her feet and stalked the edges of the solar. God, was there no one who did not want a part of her? The Knights, the Ladies, the wildfolk, the Mother, the king, the Ladies of Lutèce, and now these—they all had a use for her. She was a pawn in a vast game; for all her wealth and rank and power, she was as helpless as a rat in a millrace.

She stopped short. The rest was true enough, but helpless? Not unless she wished to be.

No mortal knew all that she was, except Gereint. Precious few knew what he was or what he was capable of, either alone or through the bond they shared.

He was the one man in the world she wanted, and the one she could not have. If she took this bargain, that could change. They could be what they were meant to be.

But the cost . . .

The Isle and all its power and the Ladies' lives and souls for one man who might not even want her if she turned traitor. And he would call her that. It would be true.

If she could convince him, turn him—

Could she? Would he let her?

She dropped into the first chair that presented itself and lowered her head into her hands. Whether she made this decision now or a fortnight from now, it would be no more difficult.

If she could enlist Gereint in this conspiracy, would she want to? Did she want what these men offered? If she could save the Isle and still have the rest, would she?

Her body ached with wanting the freedom to choose what she would be, where she would go, whom she would love. Her mind persisted in throwing up doubts.

So—and that was somewhat surprising—did her heart. These lords and mages were not telling everything they knew. They had not explained away all that the Serpent had done in its reign. Even if it had only granted mortals freedom to do as they pleased, what was to prevent the strong or the violent from overwhelming the rest?

And they would. That had been the way of the world since the beginning.

She sought no counsel from her magic. This decision she had to make herself.

She should sleep on it. Or she could do as folk did in the east: consider it first drunk, then sober. There was wine enough here, but when she went to retrieve her cup, her stomach revolted.

She could not live like this. She sent a summoning into the hall, a tendril of magic that brought them all at a dignified run.

She almost regretted what she had to say. "This is too great a choice to make in a moment. May we rest here? Tomorrow or the next day, I will tell you what I have decided."

"Of course, lady," Esteban said, though one or two of the others looked less than pleased.

To those she said, "My lords, if you have obligations elsewhere, please pursue them. When my choice is made, you'll know."

"Lady," they said, bowing. But they made no move to leave.

She wished they would. It was hard to think with the nine of them hovering, burdening her with the weight of their regard and trying to spy with their magic. She was the answer to their prayers. It was all they could do to wait for her word.

She stared until they retreated to the hall once more. Then the servants came to escort her to the room in which Jennet was still asleep.

The spell showed no sign of lifting. Averil saw the way to unravel it, as clear as a knot in a thread, but she let it be. She needed neither Jennet's questions nor her vigilance.

In the soft sound of Jennet's snoring, Averil was as truly

alone as she could hope to be. She dozed for a while in the high curtained bed, but deeper sleep refused to come. The net of silver inside her and the warm presence that never left her kept her on the edge of wakefulness.

So many things bound her to this world. However hard she tried to shake herself free of them, they clung with unshakable persistence.

So did her profound suspicion of the Serpent and its purposes. She could not forget that it was a living creature, albeit made of magic and all but immortal. Living creatures had to feed—and the Serpent fed on souls.

She knew that in the depths of her magic. Maybe this Great One as they called it might spare those who served it, but the rest of the world would serve only to feed its monstrous hunger.

Maybe there was another side to it. Maybe that wise eye and that divine peace could reconcile itself with the horrors she knew were true. Could it be both dark and light, good and evil?

Maybe so. But as she lay in that cold and lonely bed with her head full of stars and her heart full of doubt, she knew she could not go so far against all she had been raised to be. It might be false and she might be a coward for holding on to it, but she would be untrue to herself if she let it go.

13

AVERIL HAD A night and a day at most before Esteban and his allies forced her to speak. Tonight she was under light guard: a flicker of wards with a flavor of Esteban about them. He trusted her—not enough to let her be, but she could have been surrounded by guards both mortal and magical.

Her own guards were nearby, alive and coming slowly out of enchanted sleep. She wove her wards with meticulous care. Half of them she shaped into a glamour, so that any mage who spied would believe the spell unbroken and the guards still fast asleep. The other half shielded them while she unmade the spell.

Jennet woke first. She frowned as her eyes opened; Averil felt her searching through the edifice of her magic, finding and recognizing the marks of the spell.

She wasted no time in berating herself for falling into the trap. She was on her feet and gathering belongings before Averil said a word.

Averil had no time to speak in any case. Now that the wards were set and her escort awake, she had another spell to cast, one that required even more delicacy and strength than the first. She had kept the shape and form of the spell that Esteban had laid; it was woven through the wards. Now she sent it back upon the mage who had cast it.

The tide of sleep rolled out of the room in which she sat, filling the rest of the manor. Servants fell over at their tasks; guards snored at their posts. Most important of all, Esteban and his allies succumbed in the hall. Because the spell was made of their own magic, reflected at them like an image in a mirror, they never felt it before it took them.

Averil sat back with a long sigh. For a brief moment she indulged the wave of weakness that followed the working. Then she pushed herself upright and willed her legs to hold her and her mind to think.

She did not have much time. She had to escape from this room, find her guards, and be well away from the manor before the mages woke—and they would wake; Averil was not nearly strong enough to bind ten mages for a day and a night. She would be lucky to gain the rest of the afternoon.

In the event, her guards solved one problem for her: even as she unraveled the spell on the lock and opened the door, she found them running toward her. They were wide awake and in no good humor. Once she was secure with Jennet in their armored circle, they set off at a run toward the stable. She kilted up her skirts and let their speed carry her onward.

The stable was defended by a pair of loudly snoring stablehands and a sentry asleep on his feet. None of them stirred as Averil and her escort fetched their horses, saddled and mounted and rode out in silence. The spell was heavy enough that Averil caught one or two of her own men yawning in sympathy.

As they passed the gate and entered the wood, Averil held herself braced against ambush or sudden magical attack, but her spell was still holding. It had begun to feed on itself. The more the mages struggled against it, the more firmly it bound them.

Averil strengthened her own wards as much as she dared. Then she meant to crouch low over her horse's mane and let the beast carry her off to Lutèce—but as they pounded down the forest tracks, her mind insisted on spinning free.

Lutèce was no sanctuary. Esteban would only follow her there and continue his campaign against her soul. She suspected he would be more amused than angry that she had turned his own spell against him.

He would not give up until she came to the king's feast and chose him for her husband. What other choice was there, after all? None was better. Most were worse.

She sat upright. Her horse jibbed, bucked, and spun to a halt. She kept her seat almost absently while her escort roused to the fact that she was no longer riding among them.

While they reined in and made their way back to her, she reached the one decision she could make and still be Averil. It was cowardly, maybe; it might prove to be terribly, perilously wrong. But she could not do otherwise.

She looked into the faces of the men and the one woman who had halted in a circle around her. "Follow me," she said.

One or two of them might have questioned her, now they were fully awake; Jennet looked ready to speak her mind. But they held their tongues. Averil nodded and gathered the reins and rode on.

DARKNESS HAD FALLEN before they reached the walls of Lutèce. The gates were closed and the night watch posted, but the postern through which Esteban had led them in the morning was unguarded.

Averil searched long and hard with eye and mind, but no ambush waited; no spell was set to catch them as they passed. They had run ahead of both—or else all those who wanted a part of her reckoned that their quarry was secure.

She hoped she would be, though not in the way any of them might wish. Once inside the walls, she turned away from the palace toward the line of noble houses that ran along the river. Their gardens opened on one another: a peculiarity that had served many a lover or fugitive.

Averil did not intend to be the lover of any man here. She left all but two of her guards in the shadow of the bridge named for Peredur, the youngest Paladin, the Young God's beloved. While Averil's men watched over Jennet, Averil went on afoot, swift and quiet in the starless night.

She found her way by the tug of her magic, letting it lead her to one of the more distant houses. It happened to be not far from the quay and the harbor of ships that berthed in Lutèce.

Perhaps that was intentional. She opened the last gate on a dizzying waft of fragrance, a garden of roses that bloomed as if it had been high summer and not the threshold of winter. They were red as blood and white as snow, with here and there a drift of yellow gold.

In their way they were as defiant as anything Averil had seen: red for the Knights, white for the Ladies, under the very nose of the king who would destroy them all.

DYLAN FAWR WAS indisposed. The porter was pleased to admit the lady from Quitaine, and indicated that her presence was both welcome and expected. But the majordomo would not let her pass beyond the solar.

"In the morning, my lady," the man said, "he will receive you. Tonight—"

"Morning may be too late," Averil said with tight-reined patience. "Please. I must see him tonight."

But the man was obdurate. "Lady, I very much regret, but you cannot."

He was a fine guard dog and a diligent one, but Averil had no time for such loyalty tonight. She swept past him, oblivious to his sputter of protest.

Dylan Fawr's door was guarded, but the man who was bold enough to try to stop her recoiled in a shower of sparks. She had meant to open the door quietly; her magic was of another mind. The door burst into splinters.

She stood in the suddenly empty space with ringing ears and a new and deeper understanding of Gereint, for whom these eruptions were all too familiar. Not even as a child had she so lost control of her powers.

Dylan Fawr's startled eyes met hers. So did those of a young nobleman whom she had seen on occasion in the court. He was neither a delicate nor a pretty creature; indeed he was what the world would call a manly man.

In properly manly fashion, he set himself between Averil and his lover. Averil opened her mouth to speak, but Dylan Fawr forestalled her. "No, no, my dear; there's no danger. Come in, lady. You've met Baron Fourchard? Of course you have. Fourchard, put on your robe and fetch the lady a cup of wine."

Averil could only bow to the master. His composure helped considerably to restore her own; so did the wine the young lord brought, serving it with grace that befit a noble page.

She thanked the boy civilly. Dylan Fawr, who had excused himself while his lover looked after their uninvited guest, returned in short order, fully clothed and wide awake. He accepted a cup of his own and sent young Fourchard away to dress in turn, with a nod and a quick word: "It's time. Be ready."

The boy's eyes brightened. He bowed and left with alacrity.

"You were expecting this," Averil said.

"Weren't you?"

She frowned. "Not quite this way. Nor so quickly. I thought I'd have until spring."

"The king has waited a year," he said. "His patience is exhausted."

"It's not the king," she said, but then she paused. "Or, yes—in part it is. But that's not why I'm here. You promised to help me. Can you find me a ship and passage to the Isle?"

"The Isle knows what is coming," he said—not as if he meant to dissuade her, but it needed to be said.

"Not all of it, I don't think," she said. "Do you know the king has enemies who worship the same power that he claims to serve?"

His expression did not change, although his eyes darkened. "I had heard rumors."

"I have heard," she said, "that my enemy's enemy should be my friend. But I can't ally myself with these. They want it of me—desperately, it seems. Because of what, and who, I am."

At that, his brows drew together. "Did they touch you? Harm you?"

"Nothing against my will," she said truthfully enough.

His frown persisted. "Are you certain? If they worked spells—"

"I am still a maiden," she said tartly, "if that is what you are asking."

His eyes widened; a faint flush stained his cheeks. He looked as if she had slapped him. "No! No, lady. Even if that were any affair of mine, I would trust you to do what is best. I only wondered . . . that kind are notorious for working spells that play havoc with memory, and laying compulsions that make themselves known long after. They are insidious. Are you sure they didn't harm you?"

"I am sure," she said. She was proud that her voice was steady. "They were most concerned that I be whole, entire, and able to decide for myself. It must be a requirement of the magic."

"Or a matter for their honor." He met her startled glance. "Not all the Serpent's followers are either evil or dishonorable. Some truly believe in it."

"You aren't one of them, are you?"

He laughed with such lack of affectation that she believed him when he said, "Not in this life, lady. However tempting their visions of paradise may be, I fear the king's way is closer to the truth."

"So do I," said Averil. "They're not going to let me be until I choose—and if I decide against them, I won't lay wagers on how long I survive. If the king doesn't destroy me, the king's rivals will."

Dylan Fawr nodded. All laughter was gone from his face. "I have a ship: she is my own, and she rides at anchor under Longinus' bridge. We can sail with the morning tide."

Averil's brow arched. " 'We'?"

"I think it's time I returned to my own people," he said, "before winter's storms bar the sea roads."

"But—" she began.

His raised hand forestalled her. "Truly," he said. "This is not a pleasant place for any man of my nation to dwell in for long. My queen has asked that I attend her at Solstice court. I shall, of course, obey her."

"But if you leave in too much haste—"

"I've been dallying for days," he said. "My friends at court are begging me to go, if only to spare them another day of babble over it."

"My friend," said Averil, "you think of everything."

He bowed in his seat. "I live to serve, my lady. And," he added, "it gives me considerable pleasure to thwart your king—and yes, his rivals, too."

Averil returned the bow. "You have my thanks, messire, and my gratitude. If I can ever repay you—"

"Do what you can to stop what we all fear is coming. That's all I ask of anyone."

"That I can do," said Averil, "and I will."

14

DAWN CAME LATE and dark under a heavy pall of cloud, but no rain had yet begun to fall. Dylan Fawr's escort, swelled by half a dozen newly hired guards and a pair of servants, made their way by torchlight to the quay and the ship that waited there.

Cernunnos was a tidy ship, with a captain who looked human enough until his eyes caught the light and gleamed green. Averil had last seen such a thing among the wildfolk; she had never thought to find it here.

The man—if man he was—bowed low over her hand. "Lady," he said. "Such a great honor."

She bowed her head in return. His touch made her shiver. The wild magic was strong in him.

Nor was he the only one. Most of the sailors were likewise fey, and some were not as human to a second glance as to the first.

One of them, all but speechless with awe, led her into the ship's cabin and made it clear she was to stay there and quiet until they were well away from Lutèce.

She offered no argument. *Cernunnos'* protections were strong; she did not try to add her own to them. If either Esteban or the king happened to be hunting, he might catch the scent of her magic where it should never have been.

There were others who would look for her, whom she

hated to leave without a word, but Dylan Fawr had promised to see to that. She had to trust that it would be done. If she came back, and she fully intended to, she would need the help and the friendship of Lutèce's Ladies.

If they truly were her allies, they would understand. If not . . . well then. This was a test; they would have failed it.

Shut into the dark closeness of the cabin, she marked time in the pounding of feet on the deck and the calling of orders in a language she half knew: not quite the language of Prydain but one that seemed older, wilder, full of strange magic.

The ship was moving, gliding down the river. Rain had begun to fall, pattering on the roof, but no wind blew. That was all to the good: it would keep the king's watch within doors and discourage hunters from the hunt.

Averil curled into a ball on the shelf of a bed that half filled the cabin. It was much more comfortable than it looked, and its blankets were wool, well woven and warm. In a little while the tongue-tied sailor brought bread and meat and apples chopped with honey and spices, with strong brown ale to wash it down.

Jennet was asleep—again. Esteban's spell had never quite left her; even when she walked and rode and seemed awake, she looked as if she drifted in a dream.

Tomorrow they would come to the Isle. The Ladies would know how to remove the spell. In the meantime, Averil did her best to keep the gnawing worry at bay.

Averil reckoned herself a patient person, but it was agonizing to lie in the cabin, shut away from the world, and wait. She stood it as long as she could, but when her bones told her it was close to noon and the ship was well away from Lutèce, she had had enough. Surely she could open the door and let the air in, wet and cold though it might be.

As she rose, wrapping herself in mantle and blankets, a flurry of voices brought her to a halt. Someone or something had boarded the ship.

There were no cries of alarm; it was not an attack. But the tone of Dylan Fawr's voice raised the small hairs on her arms. It was soft and smooth, but the sharpened steel was perceptible beneath. Whoever had come aboard was no friend.

Averil pressed her ear to the door and focused every sense on catching the words that drifted through the hiss of rain. "Indeed, messire," the captain said, "we're sailing for Prydain at the queen's summons."

"So I see," the stranger said, "but our king begs to entertain her majesty's ambassador for a little while longer. If you and your people will come with us, we'll leave the ship free to return to your country."

"I do regret," said Dylan Fawr, "that we haven't seen more of your king; but her majesty was explicit. She wishes us to return as soon as may be."

"But surely," said the king's man, "a day or two more—"

"Alas," said Dylan Fawr, "we cannot. Will you take wine before you return to your king?"

"We will take you, messire," the king's man said.

"I think not," said Dylan Fawr. From the sound of it, he was smiling.

Averil felt the arming of the ship's wards. She knew the spell, but this was stronger and more complex than the simple workings she had seen. It forged chains of magic and focused will, surrounded the ship and thrust away whatever dared menace it.

It also thrust away the netted stars that were the Knights of the Rose. Emptiness yawned where they had been, but Averil made no move to call them back. It was safer for them all if she let be.

Just as the chains locked shut, Averil saw the gap: the weakness no broader than a snake's body. On the other side of it was a wilderness of vivid green and a single flame-bright blossom, and the king's face.

She was almost disappointed not to see Esteban—a disappointment that did not bear too close examination. This was an older if no less deadly enemy.

He looked her straight in the face. She had not thought he could see her as she saw him. Nor, maybe, had he: his eyes widened.

She flung a mist across herself, but it was too late. He had recognized her. The dart of power that pierced the wards might have been meant for the ship, but the full force of it focused on Averil.

She struck it aside. The effort nearly felled her. The ship rocked as if at a blow.

There was a long, breathless pause. The king's awareness was gone. But something else was there, something altogether different—cleaner, stronger, and far more terrible.

The storm struck like the wrath of God: a blast of wind and a torrent of rain. The sea rose to meet it. The ship, caught between them, groaned in its every timber.

No mortal magic could stand against that. Averil clung for dear life to whatever offered a hold. For all she knew, the ship was empty; the others had been swept into the waves.

She would have been mad to venture onto the deck in this. Trapped, battered from every side, locked in the dark, Averil rode out the storm as best she could.

She struggled to see beyond the walls, but magic itself was torn asunder by the power of the storm. She could only see water—water everywhere, and the wind sweeping every living thing from the face of the sea.

There was no marking time; no counting breaths over the wind's shriek. It went on forever, until she was deafened and stunned, and her arms ached with holding on to a post that she could not see.

She prayed as much as she could with her thoughts torn to shreds by the wind. She gathered such magic as she had left and held it inside her. God knew what she would do with it, especially if she drowned, but there was no arguing with instinct.

Within the magic she had gathered, a familiar presence stirred. Even the wards could not keep him out: he was part of her.

Gereint shone like a beacon in the dark. His magic was strong and pure. She caught hold of it as a lifeline and drew herself along it, out of the world, away from the king's attack.

The ship came with her, with the chains that bound it and the lives that clung to it against the torrent of wind and water. She felt the weight of it in her spirit, dragging at her body, but she held on. Gereint's strength sustained her.

He gave it without stinting, as he always had. Whatever she asked, he offered freely, never asking why. She followed the path he showed her through the madness of the storm.

Whether hours passed or moments, she could not tell. The wind was all about her, and the water's rage. The king was nowhere in this world; nor were the serpent mages who had allied against him.

This had a taste of the Isle. Had she roused its defenses, then? Fool and thrice and ten times fool, not to send word ahead that she was coming.

The ship's timbers groaned. They were made to ride out mortal storms, but this battered them with almost living malice. It smote again and again, snapping the mast with a shock that ran through Averil's own body.

Even Gereint's strength had limits. It was holding, but it was wearing thin around the edges. If they both let go, the ship would burst asunder.

There was land within reach. What land it was did not matter, if only it was not Lys. It was not the Isle; Averil would have known that from the far side of death. It must be Prydain, or far Hibernia.

No matter. She aimed the ship through the wall of wind and water as if its prow had been a battering ram. The wind fought back; the water roared against her. The tiny sparks of life that rode in the ship began to go out.

She gathered every fragment of magic she had left and cast it into the working.

The ship broke like an eggshell, spilling bodies into the sea. With her last scrap of strength, Averil dived for Jennet. Even as her arms closed around the sleep-spelled body, icy water swallowed them both.

15

GEREINT BURST OUT of the dream with a strangled cry. The nightlamp burned in the room he shared with Riquier, casting warm light on the beams of the ceiling. He listened for the roar of wind without, but here in Caermor the storm was little more than a mist of rain.

He fell back in his bed, groaning. He ached in every muscle; his lungs craved air. His body shuddered still with the shock of the wintry sea.

None of that mattered. He had lost Averil. His magic had let go; when he tried to raise it anew, his fingers scraped bottom.

She could not be dead. He would have died, too. Somewhere in that wild sea, amid a tangle of flotsam, she was alive.

Riquier was a sound sleeper: he had barely stirred for all of Gereint's noise. Even so, Gereint moved as quietly as he could, rising and pulling on his clothes and padding into the hallway.

He should not strictly be doing this, but his lessons of late had touched on it, and he had been studying as far beyond his lessons as he could. He was quiet because so many Knights and Squires were sleeping, and because it was hours yet until dawn.

There were three scrying glasses in the Knights' house in Caermor. The first and smallest stood in the schoolroom for the use of Novices and younger Squires. It could, at best, show them what passed halfway across Prydain. The sea was too great a barrier, and the land taxed its poor capacity.

The second hung in the chapel behind a wall of magic. The Knights wielded it in their great workings; through it one could spy on the whole of Prydain and across the sea to the Isle, though the mainland of Lys strained its limits.

The third was not a mirror like the others but a globe of crystal that rested in a silver bowl in Father Owain's study. It was a Mystery of sorts; no one seemed willing to explain what it was or where it had come from.

Gereint had recognized it the first time he saw it. He had a gift or curse in that direction: he could see what no one else saw. This was a great rarity, a globe of the world as it was called. A mage of sufficient power and skill could look through it to any place in the world, or any living spirit.

Gereint had the power. He was not sure he had the skill. But needs must.

At this hour the study was deserted and the passage that led to it was empty. There were wards on the door, but such things seldom troubled Gereint. Wards were woven like lacework; he simply made the gaps his own and slipped through undetected.

His friend Ademar liked to say they were all lucky he had no inclination to become a thief. He wondered if slipping into the Father General's study without permission might be construed as thievery.

It was in the best of causes. He paused inside the door to scrape together his thoughts, which kept trying to scatter. The shelves of books rose dark in the gloom. A faintly gleaming shape stood guard against the wall: a suit of enameled armor that had had magic in it once and still carried a memory of it.

Gereint moved softly past the armor, very careful not to feel as if eyes watched him from the empty casque of the helmet, and halted in front of the worktable with its carved legs and inlaid top. The crystal in its bowl rested near the far corner, as if thrust aside for more important matters: a heap of books, ink and pens and parchment with bits of spells scribbled on them, and a structure of glass rods and pendant prisms that, like the armor, begged Gereint to explore it further.

He knew from hard experience what danger there was in that. Again he shut his mind to temptation, moved on past and stopped in front of the crystal.

It was singing. The sound was audible only to the heart, a high pure note that filled the room with sweetness.

Gereint called all his wits to order and searched in his mind for everything he knew about scrying with glasses. That was not terribly much. A mage should muster his wits, call his magic to heel, and be very careful not to lose control of the vision.

He closed his eyes, resting for a moment in the starlit dark. When he opened them, a light had kindled in the glass. It was soft, at first barely to be seen, but as he watched, it swelled.

He could feel his will fraying and scattering. Images flickered, leaping from one to the next. He gritted his teeth and narrowed his eyes and called up his memory of Averil.

It was not so much her face or body, though he found both more than pleasing. It was partly her scent, like musk and herbs and fresh-scrubbed skin, and partly the sound of her voice, and somewhat the way she moved. But more than that, it was who she was: the essence of her that lived in his heart. For that he had no words, nor did he need any.

He focused himself on that and directed that focus into the glass. It resisted: it was a thing of power, and such things were not made to be blindly obedient. A mage had to earn the right to wield them.

Probably there was a subtle way to control the glass. Gereint only knew how to push against resistance until it gave way or he did. He had to find Averil. That was not a choice. He would find her.

Someone else had come in behind him. He dared not take his eyes off the glass, even for guilt or the shock of being caught. He knew the Knight's presence almost as well as he knew Averil's: it was Mauritius.

"Help me," he said.

Mauritius knew Gereint better than most. He offered no argument, nor did he rebuke the Squire for presuming to give orders to a Knight. He moved in beside Gereint, took hold of his magic as if it had been the hilt of a sword, and aimed it unerringly at the heart of the crystal.

It was not as smooth a joining as Gereint had with Averil, nor did it ever go so deep, but it matched his strength with a master's skill. Both distractions and temptations fell away. Gereint fell through deep water into sudden light.

THE WORLD WAS singing. Far away in a cold distance, waves roared, crashing on stones. Where Averil was, was luminous peace and that eerie and otherworldly music.

As alien as it was, yet it was familiar. Wildfolk were singing, strong and clear under the sea.

As Averil's eyes learned to focus in that pellucid and source-less light, she saw them floating all around her. Rather than wings and claws, as befit this place in which they chose to live, they tended to favor gills and fins. Those that favored some kind of human form were inclined toward round fishy eyes and blunt noseless faces and legs fused like rods of glass and ending in the flare of a dolphin's tail.

A school of them swam toward her and gently but inexorably tugged Jennet out of her grip. Jennet's face was pallid in the water, her dark hair floating like seaweed, her arms trailing limply. She was not breathing, but neither was Averil—or they both would have drowned.

If they were dead, how was it that Jennet still slept and Averil was painfully awake? Averil did not feel dead. She felt spellbound and surrounded by wild magic, with wildfolk beckoning, drawing her onward.

She followed because she could think of no reason to refuse. There were currents in the water, as distinct as paths in a wood. Some led downward into unimaginable depths. Others spiraled upward toward a turbulent sky.

The storm was raging still. The force of its fury touched even those below, knotting and tangling the currents. Averil's escort—guards, captors, whatever they were—guided her unerringly onward and . . . downward?

She darted free of them, aiming upward toward the storm. But even as she escaped, she paused. Jennet was still in their hands.

Averil reached out toward her in broad entreaty. The wildfolk's eyes were cold and strange. They were not human or anything close to it.

Yet they shared a part of her magic. She gave them that part, half gift and half threat. She was blessed of the Mother. They must do as the Mother would wish.

One by one and then all together they surged toward her,

bearing Jennet with them. They swirled around her, carrying her toward the fiercest roaring and the wildest waves.

The dark bulk of land rose there. It stood immobile, vast and silent, with the sea crashing against it.

A great part of Averil recoiled. On land she would lose this lightness, this freedom from the bonds of earth. She would be subject to the tyranny of breath and pulse and life. She would be mortal again.

She could stay—just as she could still submit herself to Esteban and his allies, or the king and his terrible design. She had all the choices there were.

She half turned, but as she hesitated, a voice called to her. It came out of earth and air, resonating through the water. The light flickered, then suddenly brightened.

She looked up into Gereint's face. In this light it seemed as eerie as any of the wildfolk, with its fair hair bleached to fallow gold and its grey eyes paled to silver.

He looked down as if into the depths of a well. As his eyes met hers, they outshone the light. She had to look away or be blinded.

His hand stretched down toward her. She sprang suddenly, got a grip on Jennet's wrist, then strained to catch hold of him.

Even in the water, Jennet's weight dragged at her. But Gereint held her firmly, drawing her upward into the tumult of wind and wave.

16

THERE WAS A roaring in Averil's ears. She was wet. Somehow, distantly, she knew she should be cold.

That would come when she was more awake. She rolled onto her back and stared uncomprehending at the sky.

It was the same pure unsullied blue that shone from the window of a cathedral: the most beautiful of colors and the deepest in magic. The sun was a blaze of molten gold, rising over the tumbled sea. A keen wind struck sparks of foam from the tips of the waves.

She sat up stiffly. A pale strand stretched away before her, broken at frequent intervals by jagged outcroppings of rock. Flotsam tangled among the stones; broken spars and bits of shattered timber dashed themselves to pieces.

Some of the flotsam moved. Here and there it resolved into a human figure, sitting up or staggering erect. More of them washed in as Averil stared, carried up out of the waves and laid on the sand.

She bowed to the wildfolk and gave them thanks. Gravely they bowed back. There was a debt owed, but on which side it fell, she was not entirely certain.

She rose to her knees and then, unsteadily, to her feet. Her breath hissed. Pain stabbed through her soles and radiated up her legs, as if the sand concealed a bed of knives.

She gritted her teeth and essayed a step. With each successive step the pain faded, until she allowed herself to forget.

Dylan Fawr knelt not far away, leaning on Fourchard, who was battered but upright. Their eyes were fixed on a form that Averil did not want to recognize. Jennet's sleep had passed into death. Her body was empty; she lay as Averil had seen her under the sea, with limp hands and trailing hair.

"The sea takes its price," Dylan Fawr said. He sounded ineffably weary.

"Was it the sea? Or the king's enemies who are not our friends?"

"It seems they've shared the victim," said Dylan Fawr.

Averil shuddered. "Don't say that. You don't know what the king does to his armies. How do I know his enemies are any better?"

"I do know what he does," said Dylan Fawr, "and I know his enemies haven't descended to that—yet. Will you give her back to the sea, or will you bury her here in the sand?"

Averil wanted her to be alive and both of them in Fontevrai, with no wild magic or traitor king or alliance of serpent mages to torment them. But that was cold and exhaustion turning her into a whining child. "The sea," she said. "The people there will be kind to her, after their fashion."

Dylan Fawr bowed. Unwittingly it seemed she had done a great thing.

Together with Fourchard he helped Averil to wrap Jennet in her mantle and hood as if in a shroud, bind her closely and lay blessings on her and carry her back out into the waves. Heavy as she was to lift from the earth, in the water she had no weight at all. She rode as light as a leaf.

They could not go out far; the sea was too strong still.

When the water had come to their breasts, the waves turned to glistening hands. They embraced Jennet and bore her down, carrying her back to their deep realm.

The two men drew Averil out of the water before she froze. She hardly noticed the cold. It was still warmer than her heart.

GEREINT HAD NO clear memory of what he said to Mauritius or Father Owein, or what they answered, but when his head cleared, he was mounted and riding southward toward the sea. Half a dozen Novices and Squires rode with him, and Mauritius led them.

Gereint did not seem to be in disgrace. Their errand might prove to be grim, but it was difficult to scowl on such a day. The rain had blown away; it was a glorious morning, such as one seldom saw in this misty country.

Their horses were fast and fresh, but the miles crawled past. He yearned for wings, to fly faster than any horse could gallop.

His mind kept leaping ahead, but it could not find her—or anyone else, for that matter. He was too badly rattled; he could not focus. When he tried, all he could find was a blur of watery light.

It was a stern test of discipline to endure this ride and this gnawing uncertainty. He bent over his horse's neck, welcoming the sting of mane that whipped his cheeks. The strong rocking gait, the pounding of hooves on the greenway, lulled him into a sort of clenched peace.

THE SUN WAS westering; the wind was sharp and cold, with a taste of salt. Gereint had forged ahead of Mauritius as they drew nearer to the sea. At last he ascended a long hill and looked down across a wilderness of sand and stones and tumbled waves.

There was no village here on this forsaken coast, but it seemed a hermit had chosen it for his retreat. Up against the sea-cliff, a low wall enclosed a round hut made of rough stones and salvaged timbers. Its roof was broken and its door long gone, but it was shelter of a sort.

They were there, all who had survived the wreck of the ship, huddled around the half-ruined hearth: eight men and a lone woman. Gereint hardly saw the men; their number would come to him later out of memory, because a Squire was trained to notice everything. He left his horse to fend for himself and sprang from the saddle at the run, hurdling the wall as if he had, at last, found wings.

He came down hard, staggering to his knees in front of Averil. She reached to steady him even as he reached for her.

A vast sigh escaped him. For a year he had lived without her, devoted to his duty as she was to hers. Their magic was bound wherever either of them might be; nothing could separate the parts of it. But to be here in the body, hand in hand, was a profound and blessed rightness.

He bowed low. That was proper: she was a high lady, a descendant of Paladins, and he was a farmer's son.

She pulled him upright. Her eyes widened slightly as he straightened. He resisted the urge to hunch and stoop, as if anything could make him smaller. He had grown, God help him; she was a tall woman, but her head came just above his shoulder.

It took all the will he had to let go of her. She was haggard and her eyes were haunted, and her hair and clothes were stiff with salt. But she was the most beautiful creature he had ever known.

She seemed to have forgotten him already. Her eyes had shifted from him to the men behind him. She greeted them all by name, taking their homage with a slight air of impatience. "No, don't; stop that. We're all friends here."

"If you wish, lady," Mauritius said. "Are you fit to travel? I'd not ask it, but this is a poor place to spend a night. There's a town an hour's ride east; we've bespoken beds and baths and whatever else your heart desires."

"A bath?" she said faintly.

Gereint bit his lip. Laughter would not be wise—but that was purely Averil.

It was the most natural thing in the world to see her mounted on the horse they had brought for her, and to take the place beside and just behind her that had been his before they were parted. The rest of her companions mounted as they could—some with no grace whatever; they were seamen, not horsemen. But they managed well enough.

Gereint did not take his eyes off her, even as dusk turned to dark and a wan moon cast its little light on their road. Never again, he thought. No matter what he had to do or how he had to do it, he would not be parted from her again.

FOR AVERIL THAT ride was a blur of wind and stars and darkness and Gereint's warmth close behind her. She was almost at the edge of endurance, but while he was there, she could go on.

The village was as near as Mauritius had said. It was small and very old, full of little dark people who looked like children of the wildfolk. They welcomed her warmly and gave her everything the Knight had promised.

She had thought nothing would make her forget the storm or the wreck or the deaths of her maid and all her guards, but once she had bathed and eaten and fallen into the bed that waited for her, she let memory slip away. All that was left was Gereint asleep as near to her door as he could go and still be in the hall, and a small and fugitive thought: was there something odd about the color of his cotte?

Blue did suit him. But should it not be? . . .

The rest of the thought lost itself in sleep, but when she woke, it followed her into the morning light.

"Shouldn't it be green?"

There was no one to answer the question. She lay in an oddly shaped room: the house was round and the walls of the rooms ran like spokes from the central circle of hall and hearth.

Averil rose. Their host, a widow of both wit and means, had seen to it that she had clothes to fit. They were plain, a commoner's clothes; Averil was beyond measure glad to be so simply dressed again, in clean linen chemise and deep green gown and shoes made more for use than show. She shook her hair out of the plait in which she had slept, combed and plaited it once more.

The Squires were still asleep in the hall, wrapped in their deep blue mantles. She could hardly miss Gereint's shock of fair hair: he was lying at her feet.

She sat on her heels beside him, hands folded in her lap, and waited for him to wake. It did not take long. Under the weight of her regard, he twitched, then scowled. After a handful of breaths, his eyes opened.

They warmed at the sight of her. She felt that warmth in her body, rising from her knees to her breastbone.

By the saints, if any son of Paladins could do that to her, she would marry him before the day was out. But it was Gereint; she had to steel herself against him. "You didn't tell me," she said.

He frowned. "What?"

Her finger brushed his mantle. "This."

He raised himself on his elbow. His shirt strained across his shoulders. His shape had changed: from rangy boy with a farmer's foursquare carriage to the honed strength of a fighting man.

Averil had to stop thinking about that body, or she would not be able to keep a sensible thought in her head. Gereint was still frowning at her. "I meant to tell you," he said. "There never seemed to be time."

"They tested you twice?"

He shook his head. "I thought I was testing for Novice. Then they gave me this. I did try to talk them out of it."

"Of course you did," she said. "You've been training hard. Even I can see it. You look like a Squire."

He flushed and looked anywhere but at her. "I've been trying," he muttered.

"I am proud," she said, "if you won't let yourself be."

That reduced him to complete incoherence. A few words did come out of it: "I shouldn't get above myself."

She caught his head in her hands and pulled it around until he had to face her. "You are not a farmer now and never will be again. You will be a Knight of the Rose. A Knight doesn't get above himself. He honors the order and his brothers by acting as a Knight should."

A roar of applause startled her almost out of her skin. The rest of the Squires were awake and up and grinning at her, pounding fists on benches and feet on floor.

"That's telling him, lady!" said Riquier. "God knows, he doesn't listen to any of us."

"I listen to you!" Gereint protested.

Riquier shook his head, still grinning. "You're as stubborn

as your mother's mule. Lady, we've missed you sorely. All of us—not just this great lout."

That cast Averil to the brink of incoherence herself, but she had been training to be a courtier. Words were there when she reached for them. They even made sense. "I'm honored, messire."

Riquier swept a bow. "The honor is ours, my lady. May we serve you? Would you break your fast?"

"I am hungry," she admitted—sending the lot of them on a mad race to remedy it.

Gereint could not go with them: she still held him captive. She did not want ever to let him go.

Carefully she lowered her hands. She expected him to leap up and bolt with the rest, but he stayed where he was. "You don't have any surprises for me, do you?" he said. "The man who was with you—I don't suppose—"

Averil swallowed the surge of wild laughter. "Not in this world," she said. "You see that young bull with him, who's almost as big as you?"

Gereint's brows went up. "Truly?"

"As I live on this earth," she said.

He let out a long sigh. "Well," he said. "Good, then."

His relief was so strong she could taste it. She buried it in words. "He's the queen's ambassador to Lys. Or was. I doubt he'll be allowed back after this."

"I know who he is," Gereint said. "I had to ask. Because, you know, you did go to Lutèce for that. There wasn't anyone?"

"Not one," she said.

It was the truth. She could not understand why it felt like a lie. She felt nothing for Esteban—and certainly nothing like what she felt for this great gawk of a boy.

There was no logic in it. Gereint was not helping, either. "Maybe there will be a suitable lord or prince here," he said.

"What, are you a matchmaker now?"

That brought him up short, as she had meant it to. "I'm acknowledging what is," he said stiffly.

"Don't," she said. "It's not your place."

His bow was as stiff as his tone. "Yes, your grace," he said.

She knotted her hands together before she slapped him silly. He was only doing what she had provoked him to do— what she had to do.

A year's absence had made this thing between them more dangerous than ever. He had grown and so had she; they were no longer children. He knew as well as she that her only salvation was to find a husband soon and bind him fast, and keep Gereint as far away from her as either of them could bear.

For somewhat too long a moment, she regretted that she had run from Esteban. He promised a world in which she would not be bound to marry within the blood—a world in which she could have what her heart so dearly wanted.

That was not the world she lived in. She rose and smoothed her skirts and turned her back on a worse temptation than Esteban or his plotting could ever be.

17

BREAKFAST BEGAN WITH great goodwill as they feasted on the bounty of food and drink that the Squires brought back from the kitchens. Averil sat as far away from Gereint as she could go, but no one remarked on that. He was the lowliest of the Squires; she was a duchess. Her place was between the Knight and the ambassador, partaking of fine white bread and fresh-baked fish and honeyed wine, with cakes and apples and fresh curds.

There was no dissension that morning, not where Averil let anyone see. After they had eaten, their host appeared, windblown and smelling of the sea. She did more than oversee her late husband's fleet of fishing boats, it seemed; she commanded one of her own.

She insisted that none of them ride away without full saddlebags to go with their full bellies. Her kindness warmed Averil's heart. She gave it freely, and not as if she did it out of duty; her charity was heartfelt.

Averil was almost sorry to leave that house, but more than duty drove her onward. She had not come here to dally while the world crumbled about her ears. She had done enough of that in Lutèce.

Prydain, like Dame Alison, offered Averil a warm welcome. Though winter was close and the woods and copses had shed their gold and red upon the ground, the sun was warm and the air was sweet, like a last memory of summer.

There were wildfolk in the woods—not as many as had come to dwell in Quitaine, but a fair flock, as numerous and almost as noisy as jackdaws. Averil surprised herself with pleasure at the sight of them. Lutèce had been too stark and barren a place for wildfolk, and the sea offered no haven to the folk of air.

She had grown used to a world full of them. To see them here, living as free as any other creatures of this country, made her dare to hope that Prydain could stand against the king of Lys. Not only was it an island and a sovereign kingdom; the magic here was different. Different enough maybe to tip the balance.

The Knights seemed to be prospering. They would never lose the grief of their order's fall or the horror of so much magic destroyed and so many lives and souls taken, but here they were strong. They moved through the currents of magic in this country with the fluid ease of fish in the sea.

Those currents led them northward to a city that loomed as large in the spirit as in the world of brick and timber. Its palace stood by the river's bank, watching over the low round houses and squat towers to the east of it. The soaring spires of Lys and the marble domes of Romagna had gained no foothold here. Prydain remained, as ever, itself.

A company of guards met the Knights at the gate. Their captain bowed low to Averil and said, "Her majesty welcomes her grace of Quitaine and requests the favor of her presence."

Averil was not ready to go back to courts and palaces, but this was not a choice. She was a guest here; she had duties to her host. She suppressed a sigh, managed a smile and a slight bow, and let herself be conducted through the city toward the western wall.

The streets through which she rode were wide and clean. The people who flocked in them seemed well fed; beggars were few, the markets full of both treasures and necessities. This was still a mortal city full of mortal faults and foibles, but an air of contentment lay over it.

It spoke well for the queen that she ruled such a city. Her palace was nothing like the palace of Lutèce; its splendors were the splendor of polished wood and glimmering glass, and its courtiers' dress lacked the extravagance that Averil had seen in Lys. They were not as conscientiously useless, either; those who hung about in the hall had the air of petitioners rather than idlers.

Prydain's queen was young. Averil had known it, and yet it was unexpected. Averil also had heard that she was a Lady of the Isle: that she had passed the testing and become full initiate before the deaths of father and brothers had left her the only and unexpected heir to Prydain's throne. There must have been a dispensation; she had been sent away with her vows intact, still a Lady but also a queen.

Rumor did not say whether she had been reluctant to leave the Isle. When she was called to Prydain, Averil had been a child, too caught up in her own small preoccupations to notice one Lady among so many.

Whatever Eiluned had felt when necessity forced her to leave her order and her home, clearly she had made her peace with it. She had grown in her office, but it had not sucked the life from her.

She was of the old blood, older than Paladins. Many of her kin still walked these streets: little dark people crackling with magic, some bearing the old clan-marks on cheeks and brow.

Eiluned did not observe that custom. Her broad brow was clear, her high cheeks ornamented only with their own hint of rose. She wore a crown of flowers, the last of the autumn, purple and gold and white; her gown was simple, and she wore no jewels but a belt of gold from which hung three golden apples.

As Averil approached, she rose from her gilded chair. The apples rang softly as she moved: they were bells. She swept past clerks and courtiers to embrace Averil and kiss her on both cheeks. "Cousin! Welcome. We're glad beyond measure to find you alive and well."

"Cousin," said Averil. "I'm most glad of your kindness."

Eiluned smiled. "We're pleased to give it. The world is in great danger; we need everyone who can fight."

Averil bowed to that. "Then you know, majesty: the Isle is threatened."

"Tomorrow we take counsel," said Eiluned. "Today, let my people offer you food and comfort and rest. You'll be our guest, of course."

"Of course," said Averil. It was proper; it was expected. She could hardly have thought to live in the Knights' guesthouse when there were lodgings more appropriate to her rank and gender.

It was foolish of her to be disappointed, even as weary of courts as she was. She stiffened her spine and polished her smile and gave herself up to the queen's servants.

WITH AVERIL UNDER the queen's protection, the Knights were free to go. Gereint's steps dragged. He was where he belonged: he was surer of that with each day that passed. But with Averil here, he found his heart was torn in two.

He had thought only of saving her from the sea, then of

bringing her to Caermor. He had not stopped to think that the life they had lived in Fontevrai, when he was a Postulant in service to the Lord Protector and she was a servant in disguise, was not possible here.

She was a duchess in exile. He was a Squire of the Rose. They had their spheres, and those were scrupulously separate.

She went where her duty took her. So did he. She did not look back or show any other sign of caring that he was leaving her.

What did they have in common, after all? An accident of magic had turned them into two halves of the same unnatural creature. In all other ways, they were alien to one another—and so they should stay, for her good as much as his.

THE FLARE OF temper carried him most of the way to the chapter house before it died. Then he was merely morose. No one appeared to notice: they were tired and hungry, with little else on their minds but their supper and their beds.

Gereint wanted to crawl under his blankets and not come out again until spring, but as he trudged away from the stable after the horses were unsaddled and fed and bedded down, Mauritius called to him. The Knight had been taking a turn as stablehand, which all of them did on occasion: it kept them humble.

It seemed he had been waiting for Gereint: he was sitting on a barrel with a lapful of newly cleaned harness. Gereint perched across from him and reached for a bridle that was still in need of cleaning.

Mauritius was the least pretentious of the Knights. He was a quiet man, not given to vaunting, but he was a fine fighter and a powerful mage. The web that bound the Knights in spirit and magic was partly of his making. After it was broken in the fall of the Rose, when with the help of the wildfolk the bare bones of it had been restored to those Knights who survived, he had helped to rebuild it with even greater strength and subtlety.

Gereint had known Mauritius since he first ran away to the Knights. No one had ever exactly said, but Gereint was sure the Knight had convinced the rest to accept the raw boy with so much magic that he was a danger to himself and everyone around him.

If Gereint had been less cross-grained and his nerves less jangled, he would have taken comfort in this silent labor. As it was, he hoped that all he was wanted for was to finish the cleaning; then he could escape to his room.

But Mauritius was not as merciful as that. He let Gereint take apart the bridle and scrub it in peace, but as he began to put it back together, the Knight said, "If you like, we can send you away from Caermor."

Gereint wheezed as if he has been struck in the gut. The part of him that was sensible knew he should accept. The rest could not breathe.

Sent away? Separated again from her? God help him, he could not endure the thought.

He hunted for words that would not betray the truth, but Mauritius was there before him. "Ah so," the Knight said. He did not seem angry. "I'll tell you the truth: what is between you two may be the best hope we have. But it will ask more of you than is fair or just to ask of anyone."

"I never heard that life was fair," Gereint said. "Is it for nobles, then? The rest of us aren't so lucky."

Mauritius acknowledged the stroke with a lift of the hand. "Well struck, sir! Still, you do have a choice."

"What, to let the king destroy us all?"

"There are other mages in the world," Mauritius said dryly.

"But you said—" Gereint broke off. "What am I supposed to do? We can't ever be what we want to be. We don't even dare think about it. But our magic thinks of nothing else."

"That is a difficulty," Mauritius said. "You came to us to learn discipline. This is a greater test than any of us imagined. But if the good God has set it, he must believe that you can pass it."

"Or else," said Gereint, "he's telling us the world needs to change."

"That is not for you to say, messire," Mauritius said.

His voice was quiet, but Gereint's throat closed. However sympathetic Mauritius might be, he was still bound by law and custom. All mages were, by the nature of their orders. Anything else was wild magic—and even after his sojourn in the Wildlands, Mauritius could not stretch his mind so far.

Gereint did not mean to be disappointed. Mauritius had not forbidden Gereint to bind his magic to Averil's—not that anyone could stop him, though under the law, many mages might try. The Knight was as true an ally as Gereint could have in this world.

If he was wise, he would take what he could get. The only other choice was the way of the Serpent that the prince from Moresca had offered Averil—and Gereint could not stomach that. Not now and not, God help him, in any world that he could see.

18

AVERIL HAD LOST the habit of deference. When she spoke, she expected to be listened to; when she proposed a course of action, she took it for granted that it would be done as she decreed.

In Prydain she was an honored guest, but she did not rule. Although her voice was heard well enough, it was only one of many. It was not the loudest, nor was her will the one that seemed likely to prevail.

"Lady, we understand," the queen's chancellor said with saintly patience, "and we have considered mounting a fleet and going to the aid of the Isle, but we believe the Isle is better served if we hold our ground here."

Averil gritted her teeth. For three days she had been waging this war of words, day after misty, rainy, sodden day, before the queen's privy council. She was completely out of patience, and severely out of sorts. "No, messire," she said. "With respect, *you* do not understand. I realize that Prydain must defend itself. I am asking for one ship and one crew to carry me to the Isle. Once it has done so, it can return to Prydain. If we go quickly, we will come there before the king invades."

"Lady," said the chancellor, "the Isle's wards are up. The walls of air are thrice and fourfold stronger than you may remember. Your first ship was lost when it ventured near those walls. We cannot spare another—or, my lady, you."

"This time I will pass," she said. "I was unprepared before. Now I know what I face. They will remember me; they will let me through."

"Will they?" Dylan Fawr had held his peace through all this time, but it seemed he had his limits. His voice was unusually sharp. "Lady, for all they may know, you are the king's weapon against them, and your arrival will bring down the walls of air and let in the invaders. Can you blame them for letting nothing pass? Even you?"

"I can help them," she said. "I know what is coming, and I can help to stop it. I'm no use here. Whereas there—"

"If you had been meant to reach the Isle," said Dylan Fawr, "you would be there now. The Powers brought you here. This is where you're needed."

She shook her head stubbornly. She was half mad with wanting to be among the Ladies, helping to drive back the king, and not cooling her heels here, trapped in another royal court.

She looked round the circle of courteous, impervious faces. Even the Knights offered her no sympathy. They had decided what they would do. Neither her will nor her urgency mattered in the least to them.

She left with abruptness bordering on insult, but she was past caring. Outside the council chamber, people caught sight of her face and drew out of the way.

She was in a remarkable mood; she could not remember when she had been so close to the edge. She needed to get out, to run, to do something, anything, but sit and listen to courtly nonsense. But the rain had closed in, drumming harder than ever on the roof.

Her only recourse was the library, which was even larger than hers in Quitaine, or the chapel, where the silence might teach her to be her sane and sensible self again.

Maybe Dylan Fawr was right. Maybe she did have a spell on her.

There was one person who could tell. She had not seen him since he deposited her in the queen's care, nor had he sent word, either in the mortal way or through their conjoined magic. He was avoiding her—which was wise of him, but in the mood she was in, it felt like abandonment.

ONE OF THE royal guards followed Averil out of the palace, but he made no move to stop her. She had not reckoned that she was a prisoner; still, there was a peculiar relief in this proof that she could go where she pleased.

The rain had not abated even slightly. She was damp even under the tightly woven wool of her mantle by the time she presented herself at the gate of the chapter house.

For a long while there was no response to her knocking. She began to wonder if she had come to the wrong house; even though there was a rose carved on the lintel and a taste of familiar magic about the walls, it might be a ruse.

Then the porter's panel slid back and a pair of eyes peered out. They widened as Averil slipped back her hood enough to show her face. Before she had to say a word, the man shot the bolt and opened the door.

He was a Novice, and Averil recognized him. "Ademar," she said. "I've come to see—"

"Yes, lady," he said a little breathlessly. He had been a world-weary young thing when she first met him, but the fall of the Rose and the flight into exile had struck off that jaded veneer. He smiled, transparently glad to see her. "Come, lady. There's a fire in the lodge, and it's dry."

The porter's lodge was a small room and plain, but it was warm as he had said. A pair of sturdy chairs stood in front of the fire, and a table between them, with a basket of bread and cheese and apples and a jar of ale. Averil declined to share Ademar's dinner, but she basked in the warmth of the fire.

Ademar took Averil's cloak and spread it over one of the chairs to dry. She was sorely tempted to linger, but urgency sparked with anger and burned away her lassitude. "Messire," she said, "I thank you for this, but I must speak with Gereint. Is he in the house?"

Ademar's brows twitched upward. "I'm sure he is, lady. But—"

"Will you take me to him?"

He was clearly torn. "Lady, if your man will take my post, I can, but—"

"Good, then," she said, turning toward the door.

He leaped to block it. "Lady, are you sure you should do this? Won't you talk to Mauritius first?"

"Why?" she demanded. "Is something wrong? Has something happened to him?"

"No, lady," said Ademar, "but he's under full discipline now, and his time isn't his own."

"He doesn't want to see me, does he?"

Ademar shook his head firmly. "No, lady. That's not true. He hasn't said anything about you at all. May I take you to Mauritius? Please?"

Averil sighed. "Very well," she said. She refrained from thinking about what it meant that Gereint had not been speaking of her. He was being wise, again. And she was being an idiot.

MAURITIUS, THOUGH A Knight Commander and master of all the Knights from Lys who remained in the world, was able to speak to Averil immediately—unlike the newest of his

Squires. When Ademar brought her to him, he was just emerging from a roomful of Novices. He brought with him a distinct odor of fire magic and a faint crackle in the air as he moved.

Averil flicked her hand in a counterspell that turned fire to air and water and made it dissipate into the aether. It was presumptuous, she realized as soon as she had done it, but the Knight thanked her civilly and asked, "To what do we owe the honor, lady?"

Ademar had disappeared. After Averil had had enough of wanting to slap Gereint, she would move on to him. "Messire," she said, she hoped not too sharply, "I would like an audience with your newest Squire."

"Indeed," said Mauritius. She could not read his expression. He opened a door a few steps down the passage and led her into an empty schoolroom. It was dank and cold and the light was dim, but a flick of his fingers lit the lamps above the benches and tables.

The light brought welcome warmth but no peace to Averil's spirit. When Mauritius perched on the master's stool, she paced restlessly, until with a sweep of skirts she whirled to face him. "Well?" she demanded.

"My lady," Mauritius said in a tone he must practice frequently with obstreperous Novices, "this is not a monastery. We're not keeping him from you. But is it wise? You both know what must be according to law and custom. Are you going to break his heart or only his trust?"

Averil gasped. She had not been expecting words that cut so deep—even if she had thought them herself often enough. "Messire," she said, then had to pause to draw in enough air for the rest. "Messire, I would never harm him. But the king is threatening the Isle, and this magic that we have may be the weapon the Ladies need to drive him back."

Mauritius' dark brows drew together. "Wild magic? Even more reason not to trust you."

"Not wild magic," Averil said. "Something else, maybe new in the world—or maybe so old it's been forgotten. And no, I don't mean serpent magic! It has power against that. Maybe enough to save the Isle."

"And if it turns on you and on us all and destroys what it means to save?"

"Do you trust Gereint?" she asked.

He seemed mildly startled. "He has learned to control himself. But, lady—"

"Will you at least consider what we may do? Can you unlock your mind from the orders and see the world that is beyond them?"

Mauritius had ridden through the Wildlands with Averil, had seen the wildfolk in their multitudes and tasted their magic. It had not been pleasant for Averil; for him it must have been outright pain.

Nevertheless, it had shown him the truth of the world he thought he knew. He must remember. She willed him to see, and to try to understand.

It was like battering against a castle wall. "Lady, it may well be that you are the answer to all our prayers, but we must be very sure before we let go the world we know. For myself I believe there is a middle way. And maybe," he said before she could do it for him, "that is what you have in yourselves, the two of you. But we can't take this solely on faith."

"Why not? The Paladins took the Young God on no more than that."

His breath hissed; then, as if shocked out of sense, he laughed. "My lady! Well struck. But can you understand? All of us are in terrible danger. The Isle is prepared to draw the king's wrath and, if possible, destroy him. We stand as the rear guard; if he fails with the Isle, he will come here. Then you'll have the fight you're hungry for."

"I am not—" Averil broke off. That was not true. She did want a fight. She wanted fire and wrath, and Clodovec stripped of his soul as he had done to so many mothers' sons of Lys. She wanted him to know who had destroyed him and why, with every twist of the agony that he had visited on his people.

She called herself to order. "You are well placed here," she said, "but I would serve us all better from the Isle. With the power the Ladies guard and the strength I share with Gereint, we can—"

"It's too late for that."

Averil spun. Gereint filled the doorway. His fair hair was damp as if he had run across a courtyard in the rain; his breathing came a little quickly.

He was not smiling. He seemed anything but glad to see her.

And yet he had run to this room. Ademar came up behind him, flushed and breathless, with an expression half of guilt and half of determination.

Averil would find a way to thank him later. For now she kept her eyes on Gereint. "It won't be too late if we move quickly. There's more than enough time to get to the Isle before the moon's dark."

"The Isle is closed to all of us until this war is over," Gereint said. "Don't you think we've tried to get there ourselves? It can't be done. For good or ill, this is where we stay."

" 'We'?" she asked with arched brow.

His face went still. "You were brought here, lady. There is a reason for that."

"Yes," she said. "I called and you answered. You pulled me out of the sea."

"I couldn't have done that if the Isle had taken you first. And it would have, lady, if it wanted or needed you there."

"It needs both of us," she said. "Don't tell me you can't see that."

"I can't," he said.

Damn the boy, he could look as stupid as one of his mother's sheep. It was a pity for him that Averil knew better. "Don't lie to me," she said.

"It's the truth. The Isle doesn't need us. Prydain and the Rose do. You'd see it, too, if you weren't so busy being stubborn."

"Of course I'm being stubborn! The rest of the world is blind. Why can't you see, too? You always could before."

"There's nothing to see. We are where we belong. You, too. Whatever we're meant to do, we'll do it here."

She spun back toward Mauritius. He looked like a man at a battledore match, eyes flicking from one to the other. She thought she knew which of them he wanted to win.

There was no help here. Even the one human creature she had ever truly trusted was against her. She was alone.

She walked out past Gereint, not even noticing when or how he stopped blocking the door. When she reached it, he was not there. That was all that mattered.

19

T HERE WAS NO use in sulking, or in blasting down walls with temper, either. Averil retreated to her chambers in the palace, barred the door and flung the shutters wide and let the cold and the damp blow in.

It helped her to think. She was more hurt by Gereint's refusal than she wanted to acknowledge, though she stopped short of calling it a betrayal. He was only practicing obedience to his commander.

She pulled herself up short. It was not as simple as that. He believed what the rest of them were reciting like doctrine. He opposed her from his own heart, not just his superiors'.

They had never been at odds before. There had been squabbles, yes, but they had always gone the same way in the end—her way.

Gereint had grown a mind of his own. And she did not like it at all.

Very well then, she thought as she paced the borders of the room. She was alone. She had left all allies and possible allies behind in Lys, where she might be pawn or puppet, but she was also a duchess who might become a queen. Here she was no one; she had no rank, no place, no wealth or fortune but what she could beg of the queen's charity. No one on this side of the sea would help her.

The web of the Knights was secure inside her, but it would

not yield to any will she laid upon it. The Knights had agreed: Prydain was their battlefield, and the Isle had to fend for itself.

They offered no objection to her scrying toward the Isle— and no wonder. There was nothing to see. The walls of air were raised and secured. Storms roared around them, driving ships astray and even destroying them—as she had discovered to her grief.

Nothing that she did or tried could pierce those walls. They rose in the landscape of the mind like a dome of glass, clear enough to see the loom of the mountain and the whiteness of foam about its edges, but shadowed where the Ladies' vale and the port should be. As far as she could tell, it was a deserted island of sheer black rock with a lake in its heart.

She could not find the Ladies' magic at all. It was thoroughly and completely warded. No matter how she cried out or to whom she ventured it, she received only silence.

With Gereint she might have succeeded. But he was walled off from her, too. The deepest part of him was still there, but it was mute, like a stone, heavy and impervious.

The king was going to break that dome of perfect glass, slide his serpent magic beneath it and crack it like an eggshell. And there was nothing at all that she could do about it. She could not even warn the Ladies.

"LADY?"

Averil called on all her reserves of discipline to suppress her temper, focus her mind, and greet the royal servant who bowed before her. It was hard; she felt a little strange, as if something was stopping her from reining herself in.

She thrust the thought aside. She was exhausted, she was frustrated, she was thwarted at every turn. How could she not be in an ill temper?

"Lady," the queen's servant said in her silence, "you have a message. The boy who brought it was bidden to wait for your answer."

Averil took the bit of folded parchment from Dame Grisel's hand, and nearly dropped it. It crackled with magic, a signature as clear as ink on a page.

There was something oddly familiar about it, but she could not recall where she had seen this thing before. On the Isle, she supposed—or, she thought with a slight shiver, in the Wildlands. There was a distinct air of wild magic about it; but there was a great deal of that in Prydain. "Who sent this?" she asked.

"The boy belongs to her majesty's master mage, lady," Grisel said: "the Myrddin, he's called."

Averil was intrigued in spite of herself. "Indeed? That doesn't sound like a title from one of the orders."

"It's not, lady," the woman said. She dipped in the curtsey that womenservants favored here, and withdrew before Averil could call her back.

Averil opened her mouth to do it even so, but shrugged and let it be. She dropped to the edge of the bed and peered at the letter in her hand. The seal looked like a drop of blood, glistening and alive, with the image of a hawk in flight impressed on it.

She hesitated before breaking the seal, but no storm of magic burst upon her. The letter was written in a round old-fashioned hand by a scribe of fair skill, and it was brief and to the point.

> To her grace of Quitaine, greetings and good health: We have heard of certain difficulties and besetting frustrations. There may be no cure for these, but a diversion might please you well. The boy will lead if you will follow.

Averil ran her finger along the written lines. The magic in them tingled. There was wild magic there, and no mistake.

She had never heard of the Myrddin. For all she knew it was a lie or an ambush.

The air in the room shifted. She looked up to find the doorway filled by a pair of broad shoulders in a blue mantle. Doors, she thought distantly, needed to be larger where Gereint was—or he needed to stop growing like a well-watered tree.

Half of her wanted to drive him back where he came from. The other half was far more relieved than it strictly wanted to be.

Her greeting was not precisely gracious, but she did not openly order him out. "Messire. What brings you here?"

He scowled. His mood was as confused as hers, and his temper was no sweeter, either. "You're making my head hurt. You need to stop."

"You didn't have to come all the way here in the rain to tell me that," she said. "Did your keepers let you go, then? Or are you running away?"

His jaw tightened. "I don't want us to fight. But you're being unreasonable. I know you were raised on the Isle and it's your real home, but—"

"Fontevrai is home," she said. "The Isle anchors all the magic in this part of the world. Has no one stopped to think of what will happen when it falls?"

"It's not going to fall," he said.

"The Rose did."

That gave him pause, though not for long. "The Rose was in Lys, in the king's own country, without the wild magic to help it. The Isle is in the middle of the sea."

"That won't stop Clodovec," she said grimly. "If he wakes

the Serpent, the whole world will be under its sway—sea, land, it won't matter."

"He has to find it first," Gereint said.

"If he thinks the Knights still hide it, you know where he'll come, don't you? He'll come here."

"Then the Isle will be safe," said Gereint reasonably, "and we'll be where we're most needed."

Averil bit her tongue. She had just talked herself out of her own argument.

He knew it, too. He was kind enough not to gloat.

"I don't suppose you know where it is," she said.

He shook his head. "Nobody does."

"Are you sure? Not Mauritius? Not the master of the Knights here?"

"They don't confide in me," he said fairly cheerfully, all things considered.

Of course Knights of the highest rank did not share their order's deepest secret with a newly minted Squire. Averil was foolish for even thinking he might have the answer.

Then he said, "I don't think they know. The ones who did are dead, and it seems they died without talking. That Mystery is hidden—maybe forever."

"If it can possibly be found," Averil said, "Clodovec will find it. He's calling on every power he knows—and he's not the only one. Some of the hounds that are running on the scent are Serpent's men, but they're none of his. This hunt is going to turn up its quarry or overturn the world in looking for it. Which is why we need the Isle. What else is left that keeps so much power in a single place?"

"It doesn't share the power," Gereint said. "The Ladies keep to themselves. Everything they do is secret. How does that help the rest of us?"

"They're holding the world together," said Averil.

"Do you really think they need help? Or is Ademar right? He says you want to go to the Isle and convince the Ladies to make you one of them like Queen Eiluned, so you won't have to marry."

"Ademar is wrong," she said, "about Ladies and marriage, and about me. I know my duty. I may not like it, I may pray for it to be taken away, but in the end I'll give Quitaine what it needs: a leader for its armies and a father for its heir."

Gereint had the grace to look abashed and the strength not to let her words crush him. They had been no easier to speak than they must have been to hear.

Averil was tired suddenly of running in these circles. She held out the Myrddin's letter. "Here. What do you make of this?"

The diversion succeeded. Gereint felt the magic in the letter: his eyes widened and his hand twitched. As he took in the seal, his eyes went even wider. "The Myrddin? He wants to see you?"

"Why?" Averil asked. "Do you know him?"

He shook his head. "Oh, no. He lives on a hilltop in Dyfed, away in the west of the kingdom. He only comes to court if there's great need or a great rite: a coronation, the birth of an heir, the death of a king. If he's in Caermor now, then something is happening."

"Something *is* happening," she said testily. "Clodovec wants to destroy the Isle."

Gereint spread his hands and shrugged. "Maybe that's it, lady. Are you going? The boy is still in the anteroom. He looks as if he means to wait for days."

"What if it's a trap?" she said.

"I don't think it is." He ran his finger over the parchment.

"This is strong magic, but it's clean. It doesn't smell of serpents at all."

"It could be disguised," she said.

"It's not." He laid the letter on the table by the bed. "We should go. I think the Myrddin's boy is not human, but I'm sure he needs to eat and drink and rest."

"And I am a bad host for offering him no hospitality." Averil let her breath out sharply. "We'll go, then. Both of us."

He offered no objection. Even as put out with him as she was, she felt for the first time in a year as if the world was in its proper orbit. Gereint was at her back. She was, at last, truly safe.

20

THE MYRDDIN'S BOY looked at first glance like any other noble page, but there was an odd shimmer on him. He felt like one of the wildfolk, though Averil had never seen one who chose to appear so nearly human.

He, or it, did not speak when she greeted it civilly. It rose from the bench and bowed, then beckoned.

It moved almost too quick to catch, and yet somehow it never quite eluded them. Averil took note of the turns and passages.

They never left the palace, which surprised her somewhat, but they were not exactly in it, either. They had passed through into a sort of sidewise world, or perhaps into an eddy of time. The air seemed thick, almost like water; they moved through it slowly, at the pace of a dream.

They left a maze of corridors to ascend a spiral stair. It was made of ash-wood, and the power that slept in it put Averil in mind of old tales of the World-Tree that had grown in the northlands before the Serpent fell.

There was no glass here, and no iron, either—no metal at all. It was all wood. The door at the top, as they paused to rest aching legs, was made with wooden pegs; no nails, nothing of metal or stone.

The room beyond was round and high, a tower room, and

where the stair had been all of wood, it was all of stone. No glass gleamed there, either; the tall narrow windows were open to the air, without pane or shutter. The pillars that held up the dome were carved in the likeness of trees, oak and ash and the gnarled knots of thorn. Averil could almost swear that serpentine shapes coiled through the branches.

She was seeing serpents in every long or convoluted curve. These were only stone trees, winter-bare, supporting a dome like the vault of the sky. Indeed there was sky in the center, a circle of tumbled grey.

It was a strange room, and bare, without hearth or furnishing, and yet strangest of all was that it was not cold. She could feel the kiss of rain on her cheeks as she passed by the windows, and sleet rattled on the dome, but the air was warm and sweet. It smelled like a wood in the spring.

If she closed her eyes, she could feel sunlight on her face and inhale the scent of grass and flowers. The sound of falling sleet softened into the bubble of water in a stream.

She would have preferred that world to the one her eyes insisted on seeing, but she had never been one to flinch from truth, however peculiar. She opened her eyes on the man who stood across the hall, almost lost in the dimness and the spreading mist.

That, she thought, was a distinct annoyance. He was a tall man, broad in the shoulder, dressed in plain dark clothes. She swept the mist aside with a word and a gesture, and flung a witchlight after it.

Then she recognized the man who stood smiling at her as if with pride at her little feat of conjuring. The sight of him startled her; she stepped backward abruptly, into the warm and breathing wall that was Gereint.

His arms closed instinctively around her. His surprise and sudden pleasure sparkled through her. "Messire Perrin! *You're* the queen's magician?"

"I am the hawk on the hilltop," the mage said. He seemed as pleased as Gereint.

Averil was not nearly as delighted as they were. The last time she saw this—man, she supposed she had to call him, though she had her doubts—he had played host to the last of the Knights, far away in the heart of the Wildlands. He was so full of wild magic he made her skin itch; though no one had ever said, she strongly suspected he was a Power of that country.

Gereint shared none of Averil's suspicions. He had met the creature in Fontevrai itself, wearing the guise of an herbalist. He could not understand why anyone should dislike or distrust the one he called Messire Perrin.

There was no logic in it, and no sense in the boy, either. Averil had to have enough of that for both of them. She extricated herself from his grasp and faced the mage direct.

His smile had widened intolerably. "Lady," he said. "It's well we meet again."

"Is it?" That was rude, but Averil could not keep hold of her manners where wild magic was concerned. "You're everywhere, it seems. Do you hold office under the king of Lys, too?"

"Not under this king," he said. He held out his hand. "Shall we go somewhere more pleasant?"

Averil opened her mouth to refuse, but Gereint had already taken the proffered hand. The room was shifting, the scent of grass and flowers growing stronger, and the mist rising to swallow them. By the time Averil scraped her wits together, the tower was gone, and the place they stood in was as familiar as the mage who had brought them there.

It seemed altogether ordinary: a greensward up against a wood, a kitchen garden fenced against rabbits and deer, a cottage with a thatched roof and a curl of smoke rising from the peak. The orchard was in bloom; its scent had reached her even across worlds.

It was winter in the world she knew, but here it was high spring. It had been high spring when last she was in this place, too. Maybe it always was. In the Wildlands, anything was possible.

Flocks of lesser wildfolk swirled like leaves overhead, chittering in excitement. The greater ones were not in evidence—except for Perrin, who led them into the cottage.

It was much larger within than without, as she remembered. It was odd not to see the rooms full of the Knights' gear. They were clean and empty and sunlit, with a tranquility about them that was not of mortal earth.

Perrin sat his guests down at the heavy wooden table in the kitchen and laid out a homely feast: fresh-baked bread and fresh-churned butter, hard cheese and soft curds mixed in with herbs and garlic, apples and pears and apricots that tasted like sweet sunlight. There was cold spring water to wash it down, with a taste of deep earth and high magic, and for after, tiny cups of a cordial that seemed born of honey mead and liquid fire.

Averil did not want to be hungry, but she was ravenous. She had eaten the fruit of this country before without losing her soul or her freedom; she had to hope that immunity continued.

Gereint was halfway through his substantial portion already. Averil reached for half a loaf and the pot of herbed cheese. It was good—wonderfully so; there was no taint of sorcery in it that she could detect.

Messire Perrin ate with them. It was the first time she had seen him take mortal nourishment, and it rather undid one of her more cherished suspicions.

He was doing his best to look both human and mortal: a big man like Gereint, fair-haired and grey-eyed. They might have been of the same nation, though Gereint was unmistakably human and Perrin was perceptibly not.

And yet, was Gereint as human as all that? He spoke and acted like a farmer from the west of Lys, with a broad country accent and a certain rustic innocence that a year and more among the Knights had done little to erase. He was also the strongest mage she had ever seen.

No one else had magic that ran so deep or spread so wide. It was not inexhaustible—she had seen it taxed to its limits a time or two—but he had more of it than any mortal had a right to.

Could it be because he was not mortal?

The thought gave Averil serious pause. Gereint was godborn as the countryfolk said: a child without a father. His mother had never named the man she lay with, nor had anyone claimed the son who came of it. All that was left for her was a fierce rejection of magic of any kind, and a steadfast refusal to see her son educated in the use of what he had.

If a mage had loved and abandoned her, that would explain much. If he had been more than a mage . . .

There was no such thing in these days. The old gods and daimons were gone, swallowed by the Serpent or by the Young God's Church that took its place. It must have been a wandering conjurer, or a nobleman who paused for a while in a village in the back of beyond and then returned to his proper world and place; or else a wild mage, a madman who captured a farmer's fancy for a day or a week before he blew away like a leaf in the wind of his unbridled magic.

A wild mage would explain a great deal. Averil cut an apple into careful slices and dipped each one in honey, eating it slowly, letting the sweetness fill her mind and drive out these thoughts that had no useful purpose. What did it matter who or what had fathered Gereint? He was what he was, no matter where he had come from.

He was oblivious to such maunderings. He ate heartily, laughed and jested with their host, and covered her silence admirably.

Sometimes she wished she could be as guileless as that. She set aside the last of her dinner, considered the cordial but did not dare fuddle her wits, and waited for the others to finish.

It seemed they had been waiting for her. Their sunny goodwill managed, by a miracle, not to sour her stomach.

Truth to tell, after shipwreck and grief and gnawing frustration, this interlude in undying spring was welcome. If she could let go her fears and lay aside her wariness, she might find something resembling peace.

There was peace in death. She did not want to die quite yet.

She inclined her head to Messire Perrin and schooled her face to an expression of cool civility. "I thank you for your hospitality," she said.

He bowed in return. "You are most welcome."

That dispensed with the proprieties. Averil folded her arms on the table and leaned toward him. "Now then, messire. You didn't bring us here for the pleasure of our company. What do you want of us?"

He grinned. "That felt good, didn't it? How long have you been holding yourself in?"

"Too long," she said.

"Courts are a terrible strain on honest tempers," he agreed.

He had charm, Averil granted that. She was not going to be tricked into liking him. "Will you answer my question?"

He bowed with just enough mockery to sting, but not enough to spark her into anger. "I have a question for you, lady. What do you know of the Knights' great Mystery?"

She had not expected that at all, but it seemed Perrin thrived on the unexpected. Her answer was blunt but polite enough. "Less than the Knights do, I'm sure. The king of Lys is hunting it; his rivals hope he finds it so that they can capture it. The Knights would know where it is. Have you asked?"

"The Knights know nothing," Perrin said. "Those who did are dead."

"Who did know?" Gereint asked.

Perrin answered without hesitation. "The Grand Master, his two most trusted Knight Commanders, and the Knight who kept it. Only four, and only those four, since the order began."

"So then," said Gereint, "if the king captured and killed all of them, why doesn't he have the Serpent's prison?"

"Maybe it's not a physical thing," Averil said. "If it's knowledge, or a spell committed to memory, then it's lost. There won't be any getting it back."

Gereint shook his head. "That doesn't make sense. All the magic the Knights work is tangible magic. The other Mysteries are real in this world. Surely the great one would be more real than any."

Perrin applauded him, to his visible confusion. "Well and wisely spoken! Yes, the Mystery is a thing that the hand can touch."

"You know that, and you ask me?" said Averil.

"What I know is old knowledge," he said. For the first time since they had met again, his face was somber. His eyes were the color of the rain in Caermor, greyed silver with a faint glimmer of light beneath. "After the Fall and the working that imprisoned the Old One, Melusine entrusted it to her lover, Longinus."

"Melusine?" said Averil, startled. "The Betrayer? She was never the first Knight's beloved."

"So the Church would have its children believe," Perrin said. "They teach that Longinus would not take a lover until the Lady Magdalen, whose name has since been softened to Madeleine, obeying the good God's will, reft away his wits with wine and conceived their two heirs: Gahmuret the prince and Emeraude the beautiful, great in magic. That's a pretty story, but it was never Madeleine who bore him those children. She took them after the Fall and gave them her name, knowing what infamy their mother had won for herself."

Averil did not feel anything, not yet. It was too deep a shock. She could not believe it.

"I am descended from Gahmuret," she said—quietly, she hoped, and calmly. "Are you telling me that my whole inheritance is a lie?"

"Your inheritance is high and noble," said Perrin, "and the lady who began your line made a choice that she knew would damn her in the world's eyes forever. She betrayed the Young God, yes—at his command. It was a trap into which the Serpent and its servants fell, and so they were destroyed."

Averil's head had begun to ache. "The Young God *asked* her to do it? That's heresy."

"The truth often is," said Perrin.

"Then why does the Church teach otherwise?"

"Because," he said, "she had enemies, and they prevailed. Those who told the truth were cast out or killed. Her children were safe only because they were born just before the Fall, and few knew of their existence. When Madeleine joined with Longinus to spin their tale, the world believed them. Those who doubted or who remembered the time before, when Longinus and Melusine were famous lovers, either came to mistrust the memory or believed they honored Longinus by never speaking of it."

Averil squeezed her eyes shut and pressed her palms to them. "I don't think I can believe you. How do you know this?"

"I remember," he said.

She lowered her hands and opened her eyes. He was not looking at her or at anything in this age of the world. His voice was soft and his gaze remote, fixed on things that had passed two thousand years ago.

"She was a daimon's child," he said, "with all the beauty of that blood, and all the magic, too. Her children inherited both. She died willingly, knowing what would come of it; and with her last strength she laid the Mystery in Longinus' hands. 'Guard it,' she said. 'Never let it go. If the working fails, you know what will come.'

"Longinus nearly cast it away in horror and grief, but even as she died, she held his hands over it until he clasped it close. He kept it all his life, and when he died, he passed it to his most trusted pupil. And so it passed down from generation to generation."

"What is it, then?" Gereint asked in Averil's silence. "Do you remember?"

"It changes," said Perrin. "From age to age and keeper to keeper, it takes whatever shape serves it best. It's been a necklace, a belt, a gauntlet, a helm, a dagger—different each time, but always in one respect the same."

"And that is?"

"It comes in a form that stays close to its keeper."

"Logical," said Gereint. "You know where it is now, don't you?"

Perrin shook his head. "I know where it was. After the Rose fell, it vanished. No Knight living preserves the secret. And yet someone, somewhere, has it. Someone who perhaps doesn't know what he has."

Averil's hand rose of her own accord to the pendant that she never took off even to bathe. It was preposterous, of course. It was a gift, that was all, a trinket to which she was unreasonably attached.

Gereint had had the same thought. "Who had it last? What was his name?"

"I don't know," said Perrin. "It was a Knight of rank, but he must have been old when the Rose fell: the Mystery had not moved or changed in forty years."

"Maybe it's still in one of the chapter houses," said Gereint, "or the Mother House itself. If no one knows what to look for, even the king might have passed over it."

"It is possible," said Perrin, but he did not sound as if he believed it. "Tell me, messire. Were you given a gift by any of the Knights?"

Gereint started slightly, just enough for Averil to see. His eyes darted toward her and then away. "An old man gave me a bauble," he said, "when I went from the Mother House to the duke's palace. But it can't be—"

"May I see it?"

"I don't have it," said Gereint.

"But it is here."

Averil's heart should have been screaming at her to escape while she could—for if her pretty pendant was the greatest Mystery of the Rose, this could well be a trap and the world itself could be about to fall. But she felt no fear aside from what any sane person should feel on being told that she guarded the Serpent's prison. She neither liked nor trusted Perrin, but whatever he wanted, it was not to free the Serpent. That much was clear in the eyes that came to rest on her.

Slowly she drew the pendant from her bodice, holding it up by the chain. Her hand trembled; the brightly enameled disk spun and sparkled. It felt no more magical than it ever did. No bolt of fire pierced her; no monstrous beast of ancient days rose up to devour her.

Perrin made no move to take it. "Ah," was all he said.

"Well?" she said. "Is this what you think it is?"

"May I touch it?" he asked.

She wondered at his diffidence, but again she felt no fear. Maybe it was the pendant working on her. Maybe she had gone numb with the shock of so many revelations at once.

She cupped the pendant in her palm and held it so that he could touch. He barely brushed it with a fingertip, then drew away.

She had not felt anything. The enamelwork gleamed, no more or less lovely than it had ever been. The shapes within it coiled like vines—or serpents.

She peered at it as if it had been a scrying glass. It was as opaque as ever. The vision she had seen in the cavern beneath the royal hunting lodge did not come to her here or now.

Perrin sat back and drew a long breath. "Yes," he said. "May the gods help us, yes."

21

"How can you tell?" Gereint demanded.

Perrin reached across the table, got hold of his hand before he could escape, and held it over the pendant that was still in Averil's palm.

Averil frowned. Gereint did not feel anything apart from the mingled pattern of spirit and magic that made her who she was.

The pendant made the pattern a little warmer, a little more complicated. Its colors gleamed jewel-bright. Those *were* serpents; he had always wondered whether they were leaves or vines or some pattern of the jeweler's fancy.

There was something inside. He could not quite see it, but he felt it. It coiled upon itself, serene in its bubble out of time, dreaming cold and scaly dreams.

He looked up into Averil's eyes. She saw because he did: the magic had roused in both of them, giving him sight and her understanding.

Very, very carefully she slipped the chain from around her neck and laid the pendant on the table. It lay gleaming, red and gold and green and blue, as harmless to look at as any bauble in a peddler's pack.

"I don't think I'm meant to have this," she said. "The old Knight gave it to you."

"No," said Gereint. "It's yours. Didn't you hear what Messire

Perrin said? Your ancestors had it first. It's your inheritance."

"It's not one I ever asked for," she said.

"That's often so," said Perrin. "I do believe it was meant to come to you—or, I think, to both of you. What you have between you is very like what we saw between Longinus and his Melusine."

Averil shivered. Gereint felt a slight chill himself, to think that she had come by this through the Betrayer—even if Perrin had said that the truth was very different. It still did not explain where Gereint had got it; but nothing much about that was explicable.

He seized on the one thing that he had not known. "There have been others like us? Was it the same?"

"Very much the same," said Perrin, "and none of us had ever seen its like, or thought to see it again. It may be an omen that it's come back in this age of the world."

"An omen of what?" Averil asked, almost too low to be heard. "My turning traitor and giving myself up to death?"

"I should hope not," Gereint said so robustly she started. He softened his voice as much as he could. That was getting harder the older he grew and the deeper it went. "You aren't Melusine, and this isn't the age she lived in. We're wiser in some things. Whatever we've forgotten, we've gained somewhat more. Magic is different now. You can use it to keep your soul safe."

"Maybe," she said, "but what if I have the same weakness in me that she had? Even if I believe that the Young God asked her to betray him, she consented to it. She served the Serpent. She died of its poison."

"She died when it understood what she had done," Perrin said. They had almost forgotten he was there. "The Young

God was nearly defeated. Her fall caused him to rally and strike the final blow. The eruption of her magic out of her dying body built the prison; the rest of the Ladies secured it and trapped the Serpent within. With her last breath she bequeathed it to her beloved. If she had not done what she did or died when she did, there would have been no victory, no prison, and no world as we know it." He paused to compose himself. "If that is weakness, lady, then I pray we all be so feeble."

Averil lowered her eyes. It was interesting to see how well she took the rebuke: she had got a bit above herself since Gereint first met her. Humility suited her better than royal pride.

He would hardly speak those thoughts aloud, but he thought Perrin might be thinking the same. The mage had a look about him, almost amused and distinctly indulgent. The passion of a moment before was gone.

"What was your name?" Gereint asked him.

"Peredur," he answered, simply and without hesitation.

Gereint's heart stopped. "Not—that—?"

"Yes, I am that Peredur," said the man he had known as Perrin—not so far off, after all.

The youngest Paladin, the Young God's beloved. Alive, here, showing at most thirty of his two thousand years.

"How?" asked Gereint. It came out as a gust of air, hardly a word at all.

"An accident of birth," said Peredur. "My father was a lesser god. My mother was a mistress of what you would call the wild magic."

"No," said Averil, striking her fist on the table. "Enough of that. The Paladins were mortal mages. And they are all dead. Every one."

"Not I," said Peredur, who was also an herbalist in Fontevrai and a Power in the Wildlands and the Myrddin of Prydain.

Why should he not be the last Paladin? In spite of Averil's words, nothing in doctrine said that they were all human, only that they had been powerful in magic and devoted to the Young God. Powerful this one certainly was, and he had spoken of the Betrayer with such beauty and passion that Gereint was sure he had known her.

Of all the wonders Gereint had seen since he ran away to the Knights, this was one of the greatest. But it came at a price. His finger brushed the pendant, not quite touching it. "This should be yours," he said. "You're the greatest of all of us. You were a Paladin; you walked with the Young God. You saw this thing made. Who better to guard it?"

"That task was not given me," Peredur said. "Mine is to guard the guardian."

"Why?"

"Think," said Peredur. "With each keeper, the Mystery changes. One keeper and one semblance would be too easy to find."

"I suppose," said Gereint, "but if it had been well enough hidden in the beginning, why would it need more? How can anyone find it unless he knows where it is, or knows enough to guess where it went?"

"With some part of the Serpent's body and a seeking spell," Peredur said, "it can be done."

Gereint had not wanted there to be an answer, still less one so devastatingly simple. He grasped at what straws he could. "Surely there's none of those left in the world."

"One would hope," said Peredur. His tone was colorless.

"If there is any such thing, Clodovec will find it—or his rivals will." Averil stared down at her fists, which were clenched in front of her. "Would it be safe here? No one in these days looks toward the Wildlands."

"Spells of seeking and the conjuring of like with like are older than your orders, and run deeper into the earth," Peredur said. "Wherever this thing goes, our enemies can find it."

"I was afraid you would say that," Averil said. She sounded almost resigned. "No one has ever wanted this gift, has he?"

"Or she," said Peredur. "Now and then it has passed to one of the Ladies. Both the Isle and the Rose have defended it."

"I'm neither," Averil said.

"You're both." Gereint's hands covered hers. "Lady, we'll guard it together. That's what we're for, isn't it?" he said to Peredur. "That's why there are two of us."

Peredur nodded slowly. "It would seem so."

Averil's hands were cold in Gereint's. He coaxed them out of their tight fists and warmed them between his palms. She had had enough of words for a while; he gave her silence.

It had always been harder for her. To him, all magic was strange and new and barely understood. She was used to thinking of it as something that could be framed in orders and constrained into mortal sense. Wild magic frightened her, though she would have been outraged if he had said so.

This was wilder than wild magic. There was no control on it, and no order or rule that constrained it. It was entirely itself.

She was growing warmer; the tension was draining from her. He relaxed a little himself.

Abruptly she stiffened and slid her hands out of his. She would not look at him. He might have taken her expression for anger, but he knew her better than that. She was perilously close to tears.

Damn the laws that kept them apart. Damn the tradition

that would not let them be what the Paladin and his Lady had been.

Gereint reined in his temper before it struck fire in his magic. He turned toward Peredur and did his best not to think about Averil. "What do we do, then, messire? It seems we're at an impasse. We can't go forward. We daren't go back. Where can we go?"

"I think," said Averil, "that for now we should go back to Prydain. If we act any differently, we'll arouse suspicion. We have to pretend that nothing has changed."

She had mastered herself as she always did. Her words were cool, crisp, with no apparent memory of weakness.

"Some things have to change," Gereint said. "Mauritius needs to know where the Mystery is. Father Owein, too."

"And the queen," said Averil, "but no more."

"Yes," said Peredur.

"Do they know?" Gereint asked. "What you are?"

Peredur shook his head.

"Maybe they should," Averil said.

"I don't think so," said Gereint. "It's hard enough for you. Mauritius is taxed to his limit as it is, and he has the weight of the world on him, with the Rose so broken and the Isle in such danger. If he doesn't need to know, it's a kindness to spare him."

"Secrets," she said with surprising venom. "When do they turn to lies? Why should they exist at all? This thing"—her hand flicked toward the pendant—"should not have been. Why was the prisoner allowed to live? Why wasn't it destroyed?"

"That choice was made on the Field of the Binding," said Peredur.

"But why?" Averil cried.

She was nearer her limit than Mauritius could possibly be. Gereint could not even touch her this time, to comfort her. She had spun away toward the far side of the room and pressed her back to the wall, as if she were as much a prisoner as the Serpent.

"Lady," Peredur said gently, "we couldn't destroy it. Not for lack of strength, no; we had the Young God triumphant, with all the power of heaven. When we would have raised it against the Fallen, he stopped us. 'That is not written,' he said. And that was all he would say."

" 'The world contains the seeds of its own destruction.' " Gereint spoke the words without pleasure. An old philosopher had written them; they were pagan nonsense, he had been taught, and rank heresy.

But they were taught—because, he realized, they were true. They were a Mystery, bound up in this thing that lay on the table, looking so innocent and so unmagical.

"Think about a seed," Peredur said. His warm deep purr of a voice seemed to rise out of Gereint's own thoughts. "Have you ever burned a field or a wood to make it grow greener after? The earth is richer for the fire; the grain grows taller and the trees grow stronger. Would any of us be what we are without the Binding?"

"That was great bloodshed and terrible suffering," Averil said, "and it was meant never to happen again."

"No war has ever ended war," said Peredur.

Averil lifted the pendant from the table. Her hand shook as she slipped the chain over her head; she flinched as it touched her breast, then drew a deep breath and stood firm. "When this latest war is over," she said, "we are going to destroy this thing. I don't care what it's supposed to do. As long as it exists, it threatens everything we are and can be."

Peredur spread his hands—not exactly in surrender, but the inclination of his head offered sincere respect. Gereint bowed back.

Averil did neither. "We have to go," she said. "If you please, messire, show us the way."

Peredur pointed toward the hearth, where the fire had died to an arch of ash. "There is the door," he said. "Come. Follow me."

It was a sign of how perturbed she was that she took the hand he offered and followed him without a word. She did it so quickly that Gereint was almost left behind. Even as the two of them shrank and vanished into the remains of the fire, he stepped in himself. There was a moment of dizzy nothingness; then he fell into grey light and the smell of rain and the chill of autumn turning toward winter.

22

ONCE MORE THE pendant gleamed on a table under a circle of eyes. This one stood in the queen's privy chamber, and the light that shone there was mortal lamplight. The Wildlands were far away across the sea, in another world and perhaps another time.

Mauritius and Owein and Eiluned heard the tale in silence. Averil had to tell it: Peredur would not, and Gereint had gone tongue-tied in the presence of royalty.

She would deal with those two later. On this dark and rain-soaked evening, she told the Knights and the queen all that she knew of the old Knight's gift, though not what she knew of Peredur. Then she sat in silence while they pondered it.

Even without the fact that the Myrddin of Prydain was the last of the Paladins, it was a great deal to take in. They did so without haste, warmed with wine and a platter of food from the kitchens: solid fare to fill the stomach and feed the mind.

Averil caught herself dozing off. She had not slept since the day before yesterday; she had walked between worlds and learned things that with all her heart she wanted not to know. Now, in the warmth and the quiet, she fought back sleep.

As she hovered on the threshold, dreams washed over her like slow waves of the sea. She saw ships sailing—black ships innumerable—and Ladies dancing in their circle by the lake of glass, and Knights in a tournament, breaking lances with a great tumult of clashing steel and splintered wood.

There was nothing there that she did not already know; nothing that she would call foresight. She rested her head on her hand and let her eyes drift shut.

Leaves fell through dim and misty air, rattling to the half-seen ground. They were oddly shaped and much larger than leaves were wont to be, even the broad leaves of the linden, and their color was like silvered iron.

They were scales, each as large as a small shield. They heaped against the trunks of tall stone trees. Through that strange forest she saw shapes moving, shadows with palely gleaming eyes.

One of them she recognized. It was Esteban. The dream transformed him into a devil from a church wall, with cloven hooves and clawed hands and a face burned black by infernal fire.

Even in the dream she knew that was absurd. Esteban was no demon. He was misguided, yes; dangerous, certainly. But he did not serve the lord of Hell.

He served something even more deadly. For that her mind gave him this shape. He clattered on his goat's hooves over the heaps of scales, searching for one in particular out of all the multitudes.

Before she could discover what it was he looked for, Gereint's voice spoke in her ear. "Lady." He said it softly, but then somewhat louder: "Lady!"

She started awake. The queen and the Knights were still deep in thought, but Gereint knelt beside her. He had her hands in his. Again.

He had to stop doing that. But she could not make herself pull away.

"You were fading," he said. "Where did you go?"

"It was just a dream," she said.

"Dreams don't turn a woman to glass. I could see the table through you."

Averil's stomach clenched. She knew of no magic that could do such a thing, or any reason that it should. "Wild magic," she said, almost spitting it. "It's in me somehow, doing things I can't understand."

"I do know a little of that," he said. "Tell me what you dreamed."

"Nothing that made sense," she said.

"Tell me."

"All I saw was confusion," she said with a spark of temper. "Then at the end, I saw devils with familiar faces, and serpents' scales falling like leaves. There was one in particular that they meant to find. You woke me before they found it."

"I woke you before you disappeared." He was shaking, though he looked more angry than afraid. "Whatever the dream was or meant to be, it was swallowing you."

"But why? There was no reason. It was a dream, that was all, and not even a prophetic one. I was thinking of all these things, and they tangled together until my mind in its sleep cast them out."

"There was something there," Gereint said. "Something that means more than we know. Give it to me, lady. Let me have the dream."

She shook her head so hard her sight blurred. "No! If it almost swallowed me, what would it do to you?"

"I'm warned, and you're here. Just let me see."

She did not want to, but he was too close and too strong and too damnably irresistible. The dream was still there, haunting her. As he opened to it, it poured into him.

She held fast to his hands in case he disappeared. But he stayed as he was, broad and solid, frowning at the confusion of images he had taken from her.

"You see?" she said. "It's an ordinary dream. You must have imagined the rest. Were you falling asleep, too?"

He was not listening. His brows were drawn together, his eyes like grey glass. She saw reflected in them the rain of scales and the goat-footed prince.

All the scales were exactly alike, except for one. She did not so much see it as feel it, a shard of glass in a wilderness of grey iron. It opened like an eye and stared directly at her.

It knew her. It had heard every word they spoke in that room. If it was Esteban, they were in danger of betrayal. If it was the king, or perhaps worse, Gamelin, they were in grimmer straits than that.

She threw up every wall and shield she had. Perhaps it was mere fancy, but she heard a cry of pain and felt the unwelcome scrutiny drop away.

God knew what good that would do. Gereint, quicker-witted and more ruthless, sprang in pursuit, but the spy was gone. What little trail he had left vanished swiftly, leaving nothing behind.

Gereint withdrew in frustration. Averil sat within her battery of wards, with a cold sensation in her middle and the grim certainty that she had brought destruction on them all. Someone had bound a spell to her; in the flurry of escape and flight and storm and shipwreck, she had never thought to look for such a thing.

It must be Esteban: else why had he appeared in her dream? He, canny creature that he was, had gambled on exactly what had happened. He had allowed her to escape, knowing he could follow wherever she fled. He knew what she knew, where she was and with whom—everything, all her secrets, down to the last one.

She shrank under the weight of despair. Gereint gripped her shoulders, pulling her upright with roughness that sparked her temper.

Anger burned away desolation, as he had intended. And that made her angrier. Damn these arrogant men, meddlers all and bloody dangerous with it.

Gereint, unlike her enemies, was within reach. She whirled on him.

His shields were up, impressively focused and trained, as a Squire's should be. Even now she had to bow to his skill.

He bowed back, but warily. His wards held firm.

The anger was still in her, but no longer aimed at him. "Help me," she said.

He shook his head. "Not yet. This kind of hunt is better done cold."

"We may not have that much time," she said.

"We have a little," said Peredur.

She had forgotten anyone else was there. All she had seen was the dream and the spy, and Gereint. Always Gereint, wherever she was, whether she wanted him or no.

Did she want him now?

In too many ways to tell.

She looked from Peredur to the Knights and the queen. They were watching without expression. "I'm sorry," she said to them, "for everything I've brought upon you."

"We have our defenses," Eiluned said.

Averil opened her mouth to ask what good those were if she had already passed them, but that would not have been wise. She lowered her eyes and bowed her head. It was not submission, and she knew they would not take it as such.

"The black fleet has sailed," Peredur said.

Averil's head snapped up. The rest were staring, too, as shocked as she was.

"When?" Gereint demanded.

"Just now," said Peredur, "on the evening tide."

"We're safe, then, aren't we?" said Averil. "They didn't sail because of me."

"It is unlikely," Peredur said.

Averil wanted to be reassured, but the way he said it made her back tighten. None of them was safe if the king knew where the Mystery was and who held it.

"I'll go away," she said. "I'll find a place to hide, and be sure to leave a trail, so that he—whoever he is—will follow. Maybe I can even draw the king away from the Isle. If I can borrow a boat, no matter how small, I can lead them all out to sea and let the wind and the storms destroy them."

Peredur tilted his head as if in thought. "An interesting suggestion," he said, "and perhaps even practicable. If the Mystery sank to the bottom of the sea, it might be eons before it came to light again."

"That's deadly dangerous," Gereint said with banked heat, "and a frightful gamble, too. If the Mystery is captured before it sinks, we're all done for."

"What difference does it make if I'm captured here or halfway to the uttermost west? Out on the sea at least, I have a chance of losing the thing before I'm taken."

"No one will be sailing west," the queen said. She did not raise her voice, but Averil's teeth clicked together. "You are our ally and our guest. We will protect you as best we may, and fight as we must. No one will capture or destroy you while we live to defend you."

Fine words, Averil thought, weighing the woman who

spoke them. The king of Lys would have spoken them, too, if he had had the opportunity.

This was by no means another Clodovec. But could Averil trust her? She might have her own reasons for keeping the Mystery within her kingdom.

She was a Lady of the Isle. If Averil could not trust her, then there was no one in this world to trust. She rose only to sink down in a deep curtsey. "I thank you, majesty."

Eiluned raised her with surprisingly strong hands. "Let there be no titles between us," she said. "I would be pleased to call you friend."

"And I," said Averil without pause for thought. Some part of her still harbored misgivings, but that was the remnant of her time in Lutèce. Not every court was like that one; certainly not her own in Quitaine.

It was a grim world indeed if one woman could not share friendship with another, even if one were a duchess and one a queen. Averil let go her fretting and listened for once to her heart, clasped Eiluned's hands and smiled. It was not an easy smile or a steady one, but it would do for a beginning.

23

THE BLACK FLEET had sailed. The Knights followed it in their web of scrying glasses, while the mages of Prydain did their own gazing in basins and pools from end to end of the kingdom. The wards of the realm were raised and the watchtowers guarded, and every eye that could see was fixed on the gleam of nothingness in the aether that was the Ladies' Isle.

Gereint found himself distinctly unwilling to return to the house of the Rose with Mauritius and Father Owein. He knew all too well that that was foolish. Averil was as safe in the queen's palace as she could be in this world, even with that deadly gift he should never have given her.

He should have kept it and the danger that went with it. Then if anyone came hunting, the quarry would be Gereint and not Averil.

Someone would come. He was sure of that in his bones, where the magic was. Even deeper than the magic was the certainty that that person or power would come for Averil because she held the Mystery, and Gereint must be there when he came.

The Knights were still bidding farewell to the ladies. Gereint was of little account, Squire that he was. It took a fair amount of courage to interrupt the exchange of courtesies. "Messires," he said. "Majesty."

They regarded him without anger, with even a degree of respect. That flustered him. He had to pull his wits together before he could go on. "If you don't terribly mind," he said, "may I guard the lady? It's my fault she needs it."

He was careful not to notice Averil's expression. Mauritius' was more to the point. Gereint held his breath until he began to grow dizzy; then he breathed shallowly, standing at attention as he had been taught.

The Knight frowned, rubbing the side of his long arched nose. He slanted a glance at Father Owein. The elder Knight shrugged slightly.

"There is a precedent," Mauritius observed, "but we have no house of the Rose in this palace as we did in the lady's. How will we account for you?"

"Give him to me," said Peredur. "Name him my apprentice if you will—and so he will be when he can be spared from the rest of his duties."

Mauritius' brow arched. "Indeed, messire, that is an honor. I must only ask, do you know aught of weapons? That is his greatest weakness."

"I do know somewhat," said Peredur without apparent irony.

Gereint bit his tongue. If he leaped in with what he knew, he would complicate matters immeasurably. He could only keep silent and let them settle it between them.

"One of my elder Squires will assist you with his training in arms," Mauritius said after a moment's pause. "At intervals we may call on him to be examined for both knowledge and skill."

"As you will, messire," said Peredur. Apparently he was not insulted to have his skill questioned so. If anything he seemed to find it amusing.

Then at last the Knights saw fit to take their leave. Gereint wondered even then if he would be called to follow, but apart from a glance he could not read and a nod that was clear enough, Mauritius had nothing to say. Nor did the queen speak except to bid them a civil good evening.

That left Gereint and Peredur, and Averil still seated at the table. The heat that came off her made Gereint's skin prickle. When she rose, he fought the urge to fall back a step.

She said none of the things he expected, but nodded to Peredur. "Messire," she said. To Gereint she said nothing.

When she turned and strode toward the door, he had to push himself to follow. Peredur made no move to stop him.

Nor did she. In fact she ignored him completely. That stung, however richly he might have deserved it. Still, it felt as right as it ever had to walk behind her, silent and watchful, following where she led.

AVERIL WAS NOT at all pleased to be passed from hand to hand like baggage. She was even less pleased by the leap of her heart when Gereint won leave to play guardsman as he had in Fontevrai.

None of their elders seemed in the least concerned with proprieties; and they should have been. Gereint might be a saint, but Averil was not. The colder she tried to be, the hotter she burned inside; the harder she tried not to think of him, the more he filled her mind.

It was a diversion at least from the greater fear, the weight of the Mystery that was so slight and yet so terrible, hidden beneath her chemise. She let Gereint find his own way through her rooms, while she went about her preparations for what sleep the night might bring.

Not long after she had sent the servants away with the remains of a bath, a second Squire appeared at the door: Gereint's friend and teacher Riquier, laden with Gereint's belongings and an assortment of weapons. She half hoped he would stay, but after a few courtesies and a promise to return in the morning for sword practice, he went back to the house of the Rose.

Then it was only the two of them. There were servants within call, but no maid or guard to watch out for Averil's virtue.

She would have to do it herself. The difficulty, she thought, was in wanting it sufficiently. Gereint settled his possessions in the alcove that would have belonged to the maid if Averil had still had one, but carried the pallet out into the larger room and laid it across the door.

Her bed was a room in itself, a cushioned and curtained closet with a grated window that opened on a courtyard far below. It was too small to afford escape, and its grating was wrought of iron, bolted into the wall. Only an insect or a very small and insubstantial fey could enter or leave that way.

Averil meant to retreat into that cupboard and hide until morning. Gereint stripped to shirt and hose and laid out a short sword and a knife beside the pallet. Then he knelt and bowed his head as if to pray.

She supposed one might call it prayer, if prayer was calling up powers and weaving wards around the room. It was well done. She could hardly have done better herself.

When he raised his head, she was sitting on her heels just out of reach, contemplating the protections he had raised. She pretended not to see how he frowned. Let him fret; it was no more than he deserved.

After a while she said, "You should never have done this."

"Why, did you want to raise the wards yourself? Lady, I didn't mean—"

She raised her hand. He stopped his babbling. "You know I don't care about that," she said. "Why did you insist on coming here? We were both better off with me in this room and you in the chapter house."

"Maybe we were," he said, "but that was before we knew what you carry. It needs both of us, lady. If we're separated when the blow falls, there may not be time to do what's necessary."

"What's necessary? How do you know what that is? How do you know anything?"

"Lady," he said with deliberate calm, "I do know a little now. Maybe not as much as Messire Peredur knows of weapons, but enough. The rest is in you."

"It's the rest of what's in me that troubles me," she said grimly.

It was hard to tell in lamplight, but his cheeks might have gone a few shades darker. "Surely we're strong enough to overcome that."

"Are you?"

"I have to be," he said.

Fortunate man, to see the world with such simplicity. Averil slipped the chain from around her neck and held out the deceptively simple thing that had caused such sorrow. "You take this, then. Guard it instead of me. Find someone else to take it if you can. Then when they come looking for me, they'll find nothing but a duchess in exile, looking for a man she can honorably marry."

He did not flinch at that, though she had meant him to. Nor did he move to take the pendant. "If it were that easy, don't you think the Knights or the queen would have told us to do it? This thing comes to the one it chooses. You can't give it away until your time is over."

"That may be sooner than any of us would like," she said.

"Not if I can help it."

She wanted to sneer at him, to drive him away, but she could not be that false, even to save them both. She slipped the pendant back beneath her chemise and sighed. "Do you think God is laughing at us? Or is it some other power that made us this way?"

"I don't think the Mother cares for mortal laws," he said.

"I know she doesn't. But we're mortals. We have to care."

"Maybe we're not supposed to," he said.

"Don't say that," she said.

"What if it's true? What if everything we've been taught is wrong? Why are we like this, if we can't be what we were so clearly meant to be? Are we some god's mistake?"

She pushed herself to her feet and backed away. "Stop it. You're talking like the Serpent's cult."

He blanched, but the dam had broken. He could not stop, any more than she could. "We can't go on like this, lady. I can't believe we're supposed to suffer like monks in the fasting season, tormenting ourselves with visions of banquets. There must be a reason for all of this—and a way through it."

"Maybe there is," she said. "Maybe we'll both be dead before we go out of our minds with wanting one another."

"I don't want to die," he said. "I want to win this war and be rid of the Mystery. Then I want the world to change. How can anything between us be a sin? Didn't God make us as we are?"

She pressed her hands to her ears. It did little good. His frustration roiled inside her, matching her own exactly.

"This was badly done," she said. "You should have stayed away. We're not the innocents we were. All we do is torture each other."

"Torture or no," he said, "we're safer together than apart."

"This is safe?"

"Would you rather be dead in body and soul than dishonored?"

"Yes!" she cried.

"You don't mean that."

Damned bloody peasant, stubborn as one of his own mules. Lethally clear-sighted, too. No one could see as far or as straight as Gereint.

He saw straight through her. She wanted to hate him for it—it would make matters easier. It was all she could do not to love him even more than she already did.

"What can we do?" she demanded. "What can we ever hope for? I don't want to make a noble sacrifice. I don't want to marry a noble husband, either. I want you. But I can't have you."

His eyes narrowed. "Did Longinus marry Melusine? He didn't marry Madeleine, I know that. Our priest in Rémy took great offense at it. He was always preaching sermons against following their example."

"Nor can we follow it now," she said, though hope kept trying to wake inside her.

"Why? Is there really a law written that says you have to marry? What if you take vows after all and become a Lady? You can't marry then, can you? Do the laws balance one another out?"

"You've been studying logic," she said. "Do you realize how dangerous that is?"

His grin startled her. "That's what Riquier says. He's my

best teacher. Ladies don't marry, yes? But they aren't forbidden to bear children. There's no taint of bastardy in the offspring, either, is there? Because they're Ladies. It's the same with Knights: there are lines of them in the order. Mauritius comes from one: Knight to Knight all the way back to Gahmuret. Riquier, too—he goes to blessed Ilderim. Aren't there lines of Ladies as well?"

"Has no one taught you the truth?" she said with a hint of sharpness. "Ladies can win a dispensation to marry if their rank or bloodline requires it—or they can bear a child without taint of bastardy. My mother was a Lady. I still can't marry you, even if you happened to leave the Knights. I can never marry you. That is the law and it is written. Noble and common cannot be joined in honor, whatever they may be in love."

"That is a very bad law."

"It protects the blood from dilution," she said, "and preserves its holiness. It's a sacred thing. The sacred is not logical."

"There is nothing sacred about ink on parchment," Gereint muttered. "I'll tell you what is holy. When I look at you, I see the glory of the God who made you. I bless Him for it— or Her; who knows? He made us for one another. Our magic is two parts of one whole. Our hearts are the same. Our bodies would be if we weren't shackled by mortal foolishness."

"And that is why you can't stay here," she said, though her throat was trying to close. "Foolish or no, it's what is. I can't offer my suffering to God. I'm not that close to sainthood."

"Then don't," he said. "Grit your teeth and bear it. Because I'm not leaving you. We need each other. Our magic needs us—and so does this kingdom. Will you see it destroyed because you can't stand the sight of me?"

"It's not that I can't stand you," she said in a kind of despair. "It's that I like the sight of you too much."

"Why? I'm not even pretty."

He might never understand why she burst out laughing. It was that or cry herself into a fit. She rather hoped she had offended him, but he was not as fragile as that.

When she could speak again, her words were vastly unwise. "If I wanted pretty, I'd have taken the prince from Moresca—serpent magic and all. Pretty is not my weakness. Big and foolish clearly is. And strong. And stubborn. And sometimes downright hateful."

That did sting him. "I am not—"

"You are human," she said. "And flawed. And so perfectly a part of me that before God and the Mother, I don't know what we're going to do. Because this world isn't made for us, and the one that is, is the one we're trying our hardest to keep from being born."

"Then we need to make a new world," he said. "One that isn't enslaved to either Church or Serpent. Where the laws are few and sensible, and love can be what it's meant to be."

"Can such a world exist? Won't it tear itself apart?"

"Wouldn't you like to see?"

She shook her head. Her eyes were full of tears. She was exhausted and she had brought a spy into this haven and she had discovered that the trinket she cherished because it was his gift, was the most terrible thing in the world.

She willed Gereint not to touch or comfort her—then when he kept his hands to himself, she came near to hating him for it. "Go away," she said.

"I can't." He sounded as overwhelmed as she felt, but it was not enough to shake his resolve. "Please, lady. Go to sleep. Let me do what you know I have to do. Let me guard you."

"Will you guard my bed?"

"No." He rose, looming over her; then he shocked her speechless by sweeping her up with barely a grunt of effort and depositing her unceremoniously in the bed. "Good night, lady," he said firmly.

She stayed where he had left her, not because of any inclination toward obedience, but because her body would not move. The featherbed was soft and warm; it tempted her with comfort even in the midst of her anguish.

It seemed she had let go the worst of it. The rest was just bearable enough to let sleep wash in like a tide. She tried to fight it off in fear of what dreams it might bring, but all her strength was gone.

She would have to trust that Gereint would protect her even on the other side of sleep. She could feel him there, standing guard like a stone knight in a cathedral. Far more secure than she wanted to be, and far more reassured by that unrelenting presence, she let herself fall as into deep water.

24

RIQUIER WAS AT the door before dawn, calling Gereint to the morning's exercises. Gereint had hardly slept all night, and not only because of the words he had exchanged with Averil. But nothing had threatened either of them.

He was tired and slow-witted as he got up and washed in the basin and put on his clothes, but Riquier gave no quarter and Gereint asked for none. As he retrieved the bundle of practice blades from the alcove, he turned and nearly jumped out of his skin.

Averil was up, dressed, and wide awake, with her hair plaited and a look of grim determination on her face. She was prepared for a fight. He was half inclined to give her one, but in the end he decided against it. She could watch his morning humiliation; it might coax a smile out of her.

Riquier raised a brow but offered no objection, either. The three of them left the room together, with Riquier leading.

Gereint had expected him to go as far as the chapter house, but he stopped well short of it. Near the palace wall was a guardroom, empty of men but well equipped with weapons and accoutrements. The center of it was a swept and sandy floor, lit by a circle of windows in the walls above.

The sky was still dark, the dawn barely broken, but there was light in the circle and a figure in it, armed with a sword.

He had no opponent but his shadow, and yet he was doing battle with rhythm and cadence and breathtaking precision. It was a dance of edged steel, beautiful and deadly.

Gereint stopped to stare, with Averil close behind him. Riquier moved out onto the sand as if stalking the dancer, so intent he seemed to have forgotten anything but the dance.

The swordsman was Peredur. Gereint was not the best judge of the art, but if he had needed proof that the man was a Paladin, this would have been enough.

Riquier studied the dance for a long while. Then he raised his sword and ventured one of the movements, mirroring Peredur's; thereafter he tried another and another, finding the rhythm with the ease of a born fighting man.

Little by little Peredur shifted his own rhythm until they were dancing together, stroke and stroke and stroke again. The touch of blades at first was light, but as the dance went on, they engaged in earnest. Riquier was a noted swordsman, but Peredur matched him easily, with grace and strength that seemed more than a little inhuman.

He was not trying to defeat Riquier, only to test his skills as far as they would go. Riquier's face gleamed with sweat, but Peredur was as cool as ever. He was smiling. So was Riquier—though his smile had stretched into a grimace.

At last Peredur had mercy on him. He slowed the dance until Riquier's breathing quieted.

It was slow enough and simple enough that Gereint felt moved to follow it himself. So, he noticed, did Averil. She had a blade of her own, which he had not even known she had.

She had more grace than Gereint, and more skill, too. It was a strange and heady sensation to dance with her, separate and yet bound by the movements they shared. All four of them matched pace and pace, with Peredur leading so subtly that his guidance was almost imperceptible.

It was a kind of magic. It absorbed the whole body in a trance of motion, shaped and molded it until it could move in one way and no other. Gereint's center was deeper than it had ever been, his understanding more complete.

For the first time this was more than rote exercise. He had had a taste of it when he was tested, when he fought against himself and wrought a great working out of it; but this was stronger. It almost made him think that he could be a swordsman.

He was sorry when it ended, and startled that he was running with sweat, with muscles aching that he had not known he had. They all united in a salute, then lowered their blades. Gereint's shook the worst. Averil's was almost steady.

She was beautiful with a blade. So was Riquier. Peredur was beyond beauty.

In two thousand years, a man could become a master a hundred times over. Gereint wanted what Peredur had, though it be only the tiniest fraction.

He was exhausted but exhilarated. Every day he could have this. Every morning, if his body could stand it.

It would. He would make sure of that. So, he knew, would Peredur.

Peredur had taken Gereint in hand—for what reason Gereint did not know. His excess of magic, he supposed. Mages were unduly fascinated by that. And he had kept the Mystery for a while, and he was still part of Averil, who kept it now. He supposed he was interesting.

Riquier had his breath back, and his voice, too. "Messire, I must apologize for my superior. To think I could add to anything you have to teach—"

"Your commander is a wise man," said Peredur.

Riquier's eyes widened in surprise.

"It's the learning that matters, messire—whoever does the teaching."

"Will you teach me?"

"Gladly," Peredur said.

Riquier bowed to him with respect bordering on awe. He had no need to know what else Peredur was, only that he was a master of the sword.

There was a lesson in that for Gereint, though it did not help him with Averil. She had not said a word to him yet this morning, nor spared him a glance. He understood that, though he did not have to like it.

He followed the others from the guardroom in the morning light. Peredur had the library in mind, and further instruction; Riquier should have returned to the chapter house, but could not tear himself away. Averil seemed determined to stay with them wherever they went.

Gereint must have acquitted himself decently with the books: none of them took him to task for inattentiveness. Averil, similarly distracted, received a gentle but firm rebuke. Gereint nearly leaped to her defense before he remembered that he was not her guardsman here; by her apparent choice, she was a pupil as he was.

So was Riquier, and that was a little disconcerting. In Gereint's world, Riquier had always been the teacher. As young as he was, he was well up the ranks, almost within reach of becoming a Knight.

Before Peredur he was nearly as much of a child as the others—and he seemed glad of it. Peredur knew more than the sword. He had a clear eye and a deep understanding of magic.

That first day he did nothing overtly magical. He taught them not from books, though they sat together in the queen's library, but from memory. He spoke of Paladins and Ladies and the Young God before he bound the Serpent.

It was nothing they did not already know; Gereint had heard it all from the priest in church. And yet Peredur told it as one who had been there. "In those days, no man's soul was safe, and no woman could hope to escape from the breeding of sons to feed the Serpent's hunger. The last mages, the Young God's allies, had to gather such magic as was left in earth and air, conceal it from the Serpent's slaves, then wield it against all odds and in the face of potent opposition. They were masters of wards and concealment—by necessity—but they had no surety that they would succeed. They lived in fear: of loss, of betrayal, of their souls' destruction."

"You think we're soft and spoiled in these days," Averil said.

"Maybe we have more to lose," said Gereint.

She took a dim view of that, from her expression, but Peredur nodded. "The world has become richer and in many ways stranger. For all the things it has lost, it has gained at least as much more. We have more to defend, but also less knowledge of what we fight against."

"There are some who know," Averil said. "They've kept the serpent magic alive for all these centuries. How is it that no one ever found them? Did they take on the Paladins' arts of warding and concealment? Or were they allowed to live? What do we not know, that for our lives' and souls' sake we should?"

Peredur eyed her narrowly. "Have you had a foreseeing, lady?"

She shook her head. "My bones itch. That's all. Something is out there, and we're missing it."

"That's what wards are for," Gereint said: "to protect against the unexpected."

"They haven't protected us against Clodovec."

Gereint acknowledged the stroke with a swordsman's salute. "Do we want to scry, then? Or learn a new way to search for what we can't see and aren't sure of?"

"Search your heart," Peredur said.

She rolled an eye at him. "That's not where the truth is."

"On the contrary," he said. "The truth is always there. You only have to find it."

"My heart has put us all in danger," she said bitterly. "Why should I trust it?"

"What else is there to trust?"

She shied like a startled horse and bolted. Gereint barely had time for a glance of reproach before he darted in pursuit. Peredur looked not at all repentant, and not at all surprised, either.

Maybe Averil was right about him. Maybe he was as dangerous as she feared.

But then she feared she was worse. Gereint had no choice but to follow his heart—and that persisted in trusting them both, no matter what they thought of one another. If that made him a gullible fool, then so be it.

25

AVERIL'S WORLD WAS out of joint. Everything she had set her hand to had failed. All she had left was exile, betrayal, and a man she could not have.

Even while she wallowed in her failures, she knew she should pull herself up and face what had to be faced. It was not her way to indulge in self-pity. But Peredur had set a barb in her heart. The more she fought it, the more ruthlessly it tore.

Her flight carried her out of the palace past guards who made no move to stop her. Caermor's streets were full of people taking advantage of a day without rain: clear sky and bright sun and startling, wintry cold.

Gereint caught her near the clothiers' market and flung a cloak over her shoulders. He must have conjured it out of air: she did not recognize it and he was too tall for it. She wrapped herself in the thick deep-green wool, basking in its warmth.

He had the sense not to say anything. She let her feet take her where they would, wandering through the city with Gereint looming large and silent at her back.

She had seen precious little of Caermor since she came here, and that only around the palace. It was a larger city than she had expected, and parts of it were distinctly odd.

Because there had been no flocks of wildfolk crowding the

palace, she had come to think that kind did not live in cities here, though they existed in plenty beyond the walls. As she made her way through the streets and alleys, the market squares and even the cathedral close, she realized how wrong she had been. Like Dylan Fawr's poor lost ship, this city was full of people who were not precisely human.

It was not always obvious. The wildfolk across the sea were as odd as living beings could be; few of them chose to look more than vaguely human. These of Prydain seemed to have agreed that it was better to match the populace than to outrage it with strangeness. It was only out of the corner of her eye that she caught the oddities: a cat's eye in a round brown face, an ear as delicately curved as a leaf half-furled, a man who stood no higher than her waist but bulked as broad as Gereint.

They lived and worked and drank and chaffered as freely here as any human folk. When she paused, lured by the rich smell of meat pasties baking, Gereint bought a napkinful for a copper penny. The baker was a very tall and willowy person of ambiguous gender, with eyes as pale as water. When he or she or it smiled, there were a great number of teeth, and they were very sharp.

Averil had welcomed the wildfolk into her duchy for honor and duty and for the defense of her people. She never had been completely comfortable with them. These in their greater humanity were almost reassuring—but only almost. She was still at heart a child of the orders.

Gereint had no such discomfort. He walked as easily among the strange ones as among the indisputably mortal citizens. There was no doubt as to which of the two he was, but in his magic he was more like the wildfolk than a mortal mage should safely be.

She ate a whole meat pasty and most of another: they were rich and good and filled her belly with warmth. As Gereint finished off the rest, she wandered off toward a church that stood on the corner opposite the baker's shop. It was small and immeasurably old, with a low square tower and a stone arch above the door.

That door was open. She passed under the arch into surprising warmth and dim light. The windows were high and narrow and inlaid with jeweled glass in the style of half a thousand years ago.

That was old enough, but the stones underfoot, as worn as they were, were much older than that. She walked slowly down toward the altar. It was made of the same pale gold stone as the paving: a table on a pedestal, very simple, with a vigil lamp flickering over it and a golden reliquary gleaming on it.

On the wall behind, the image of the Young God was painted in faded colors. The twelve Paladins surrounded him and the nine Ladies bowed at his feet. In his hand he raised the Spear, and over him bent the Serpent, great jaws wide, curved fangs dripping venom.

Averil peered at the Paladins. The youngest and best beloved always stood on the right hand, holding the Young God's sword and helmet in the manner of a squire. He was fair-haired and smooth-cheeked as she had seen him wherever he was painted.

He bore no particular resemblance to Peredur. She marked Longinus, dark and saturnine, with a spear in his hand, and the Lady Madeleine with a golden cup and the folded bundle that would be the Young God's shroud. Melusine stood well to the side as she always did in such portraits, with her face veiled and her body half turned away, reaching toward the Serpent.

There would be no answers here, not to such questions as

haunted Averil. She settled for the peace that dwelt in the place, as dim and quiet as it was, with the flicker of candles and the scent of incense sunk into the stones.

She knelt near the altar and bowed her head. As she did, she realized that the floor was not simply worn and uneven stone. It was carved with images that looked and felt unimaginably old.

Often in such churches, remnants of older shrines went into their building. This one was built on top of such a one: those were the carvings of its uppermost reaches. They were so worn she could see no more in them than curves and protruberances.

She followed them down the front of the church past the altar to a low, narrow door. The odor that wafted from it had a distinct edge of damp earth and old stone.

She shivered deep inside, but the urge to descend into the crypt was more than she could resist. She glanced back. Gereint was still behind her, saying nothing and making no move to stop her.

God knew what she would find down below. Old tombs, most likely. She called a light into being to illuminate the steep descent.

The door was almost too narrow for Gereint. He squeezed himself through without complaint.

The crypt was round and low-vaulted, with pillars marking niches around the edge. There were stone tables within and stone effigies lying on them, stiff and ancient figures with hands folded on cold breasts. Beneath each pair of hands rested the hilt of a sword.

These were Knights of ancient vintage. The Rose was carved on each tomb. Names were carved, too, worn with years: Pelagius, Orosius, Gereint.

"Look," said Averil.

The living Gereint bent to peer at the carved face. It was stern, long-nosed and long-bearded: nothing like his blunt honest features and still beardless cheeks. "These are the first Knights after the Paladins," he said in wonder. "How did they come here? I thought they were all in Lys."

"They began there," Averil said, "then came here to spread the Young God's faith. It spread differently on this island, as you can see, but it was strong. It lasted."

"Maybe we can learn from that." He left his namesake to wander around the circle of tombs. On the far side of the crypt he paused. "Come here," he said.

He sounded odd. Averil did not hurry, but she moved more quickly than she might have done otherwise.

The tomb in front of which he stood was blank. No effigy lay on it. The name that had been carved on it had been hacked away. And yet when he touched the place where it had been, pale blue light glimmered under his fingers.

The name was still there for all that time and malice had tried to do to it: *Melusine*.

Averil drew back a step, but she was done with running away. She made herself move forward.

Gereint's hands traced the shape in air where the effigy had been. Like the name, it was still there for those who could see.

"They brought her here," he said softly, as if she could wake to the sound of his voice. "They knew; they remembered what she was. They venerated her."

It did seem so. The image was lovingly carved, more life-like than any of the stone Knights. Averil recognized the face: she saw it in the mirror every day.

That did not horrify her as much as she might have expected. This crypt, this shrine with its deliberate reverence, did more than any words to convince her that Peredur had told the truth. The Betrayer had never betrayed her god. All that she had done was for love of him.

The image was as solid to the touch as to the eye. Instead of a sword, its hands clasped what looked at first like a strange dagger.

With a deep shock, Averil realized that it was not a blade, nor was it anything made by human hands. It was long and curved and pale, less like bone than milky glass.

Gereint's voice seemed to grow out of her own thought. "Is that what I think it is?"

She nodded. Her throat was too tight for speech.

His breath hissed. "It doesn't have to be a scale. Does it? It can be a bone. Or a tooth. Any part of the Serpent will do."

Averil did not want to look at it, but her eyes would not turn away. It shimmered like pearl, a living luster that belied the eons it had been separated from its body.

There were images in it, a world opening through the narrow gate: a storm-tossed sea and a fleet of black sails and a loom of black peak against the tumbled sky. There was nothing remarkable or unexpected there—except that every mirror and pool and scrying glass saw nothing where the Isle should be. In this strangest of magical instruments, it was as clear as if the walls of air had never been raised.

Maybe it was another fleet and another time. But Averil dismissed that as soon as she thought it. This was a true seeing, today, as it happened.

The Isle rose stark and sheer out of the sea. From this side there was no harbor to be seen; the Ladies' vale was hidden deep in the mountain's heart. There was only the black rock and the dash of spume and the sleet lashing hull and mast. Ice hung glittering from the rigging of each ship.

If they were hoping to lay siege to the Isle, they were going about it in a peculiar manner. The ships sailed in as close order as the storm and the heaving seas would allow, but none of them aimed either toward the Isle or on any track that would surround it. They were sailing past it.

Surely they could not be oblivious to it. Such mages as sailed in those ships could perceive the walls of air and mark the disturbance they caused in the aether. And yet the king's mages were making no effort to assail them.

"They're coming here."

Gereint had always seen more clearly than anyone else. Still Averil said, "You can't know that."

"Isn't that the northern edge of the Isle? And aren't they sailing slightly westward past it? If they're not aiming for Prydain, there's nothing else but open sea and the world's end."

There was no denying that. Averil's heart had sunk as low as it could go. "They're coming because of me."

No one could deny that, either, and Gereint did not try. "We have to tell the queen. I don't think anyone knows what they're doing. If they're using the Isle's protections to hide them, no mage here will see them until they're ready to land."

"It's my fault," Averil said. The pit yawned in front of her, inviting her to fall into a deep wallow of despair.

Before Gereint could say it, she said it for herself. "That's not useful, is it? Yes, we should tell the queen, and pray she believes us."

"She will."

His confidence was bracing. It felt honest, too. Averil

paused, more than half tempted to bring the tooth with her for proof.

That would be most unwise. It had rested here, unknown and unfound, since the Rose was new. Best it stay. She had enough to do with keeping the Mystery safe—and all the more so, now she knew that she had brought it within reach of the one thing that could destroy it.

26

QUEEN EILUNED RECEIVED Averil at once. It was the hour between the royal council and dinner in hall, when she took her ease in a privy chamber; when Averil was admitted, Eiluned lay on a couch, wrapped in a soft robe, while Dylan Fawr read to her from a book of old legends.

There was another man with them, a young one, no older than Gereint; his fine dark features and slight stature were strikingly like the queen's. This was the queen's elder brother's son, the prince Goronwy. Averil had been introduced soon after she arrived in Caermor; she had not found him congenial, though at least a few of the court had thoughts of a match between the queen's heir and the duchess of Quitaine.

She was not pleased to see him now, but she could hardly ask that he be dismissed. She inclined her head to him as was proper. He acknowledged the gesture with a flicker of the eyelids.

Arrogant child. She turned slightly but distinctly away from him toward Dylan Fawr. He smiled as he read, warming her with his regard: a fair antidote to the chill that emanated from the prince Goronwy.

The legend he happened to be reading was very old: the tale of two lovers before the Serpent's fall, who opposed their kin and defied the masters who would take their souls. As

Averil recalled it, they had died together but with their souls intact.

It was not the story she needed to hear on this particular day. She was glad that he stopped, with a glance of inquiry at the queen, and was not bidden to continue.

Eiluned sat up. Her eyes were tired but her smile was genuine. "Cousin! Welcome. Is everything well? Are the servants treating you properly?"

"Your servants are impeccable in their duties, cousin," Averil said.

Eiluned tilted her head. "And yet?" She patted the end of her couch, inviting Averil to sit.

Averil did not dare. While she stood, she could keep herself steady; if she relaxed at all, she would collapse in hysterics.

"I have no complaints of your hospitality, majesty," she said, "and none of your kingdom, either. But I do fear for it. The black fleet has passed the Isle without pausing. We believe it's coming here."

That brought the queen to her feet. Dylan Fawr stiffened. The boy, Averil noticed, did not. His brows drew together, but otherwise he sat still, watching and listening, as lazy and yet as alert as a cat on a doorstep.

Both Eiluned's ease and her air of weariness were gone. Her voice was clear and crisp. "You know this for certain?"

"As certain as I can be," Averil said. "We scried, the Squire and I, and we saw the ships sail on past the walls of air. They're sailing north and west."

"Could it be a diversion?" Dylan Fawr asked. "As obvious as it might be that Clodovec means to take the Isle, he might think to deceive us into raising all our defenses, then turn and mount the attack."

Averil shook her head. "He knows what is here. He wants that more than he wants the Ladies—and once he has it, he can destroy anything he pleases."

"Only if he can wield it," said Eiluned. "In itself it's nothing useful. It seems to have no magic, let alone any properties as a weapon."

"First he has to take it," said Dylan Fawr. "We have our own defenses, lady."

"So you do, my friend," Averil said. "Will they be enough?"

"What do you see?" Eiluned asked her.

She was not asking what Averil had seen when she scried, nor had she asked how Averil could have seen that much when no one else could. Either that was great trust or she knew more than she was letting on.

Averil closed her eyes. In the dark she felt the world tilt; she swayed. Gereint's hands came to rest on her shoulders, steadying her.

She was aware of the queen's eyes on her, and the others', too. If she opened the eyes of the mind just so, she could see herself standing in her plain dark clothes, cheeks reddened with cold and hair ruffled out of its plait, with the big fair man standing like a wall at her back.

The vision shimmered like an image in a glass. Through it she saw again the sea, the walls of air, the fleet. The storm had grown in ferocity. Some of the ships wallowed, half-foundered in the swell, but the rest pressed on.

More than wind was driving them. The magic that filled them owed nothing to the powers of air and water. The wind that bellied the sails blew aslant from the wind of the world.

Without opening her eyes, Averil asked, "Do the Spear and the Shroud carry any magic of their own?"

It was Eiluned who answered, though Averil felt Gereint

stir behind her, and his fingers tightened slightly. "It is said on the Isle that the one is a weapon and the other is a shield, but no one in memory has used them so."

"Yes," Gereint said: "we've kept them as relics but never waked the magic in them. Some say that's because they have little that's worth using; their value is in memory, in what they mean to the order. But others say they've never been wielded because they're too strong, and no one has the power to wake them without risking us all."

"That's more likely, don't you think?" said Averil.

She felt him nod. "The king wouldn't have wanted them so badly if they were only keepsakes. They have the Young God's blood on them, and the remnant of his power. I don't know all of what they are: that knowledge isn't given to anyone of my rank. But I think that when all the Mysteries are together, they strengthen one another. If he gets his hands on the third, even if he can't break the binding that's in it, he'll still have more power than any one man should dream of."

"Clodovec dreams of ruling the world." Averil opened her eyes. She could still see the ships coming, breasting the sea like a flock of water snakes. The pendant under her shift felt suddenly heavy, as if it knew what came to threaten it.

She stepped away from Gereint toward the queen. "Cousin, I know you've forbidden me to leave here, even to save your kingdom. But mightn't we try our own diversion? If we send a ship and I seem to be on it, maybe he will follow."

"Maybe," said Gereint, "or maybe, if he knows how to use the other Mysteries, he'll track the one you keep and know it's a deception."

"It is worth trying," said Dylan Fawr. "We don't know how far he can use the magic he's seized."

"It shall be done," the queen said. "A glamour, an illusion, a hint that the Mystery is there—it's well thought of."

"And if he doesn't take the bait?" Gereint demanded.

"Prydain will be more than he can swallow," Dylan Fawr said. His smile was edged, like steel.

Gereint was still bristling, crackling with magic as Averil had not seen him do since he was a Postulant in Fontevrai. She braced for the eruption, but he had grown past that. He subsided slowly, folding his power like wings and tucking it away.

The others were somewhat white about the eyes. Averil took particular note of the boy Goronwy, how he blanched and shrank back. He was no feeble mage himself, but next to Gereint he was a flicker in the dark.

His elders responded much less obviously, though Averil suspected Eiluned would have something to say later. For now she was content to let it go.

Averil reached within herself for words that were both polite and empty: courtier's words, thanking the queen and bidding her farewell and extricating them both before the questions could begin. If Eiluned had wanted to stop them she would have. She inclined her head, as gracious as a queen should be, and allowed them to escape.

IT WAS A day for odd sanctuaries and peculiar revelations. This one Averil found high up on a tower in the frosty sunlight, looking down upon the grey and glistening curve of the river.

She had always sought high places for clarity of mind. She had wallowed enough. Now she looked past self-pity and fear to what she had to do.

The queen would see that the ship and the glamour were

made and the bait set, sailing west over the edge of the world. The queen's mages and the powers of Prydain were laboring even as Averil stood there, raising walls of air that rivaled those of the Isle. To the eyes of her magic they rose out of the sea, curving to heaven and meeting overhead with a sound like shivered crystal.

It was pure illusion, but when the dome completed itself, Averil gasped. For a moment she could not breathe. There was no air.

The moment passed. Air filled her lungs again. Prydain remained Prydain. All without was closed away, but in her heart she still felt her own land of Quitaine. That was in her always, no matter where she was.

She turned to face Gereint. "They trusted me," she said. "They never asked how I knew when no one else did."

"I think they already knew." He leaned on the parapet at some little distance from her, frowning down the length of the river. "Magic is different here. Maybe not as different as ours, but it's not all the work of the orders, either. I think they can see slantwise and round about."

"The queen is a Lady of the Isle," said Averil.

"Yes, and are the Ladies locked in chains of glass? They go back to older powers, I've heard. The orders can't rule them and wouldn't dare to try."

"Their magic's heart is glass—just as it is for the orders. The Isle itself is made of glass."

"Even so," Gereint said, "can't they see past their own walls? Look around you. If the queen were bound by the orders, would she allow the wild magic the freedom it has here?"

Averil opened her mouth to argue, but there was a certain logic in what he said. She had never been initiate; she had studied wide and deep as all the Ladies' pupils did, but what did she know, truly, of the Isle's secrets? She knew more of the Rose, because of Gereint and his strangeness, than she did of the Ladies who had raised her.

She could wallow again, this time in resentment, or she could try to see her way through the maze. So many secrets resided in her now. The Serpent's tooth, the Mystery to which it was the key—did the Ladies know any of this? Did they want to?

She had said nothing of the tooth to the queen, and Gereint had not pressed her to try. She regarded him sidelong. He was absorbed in his own thoughts, frowning into the clear cold air.

Memory took her unawares, of a dream they had shared in which they stood atop a tower and spoke of difficult things. It could not end in a kiss in this world as it had in that one—no matter how tempted she might be. She had to settle for tracing the line of his profile with her eyes.

She turned away firmly and made herself focus on the city and the river and the sky. Part of not wallowing lay in, if not accepting what had to be, at least enduring it.

Someday, she thought, *it will change.*

The thought felt like shards of jeweled glass coming together in her heart, joining in the matrix that was his deep-rooted strength. This was the man she wanted. If she had to move heaven and earth to make it possible, she would do it.

Even if she had to wake the Serpent?

She shuddered so hard she nearly fell. No. Oh, dear God, no. She would not go that far. But anywhere short of it, most certainly, yes.

27

T HE COLD HAD set in hard and clear. The sun was
bright but devoid of warmth; the stars by night were
chips of ice in a vault of black glass.

On such a night, three days after Gereint found the Serpent's tooth, the queen and a handful of her mages and a small company of Knights stood with Averil by the quay of Caermor. The ship they meant to launch was much smaller than Dylan Fawr's *Cernunnos*, hardly more than a fisherman's coracle. Half a dozen sailors manned it, running up the crimson sail on its single mast and sleeping under a canopy on the deck. For its supposed noble cargo there was a little shelter of wood amidships, up against the mast.

It was a pretty boat with a carved sea-drake on the prow and a clear air of magic about it. The folk who sailed it wore human form for the moment, but out of the corner of his eye Gereint could see webbed fingers and round fishy eyes. They would take to their native element once the enemy swallowed the bait—far out to sea, they all prayed, and far from any return to land.

Most of the spell was woven, a fabric of illusion laid over the ship. It made the sailors seem even more human and set a familiar figure within the shelter, tall and slender but womanly in shape, with a curl of red-gold hair escaping the dark hood.

Its living image stood beside him. The last part of the working had to be hers: binding the essence of herself to the image on the deck and imparting to it a sense of the Mystery she carried. She was calm and focused as befit a mage of her training, but her heart was like molten glass.

He knew better than to hover and fret, but he kept a close watch on her. She was as dangerous in her way as he used to be before he learned to master his magic.

Something in her had cracked or broken, some part of her that had rested secure in the solidity of the orders. Reft away from those, infected with wild magic and tempted by the various cults of the Serpent, she had lost her bearings. Gereint was doing what he could, standing guard and trying not to remind her of what else they could have been to one another, but the longer it went on, the harder it was to keep his distance. He wanted most of all to hold her in his arms and kiss the troubles out of her and teach her to see the world as he saw it: bright and splendid and full of manifold wonders.

It took all the discipline he had learned through a hard year to keep himself from doing that. He protected her as best he knew how, made sure nothing magical or human intruded on her, and made especially sure that he did not trouble her any more than he could help.

The spell was nearly finished. She drew the pendant from beneath her gown and cupped it in her hands, breathing on it. Its gleam was dulled in starlight and torchlight, the bright enamel turned dark and the golden traceries glinted fitfully.

She blew the memory of it toward the ship. Her breath caught and held within the structure of the magic, secure in its heart. Without thinking, Gereint wound it with a bit of his own, a thought and a wish and a hope for what might be.

Too late he tried to snatch it back, but it was gone. Averil's spell had woven itself around it.

No one else seemed to have noticed. He wondered uneasily if they should have—or if he should mention it. But it seemed to have done no harm. He held his tongue and let it go.

The ship slid away from the quay. No oar drove it and no wind filled the sail, but it moved smoothly out into the center of the river. There the current caught it and carried it away toward the sea.

Averil swayed, but before Gereint could catch her she steadied. Gereint felt the same sudden malaise in himself, as if part of him had gone away with the ship. He reached into the earth that had always sustained him; it responded as generously as ever.

He breathed thanks to it, catching himself for an instant: it was a thoroughly pagan thing to do. But he had learned to be gracious, no matter what or who offered him help.

Averil had gained strength through the bond that was always between them. The queen and the mages were moving, leaving the quay. She began to walk with them.

Gereint was drawn to follow, but the quay wanted to hold him. The ship was still in sight, a shadow on the starlit river. He saw it through the cloud of his breath as if through a dark glass.

The spell on it was visible, an obvious and unmistakable glamour. All the effort that had gone into the working had drained away into the water.

It had gone too far for Gereint to touch. He was a power of earth; water resisted him, and the wildfolk that lived in it blurred and confused his magic. He hung on his heel, torn between calling out to the mages and letting be.

He would tell Peredur later—but not too late. If the spell had failed, they all needed to know, in order to mount the defense of Prydain.

The shadows and the torches had almost reached the end of the quay. Gereint loped after them.

NOW THAT THE bait was cast and the walls were raised, the powers of Prydain settled to wait. Gereint tossed all night on his pallet, but when morning came with the passages at arms that had swiftly become a ritual, he said nothing to Peredur. It was his strange sight again, that was all. He could see magic. No one else could.

The ship had made its way to the sea. If he looked inside himself he could find it sailing on the map of his memory. The black fleet was still coming, battered by wind and storm but grimly persistent.

Without those defenses it would have made landfall in the night; but it was still beyond the walls of air, tacking along them as if looking for a way in. If the queen's mages had calculated properly, the enchanted ship would pass the walls just as the fleet came in sight of it.

Meanwhile the life of the kingdom went on. There were movements of the sword to learn, books to study, magical workings to learn the refinements of. It all passed through Gereint's mind without lodging there.

Averil seemed as distracted as Gereint. Toward noon Peredur dismissed them. "Come back when you find your wits again," he said. He sounded more amused than angry, but Gereint thought his eyes were sharper than usual.

Whatever Peredur saw, he said nothing of it. He did not send a spy or a spell after them, either. They were free to do as they would.

Averil took it into her head to attend court. That was a
duty she loathed, but today she took evident pleasure in calling for servants to dress her in a gown of breathtaking extravagance. It was all gold, with emeralds; when she stood
up in it, with her hair coiled and plaited with jewels and
crowned with a golden coronet, she looked like no one Gereint knew.

He had nothing to do for himself but put on his best cotte
and try not to look excessively foolish. Averil made a show of
ignoring him. She swept out of the room and down the passage that led to the hall.

Servants scuttled out of the way. Lesser courtiers darted
into corners and doorways, bowing as low as their girth or
balance would allow. None of them, Gereint noted with interest, seemed at all discommoded.

People liked arrogance in their royalty, if it went with
beauty and a certain wild gleam that was both alarming and
irresistible. Gereint was not immune to it, either, though it
made him want to shake her.

She blazed through the court like a firebrand in a dark
night, danced with every man who had the courage to ask
and not a few who hung back blushing and stammering, and
drank enough spiced wine both hot and cold that Gereint
took to steering her away from the prospect of it. She continued to pretend that he did not exist, which was probably to
the good—until she reached for a passing cup and he inter-
posed himself once more.

Her eyes ran up the length of him, taking their time about
it. He could tell she meant to be hard and wounding, but the
magic inside said otherwise. True hatred would have called
him all the things he was: great baseborn lout who never
knew his father. She never even thought of it.

That only made him love her more. Her eyes narrowed and her face went tight. There was no hiding from one another, no matter how they might try.

She spun away into another man's arms. That was meant to hurt, too. It did sting, but Gereint could not help knowing why she did it.

He took station by the wall where he could watch the whole of the court and intercept her if she tried to slip away. Somewhat to his surprise, Riquier came to stand beside him, then Peredur.

They watched in silence for a while. Gereint began to wonder what he had done wrong, but while both looked rather somber, he saw no anger there. He began to breathe again, though he did not relax his vigilance.

When Riquier's hand closed on his arm, he started. The Squire said in his ear, "There's still a spy here. Look."

Gereint glanced at Peredur, who nodded. He looked where they were looking, inward and outward at the same time.

It was somewhat disorienting, not unlike what he felt so often with Averil. In the world of the body, the court glittered and chattered and spun through a vigorous dance, with Averil in the center of it. In the world of the spirit, the walls of air englobed them all.

There was a crack in the globe, so subtle he could barely perceive it. As he opened his eyes to it, it came clearer. Somehow, someone had wrought or exploited a weakness in the defenses.

It was not Averil. The spell that had lain in her was gone. Someone else wished ill to Prydain: someone with the power to both weaken the walls and hide the working from those who sustained them.

"How did you find it?" he asked Peredur, more in thought than in words.

Peredur's answer had no words in it at all. Gereint saw and felt the dance of the sword from which Peredur and Riquier had just come, the purity of movement and the shapes it transcribed in the living air. Those shapes were an image written in magic of the isle of Prydain.

One of them had not been as it should be. It was barely perceptible, but when Peredur had focused the dance around it, the rest of the pattern had stretched and frayed.

He had never let Riquier's blade pierce his guard—and not for any great increase in skill on Riquier's part. Riquier's agreement was somewhat wry. "I'm not even close to winning a match myself yet. This was coming from outside. We tracked it, and it seems to be focused here, around the queen."

Gereint nodded. He could see that, too. There might be others in the kingdom who wanted to betray it to its enemies, but none strong enough, except here. Somewhere in the court or the palace was a spy who was aware of what he did—unlike Averil who had carried the spell with her from Lys.

Once more Gereint assured himself that she was safe. She was, completely. And yet the weakness had a flavor of the spell that had lain on her. Esteban the Morescan's alliance must extend even into Prydain.

It was of that kind, not the king's. Gereint made sure of that, too. The various orders of magic were as distinct as roundels in a rose window: alike in shape but different within each circle.

He stopped himself before he sank too far into the wonder of the magic. It was somewhere in this hall, which was full of mages. Most of the nobility of Prydain had some degree of magic, and the queen's mages were numerous and varied and not always bound to the orders.

A shepherd could find one sheep in a flock of a hundred. Surely Gereint could find a spy among all these lords and mages. The taste of it was male: half a hundred, then. But he had to be quick. The fleet was coming, seeking out the weakness in the wall.

28

AVERIL HAD SPUN into a world of wine and frivolity, but like the self-pity she had wallowed in before, this was no true part of her. The men with whom she danced were a blur of faces forgotten as soon as they had passed. There was no face in the world for her but one, and she refused to look at it.

She could not get him out of her heart. She was not in the least surprised between dances to find herself in front of him. He had reinforcements: Riquier and the mage who claimed to have been a Paladin.

She trusted that one no more now than she ever had. He was not human; how could anyone be sure he truly cared for mortal troubles?

They surrounded her and herded her out of the crush of the court to the relative quiet along the wall. The next dance began without her; her erstwhile partner looked briefly forlorn, then wandered off toward the wine.

"There's a spy," Gereint said.

He never had seen the use in talking roundabout. Riquier winced slightly, but Peredur looked merely interested. Averil delved into herself in a kind of panic, but all she found there was Gereint, staring back at her.

"It's not you," he said. "Someone else is weakening Prydain's defenses. It feels like another of the Morescan's allies."

"It's my fault somehow, isn't it?" she said.

That was the wine talking. None of them took the bait. She felt cold suddenly; her head was clearer than it had been in days.

"Will you help?" Gereint asked her.

"What can I do?"

He did not take it as a cry of hopelessness, but answered it as the honest question it was. "Help us find him."

She could refuse. They did not look as if they meant to force her. But she had much to atone for, and she had danced most of the foolishness out. "What, you'd like me to scry for him?"

Gereint shook his head. "You've been dancing with every man here. Will you finish what you began? I'm thinking that if you're close to whoever it is, you may be able to sense the working in him."

"What if it's someone I've already danced with?"

"We'll take care of that," said Peredur.

She felt her spine stiffen. Her dislike of him was so strong she was surprised he did not fall back a step. "Should I dance with you, messire?"

He grinned. "I'll be honored, my lady."

She examined him closely for any sign of guilt or deception, but there was nothing. Not that she expected there would be. He was too powerful a mage to give himself away.

Still, she thought, why not? She might detest him on principle, but he was a comely enough creature, and God knew he was light on his feet. She held out her hands for him to take.

He took them with good will, then bowed and spun her back out into the hall.

IT WAS NOT Peredur. As much as she would have liked him to be the traitor, it seemed he was honest in that much at least. He handed her off to an eager princeling from some unintelligible backwater of Prydain, who was not unpleasant to look at, but she was blessed if she could understand a word he said.

She lost count of the dancers but not of the time. That was advancing rather quickly toward the day's meal; already a fair number of the court had withdrawn toward the lesser hall and the banks of laden tables.

Occasionally she caught glimpses of the two Squires and the Myrddin weaving through the courtiers. They had found nothing. Nor, unfortunately, had she.

She was tiring with the exertion of balancing both dance and magic, and the lack of sleep and food, and the aftermath of her wild mood. Gereint fed her strength, but his was not inexhaustible, either. She was close to giving up and leaving it to the queen to discover the worm in the palace's heart, but even on the edge of exhaustion, Averil was too stubborn to let go.

It did not help, either, that the part of her that still rode with the ship was sending her images of sea and storm and black sails thick on the horizon. The diversion was closing on its target.

At first she thought she was imagining things: growing confused with weariness. The man who guided her through a stately pavane was as innocent of magic as a noble in Prydain could be. She had been finding him frankly restful, until with a turn of the dance she looked past him to the queen.

Eiluned had been dancing with the rest of them, but she had retreated to her throne for this little while. She looked as if she might be thinking of rising and bidding the music stop and dispersing the court to their dinner. But that was not what caught Averil's eye.

The prince Goronwy stood beside the throne, leaning on its arm with an air of studied elegance. He was dressed all in black, which suited him; it was striking beside the queen's elaborate gown of blue and silver.

He had not asked to dance with Averil. She was not sorry for it. But as her glance passed over him, it caught on something strange.

It looked like a thread, so thin it was nearly transparent, like a strand of spider silk. If she had not been looking for it, she would never have seen it. It stretched through the layers of the world toward the walls of air and grew like a root into the world beyond.

Averil stumbled. Her companion caught her with words that were both gracious and kind. She realized that she could not remember his name and could barely remember his face.

There was no time to linger. She babbled something that she hoped was suitably grateful and escaped toward Gereint.

He already knew, because she did. Her legs would barely hold her up. He lifted her in his arms and carried her away to blessed quiet.

THE QUEEN WOULD not hear it. Even Peredur could not make her listen.

Gereint was too shocked to speak. He was no stranger to blindness, but this was deadly.

Eiluned was adamant. "Whatever our cousin believed she saw, our nephew is innocent. If there is a breach in our defenses, our mages will mend it. We do thank you for drawing our attention to it."

She was speaking as queen, with stiff formality. That was anger turned to arrogance. Gereint had not realized Eiluned was so besotted with her brother's son.

Nor, it seemed, had Peredur. "Majesty, as much as you love him, you know how human he is—and humans have weaknesses. I'm sure if you press him, he'll be able to explain. It may be he suffers from the same ensorcelment as your cousin, and can be healed as easily. Or maybe—"

"We shall consider it," she said, stiffly still.

Peredur bowed. Gereint might have argued further, but that was not his place.

AVERIL WAS ASLEEP in her bed, with Riquier watching over her. Her sleep was deep and full of dreams. Gereint felt the tug of them like a tide of the sea.

The enchanted ship had found the fleet and sailed past the leading edge of it. Voices called out; feet thundered on decks. A flight of arrows flew, but none so much as pierced the sail.

The image on the boat emerged from its shelter. The wind blew back the hood from its bright head. It stared as if astonished, then darted back into hiding. Surely it was only Gereint's eyes that saw through it as through a clouded glass.

The fleet seemed suitably impressed. As the boat veered to catch the wind, a serpent of flame uncoiled from the foremost of the ships. It lashed through the blood-red sky and struck the ship full on. Timbers and enchantments alike burst into flame.

The crew dived screaming into the sea. The flames caught their hair and the trailing edges of their garments before the waves swallowed them.

The ship sailed on, burning slowly to ash, until the prow of a black ship rode over it and drowned it. The last of its embers died in the last of the light.

The fleet had drawn up like the ranks of an army. The wind shrieked. A wall of icy rain swept down upon it and splashed back as if from a wall of glass. The sails were full, but not with the wind of the world.

The sea around the ships subsided. The great waves that rose above the masts died to a slow swell beneath the black hulls. To Gereint's eyes the water had a peculiar shimmer, like scales on a sinuous dark body.

He knew that vision all too well. As he looked up from Averil's face and her dream, he found the same vision in Peredur's eyes.

No one but Averil had ever been able to see as he saw, unless Gereint was there to guide with words and magic. Peredur needed no help. It was a little disconcerting, and in an odd way comforting.

"So," the mage said. He sounded satisfied. "He's taken the bait."

That set Gereint back on his heels. "But—"

"He's spent a good share of magic on our diversion," Peredur said, "and we know where he'll strike with the rest of it. He'll aim for the gap in the wall."

"Did you plan that, too?" Gereint asked. He would not have said he agreed with Averil that Peredur could not be trusted, but he did wonder a little.

"A wise commander plans for everything," said Peredur. "Go, sleep if you can. Both of you. Be ready to ride in the morning."

Gereint did not need to ask where. What doubts he had had were gone again. So was Peredur, so swift he seemed to vanish into air.

29

AVERIL'S DREAM BECAME the waking world so smoothly and inevitably that for a long moment she wondered if she had waked at all. In the dream the black fleet sailed on its shield of calm toward the walls of air, turned that shield into a battering ram and struck again and again at the weakness in the wall. When she woke to a frosty dawn, servants waited with a bath and breakfast and clothes fit to ride in. They even had weapons for her: a hunting bow and a long knife and a sword that balanced well in her hand.

Gereint and Riquier were already clean, dressed, and fed. She could have battered them with questions, but the answers were all there in her dream.

The queen's guard gathered in front of the palace, down by the edge of the river. Boats waited, full of armed men, and a tall ship with a golden prow that flew the queen's banner and—to Averil's astonishment—the silver swan of Quitaine.

"No more secrets," Gereint said as if to himself.

She wondered how wise that was. But she had not spoken since she woke, and no words came to her now. In silence, surrounded by guards, she embarked on the ship.

She did not feel like a prisoner. Everything she had done since her memory began had led to this. Her silence was not passive; it was the silence of waiting, of gathering strength and remembering every scrap of knowledge and skill and wit she had.

Her feet rang solidly on the deck. The queen's mages were there already, with Peredur in their midst. He wore armor like a knight—or a Paladin.

There were Knights of the Rose, too, with Squires and Novices in attendance. More of them manned the boats behind, among the knights and men-at-arms of Prydain and companies of oddly shaped and accoutered creatures who conducted themselves as if they had every right to be there.

So they did. This was their realm, too.

It was a simple thought and perfectly logical, but as she thought it, something profound shifted. She had a long way to go before she fully accepted the wild magic or its people, but the deep discomfort was gone. She would be not only obliged but honored to fight beside these wildfolk, if it came to that.

The queen was the last to arrive, but only by a few moments. Like Averil she was armed and dressed to fight. Among the men at her back was her nephew Goronwy.

Averil's shoulders tensed, but as she caught Peredur's eye, he nodded just visibly. The mages would watch him. She was not altogether comforted, but she was more at ease than she had been—especially as she felt the rising of Gereint's vigilance.

Gereint, she trusted. If he was on guard with the powers he had, they might possibly be safe.

SUNRISE FOUND THEM well down the river from Caermor, riding a swift wind toward the sea. It was a swifter wind than blew in the world's air, and the river's current had ample help: folk of the water bore the ships onward.

The queen's fleet grew as it sailed, until at midmorning it stretched as far back as the lookouts atop the mast could see.

People lined the banks to cheer it on. There were no flowers to cast on the water, so close to the door of winter, but they flung wreaths of holly and bay and stalks of mistletoe, laden with old magic.

One wreath caught a vagrant breeze and came to rest on Gereint's head. He reached to pluck it off, but one of the queen's men stopped him. "That's the luck, lord," he said. "You don't want to turn it away."

Gereint did not know what the man meant—if he was a man: he had a certain look to him that said otherwise. But he sounded so sure of himself that Gereint shrugged and let be. The sharp-sweet scent of bay wafted around him; the air seemed rather brighter and a fraction less cold.

Maybe there was luck in the thing. They could use all of that that they could get.

The walls of air were still holding, but the enemy was re-lentless. The fleet raced to reach the sea before the king's ships broke through and came to land.

Gereint had never known a ship could sail so fast. The tim-bers creaked with the force of their speed; the wind whipped his face. It caught the garland of bay and plucked it off.

Too late he snatched at it. It was gone. He hoped the luck had not gone with it.

They made their own luck. He straightened his back and wrapped his mantle tighter around him.

Many of the queen's mages had taken shelter below, out of the bitter wind, but the queen stood with Averil as near the prow as they could go. Neither seemed to feel the cold. Averil's red-gold plait and Eiluned's coal-black curls streamed out behind them. Gereint could not hear what they said to one another, but Averil's joy in the wind and the speed sang in his heart.

It was a kind of healing, and she had needed it. She always had been happier running toward danger than away from it. It seemed Eiluned was of the same mind.

They had left the mortal world some time since. The river had turned to a stream of silver, and the wild magic flowed through and beneath and above it. They sailed between worlds, as once Gereint and Averil had ridden with the remnant of the Rose through the heart of the Wildlands.

Then they had been fleeing a battle; now they sailed toward it. Gereint hoped it was a good omen.

There was no better or faster way to come to the sea. The river was molten and the sky was full of light. Peredur beside him stood taller and fairer and far brighter than he ever stood in the plain light of day. It almost hurt to look at him.

Everyone was shining, even the most mortal and least magical of them. The strongest mages and the wildfolk were shapes of light. Gereint looked down at his own hands and blinked: they were as bright as Peredur's.

They were all drinking magic as they sailed, drawing in the strength of the land and the water. Gereint wished for earth to set his feet on, but that would come soon. The sea was a spreading brightness ahead of them.

It was barely noon, and they were nearly there. The river lost its molten look and turned again to dark water flowing between winter-bare banks. It was broad now, threading through a wilderness of sand and reeds. The air smelled of salt and spume.

This was a desolate country, and yet it was rich in magic. Wildfolk loved such places, where humans were loath to go but their own kind could thrive.

There were few left here, with the walls of air trembling and ready to fall and the black fleet nearly upon them. They had fled to safer shores—and so, perhaps alarmingly, had the gulls that in gentler times flocked the strand. In their place stood ranks of the queen's levies, mortal and otherwise, gathered from the towns and villages of this southern coast.

They had taken their stand in and around the squat bulk of a tower that stood on the last low headland. From there, the queen's men said, the tribes of ancient Prydain had beaten back Romagna's invasion and driven it clear across the sea to Lys.

They would do it again, God and the old gods willing. The queen's fleet emerged from the mouth of the river, drew up in a wall along the shore and dropped anchor.

The sea that could have battered them to bits was a slow and gentle swell. All the storm and tumult raged just past the horizon, where Prydain's great defense rose invisibly but palpably to heaven.

THE QUEEN'S MAGES reckoned they had another day at most before the black fleet battered its way through. They gathered from all the ships and the army and met in the tower, in a high round chamber full of firelight and warmth.

The warmth was welcome. Cold seldom troubled Gereint, but the wind off the sea was edged with ice. It was a relief to be out of its reach.

This was a guardroom, ringed with benches, with a long trestle table by the hearth in the center. There the mages sat with the queen at their head, filling their bellies with brown bread and strong yellow cheese and drinking the guardsmen's ale. A scrying glass stood on the table near the queen; it looked out like a window on the black fleet.

Gereint could see the fleet without the aid of a glass. So could Averil. She sat near the queen, listening and saying nothing, while the mages debated strategies.

Some wanted to bring down the walls and loose the queen's forces upon the enemy before this day waned; to strike while the land's magic was at its height. Others preferred to let the black fleet exhaust itself in breaking the walls, so that when it came, it would find the defenders fresh and strong.

Both arguments had their merits. Gereint was not a general, but he was a mage, and he was Averil's protector. He watched her, not exactly uneasy, but not in comfort, either.

She had been close to breaking since she escaped from Lys. Her mood was less chancy now that she was freed of the spell, but that might be more dangerous rather than less. She had the too-perfect calm of a woman whose mind was made up.

He could not tell what she was going to do. That disturbed him. By the nature of their magic they could have few secrets between them, but she had found a way to keep a part of herself hidden—which meant that whatever she was contemplating, she knew he would object.

He could only guess at it and stay close. When she rose under pretext of needing the privy, he followed. She could hardly have failed to expect that: she sighed where he could hear it, but she did not try to send him away.

Her excuse had been genuine enough. When she emerged, she descended the narrow stair past the guardroom to the lower hall, then out of the tower.

Even though Gereint had been braced for it, the wind took his breath away. It blew off the land, which explained why the same powers that had calmed the sea had made no effort to quiet the gale. Even if the black fleet broke through, it would be hard put to sail to shore against the force of that blast.

Gereint wrapped his cloak as tightly as he could and took

comfort in the solidity of earth under his feet. He was no sailor and never would be.

Averil did not go far: only to the edge of the sandy shore, where reeds lay flat in the wind and the waves rolled sluggishly in and out, smoothed and flattened by the magic that lay over them. One of the smaller boats from Caermor was drawn up there, tipped on its side for a sort of shelter, but its crew had gone off elsewhere.

Gereint suspected they had gone into the water; a fair few of the others had done so, seeking their own element to escape from the wind. Now and then as he looked out over the sea, a sleek head broke the waves, looked about as if to get its bearings, then submerged again.

Most of battle was waiting. Gereint had learned that lesson in the flight from Lys. Along the shore, men and creatures not quite men took what shelter they could, rested and played at dice or knucklebones, or gnawed on rations, or tended fires in the lee of their boats.

While Averil sat with knees drawn up, clasping them and frowning at the sea, Gereint gathered the odd bit of flotsam and an armful of seaweed, dry and crackling, and woke fire in it. The fire he set would burn slow and long and magically warm.

She sighed as that warmth crept over her, a different sigh than had come out of her in the hall. Gereint squatted on his heels and spread his hands over the flames, letting them lick his fingers. "Whatever you're up to," he said, "at least let Peredur into it. He's stronger than both of us put together."

"I don't think so," she said.

"I know you don't like him," Gereint said doggedly. "It doesn't matter. We can't do whatever you want to do alone."

"I don't think he's stronger than we are," she said. "I don't think anyone is."

"He's forgotten more magic than we ever knew."

She shrugged, dismissing Peredur from her mind if not from Gereint's.

He was not ready to give up, at least until she told him what she wanted to do. "The queen, then. Or Mauritius. You trust Mauritius. He's a master; he knows what we are. If he brings in the rest of the Knights—"

"They have their own battle to fight. All of them do. Except us."

"We're as much a part of the war as anyone else."

"Yes," she said, "but what have they asked us to do? Nothing. If it weren't for us, they wouldn't know what was happening even now. We might not even be here."

"Well," he said, drawing out the word until she looked sharply at him. "We are young, and there are master mages everywhere. Even Mauritius doesn't know everything we can do. Peredur does, I think—but he's not going to betray us to the others. He'll expect us to do that for ourselves."

"I don't intend to." She hugged her knees tighter. "Will you fetch Peredur? I think I know what we can do to stop the fleet."

It was a noble effort, he granted her that. If her voice shook, she could blame it on the cold.

But she could not hide what was boiling up so strongly from the heart of her. The harder she tried to conceal it, the less she succeeded.

"Oh, no," Gereint said. "You're not leaving the Mystery here and working up a glamour in the shape of it and handing yourself over to the king. That is absolutely mad."

She did not seem perturbed that he had seen through her so easily. "Why? It's the only logical thing to do. If he has me, he'll abandon Prydain. He'll take me back to Lys and return me to much the same life I had before. I'm still the only heir he has. He'll marry me off promptly to one of his loyal servants—no illusion of choice this time, and no chance of escape. But I'll be safe."

"Certainly you'll be safe," said Gereint with a twist of disgust, "until they find the glamour and kill you for it. Which will be the moment after they see you. You've played that trick too often; they'll be looking for it."

"They won't kill me."

"Not your body, maybe. They do need that to breed royal heirs. Can you be so sure of your soul?"

At that she blanched. He pressed the advantage before he lost it. "Didn't you learn anything from what they did to the ship? They'll simply take you, burn away your soul, and keep on coming. The king wants the Mystery; he'll stop at nothing until he gets it."

"Yes," she said in such a tone that his hackles rose. "I'm going to stop him."

"No," he said as understanding dawned. "Oh, no."

"Why not?" she demanded. "It doesn't matter what happens to me, if Clodovec is dead. Maybe I'll only be close enough to him for a moment, but a moment is all I need."

Gereint sucked in a breath and did his best not to bellow at her. "You are not going to kill yourself in order to kill the king!"

"I would hope to escape," she said, "but if not—"

"No. No, and no. Even to save Prydain, you can't destroy yourself."

Her mind was like a castle under guard, with the gates barred and the portcullis raised. Gereint did his best to storm the walls. "What good will killing one man do, even that one? He's far from alone—and there's the Morescan with his own unholy alliance. If you dispose of Clodovec, you'll only free the others to be worse."

"Maybe," she said, "if there were a working set to destroy all of the Serpent's slaves when that one dies . . ."

"There probably is," he said tightly, "but if it does exist, it likely takes more art and skill than either of us has, and more time than is left to us. Please, lady. There's a battle coming, and it needs us both. Not you alone—and most of all, not you dead."

She was wavering. Gereint opened his mouth to press harder, but thought better of it. It would be better for them all if she found her own way to sanity.

30

IT HAD BEEN a lovely plan. Averil had seen it as clearly as in a scrying glass. Most likely she would die for it, but she told herself that did not matter.

Gereint dragged her back to cold reality and a less palatable truth. He had a way of doing that. She did not have to be pleased, but she could concede that he was, on occasion, wise.

She was still contrary, and wild enough to lean across his bit of half-magical, half-mortal fire and catch his face in her hands and kiss him until they were both dizzy. There was no thought in it to speak of, and no wisdom whatever.

She sat back abruptly on her heels, breathing hard. "That was for luck," she said.

He mirrored her posture, but he seemed to have forgotten the kiss as soon as it was over. Even as she sparked to temper at the fickleness of the male, he said, "Do you feel that?"

"What?" she said nastily. "The way I just did that, and you barely noticed?"

His brows drew together, but his attention was still elsewhere. "Look," he said.

There was no escaping it: his magic coiled itself around hers and forced her to see. The heat of her temper went cold.

Things moved deep in the earth, flexing supple bodies far below the world of light. Powers were awake and coiling upward. The walls of air guarded sea and sky, but there were no defenses beneath the earth.

Prydain's mages, whether of the orders or the wild magic, had committed a signal error: they had looked outward and upward, but not downward. Serpent magic was magic of the deep places, of rivers flowing underground and caverns beyond mortal knowledge. It crawled beneath the walls and drew up strength from the earth's heart.

"The fleet is a diversion," Averil said. She was less shocked than wry. "The real attack is coming from below."

Gereint sprang to his feet, pulling her up with him. "We have to warn the queen."

Averil could not argue with that. When he would have let go her hand, she knotted her fingers more tightly with his. They ran back together into the tower.

THEIR ARRIVAL INTERRUPTED an argument that had not changed or resolved itself since they left. Averil cut across it unceremoniously. "Never mind the fleet," she said. "Look below."

Some of the mages and generals would have turned their dissension on her, but she ignored them. The only ones who mattered were the queen, the Knights, and the mage whose proper name was Peredur. For them she cast what she knew into the scrying glass on the table.

The rumble of outrage died abruptly. In the silence, Eiluned's indrawn breath was unexpectedly loud. "Ah yes. Of course. Why should he do more than pretend to challenge us with a fleet when he can wield the deep magic?"

"You know of such things?" Averil asked.

The queen nodded. "We thank you for this."

"Let us help you," Averil said.

"We will need all the help we can find," said Peredur before the queen could say otherwise—and she did mean to: that was clear in her eyes. If she had had her way, Averil would have been carried off to safety with the levies and, most important of all, the Mystery that must not fall into Clodovec's hands.

But Peredur forestalled any such word. His calm stare dared the rest to disagree.

No one did, not openly. Even now, after the fall of the Rose had taught the orders a terrible lesson, it was difficult for them to turn their minds toward the ways of the Serpent. Averil was no different, but fate and chance had set her in the vanguard of the battle. She had to face what she had never been raised or trained to face.

Without Gereint she would have been as much at a loss as any of them. Magic was all the same to him, and no part of it troubled him more than any other. She had to cultivate that, for her own safety and the salvation of them all.

Through him she felt the slow surge and roll of the powers beneath. At the same time she was aware that the kingdom's defenses were buckling. All too soon they would fall.

"When the deep rises," Gereint said, "the sea will overwhelm the land. Your fleet may be able to ride it out, majesty, but is there room on the ships for your levies?"

"How much time do we have?" Eiluned asked.

She did not demand to know what a Squire was doing, speaking out of turn. That was not only wise, it was gracious.

Gereint bowed to it, even as he said, "Until nightfall at the most."

Eiluned nodded. Her face was grim. She turned to the commander of her fleet, a sturdy, weathered person on whose cheeks was a faint sheen of scales. "My lord, do what you can."

"At once, majesty," he said, and was gone as quickly as a fish darting through bright water.

The commander of her levies was on his feet already, as human as her admiral was not. "I'll move the rest as quickly as I can," he said. He slanted a glance at the mages. "With such help as these may offer."

"The paths between the worlds will open for you," said Peredur.

When the general withdrew, a handful of mages went with him, but Peredur stayed. Averil surprised herself with relief. Whatever she might think of him, he was a great power. She wanted him nearby, and not focused on duties that lesser mages could perform.

There was still that gnawing doubt and that inborn unwillingness to trust him. As they dispersed with dignified haste to the army or the ships, Averil deliberately chose to be the last to leave. Gereint waited for her—and so, as she had hoped, did Peredur.

When the hall was empty but for the three of them, she faced him directly. "I suppose I owe you thanks for not sending me packing—though one might question your reasons for doing so."

"One might," he granted her. "Or one might reflect that even if we sent you away, you would escape and come back. You're bound to this as we all are."

"Even with what I carry?"

"Especially for that."

She paused. Her hand wanted to clasp the Mystery beneath her chemise, but she clenched it tightly at her side. "Tell me now," she said, "and tell me true: You knew this would come. You waited for us to discover it for ourselves. Why? Don't tell me we had a lesson to learn. I take a dim view of lessons that destroy kingdoms."

"Lady," he said, "I knew this was possible, but I hoped our

enemies would not. I didn't think they had so much power or such knowledge."

"What was it you taught us not so long ago?" said Averil. "Never underestimate your enemy."

He acknowledged the stroke with a swordsman's salute.

She was not charmed, nor was she amused. "I must know. If you are not going to fight on our side, if you are going to withhold knowledge that will save us, or worse, pass that knowledge on to our enemies, simply to teach us the error of our ways, I don't care what the queen thinks of you. I will do my best to have you banished."

"I know you will, lady," he said. He was as sober as he could be, which was not very. For a being so purportedly old, he had a remarkably light heart.

"Tell me, then," she said. "The truth. Have you betrayed us to Clodovec?"

"Lady," he said, "I have not and will never betray you to the Serpent's slaves—unless you ask."

Averil's breath caught. She could persist in disbelieving him, or she could gamble that Gereint was right: Peredur was their strongest ally.

Time was flying; the ships were nearly ready to sail. She let her breath out sharply. "Can you stop this?"

"Alone, no," he said. "With you two, maybe."

"We have to try."

"Yes," he said.

She nodded with swift decision—and no misgivings that she would allow herself to feel. Gereint was halfway to the door already. She strode after him.

THEY WERE THE last to board the queen's ship. The sun was riding low, though there were hours yet to nightfall. On the shore, the levies were ranked and marching, beating a rapid retreat from the sea.

Even under the spell that bound them, the waves were higher, a slow ebb and surge like the breathing of a vast beast. The power beneath was rising inexorably. The black fleet had nearly broken through the walls.

The queen's mages had scattered themselves through the fleet. A spell much like that which bound the Knights connected them one to another, woven through a shard of glass that each carried. The queen had sacrificed a goblet willingly to the cause.

The Knights had woven this new web into their own. They were scattered, too, so that every ship of any size had a Knight or a mage to guard it, with smaller boats within its orbit. Mauritius remained on the queen's ship with Father Owein and Riquier.

They raised anchor all together, even as the last of the levies disappeared into mist and light. The tide tried to sweep them to shore, but the sea-folk helped carry those that had to rely on sail rather than oar.

The sea's children might not be able to stay once the deep rose. All that did not fight for the queen were already gone. Like the levies, they had fled as far as they could go, well away from the thing that was coming.

For the moment those who remained held on, and the fleet held its line. The Archbishop of Caermor sang a mass; the slow and sonorous notes of the psalms echoed over the water.

The sea-folk did not flee from the constraints of the ritual. Averil took note of that. They floated in the sea, eyes glistening. If they had ears, those pricked toward the sound of chanting; such nostrils as they had flared at the smell of incense.

A few even signed themselves with the Young God's spear, tracing the shape of haft and guard in a blessed cross.

The waves were rising higher now. The spells that bound them were slipping free. The queen's mages made no effort to hold them, nor to strengthen the walls of air.

Averil had taken station by the prow. One of the queen's maids brought a fur-lined cloak, for which she was grateful. Warm and protected from the wind, she looked not across the sea but into the depths of her magic.

Gereint was there as always, but in body he stood with Peredur and Riquier and Mauritius, close by the queen. If Averil wished, she could hear what he said.

"It's not another Serpent, is it—what's coming up from below?"

"There is only one of that kind," Peredur answered, "but it is a sort of serpent, yes: a cold-drake from the deep places of the earth. When it rises, it will lift the sea's floor with it."

"Unless we stop it."

"Just so," said Peredur.

Gereint went silent. Peredur had told them what he meant to do. His words coiled inside of Averil, ready to strike when the moment came.

She was afraid—terrified—but that fear was far away. For the moment there was only the wind and the cold and the fading sun, and the sound of ships battering a wall that was made of magic instead of stone.

She was ready when it fell, and yet it was a shock, snapping through her body. The great defense collapsed. Black sails filled the horizon, just as the sun touched it. On each sail was a sinuous shape, a silver serpent, turned to blood by the sunset light.

31

THE LOOKOUTS' CRIES were like the wailing of gulls. No sound came from the black ships.

Gereint remembered that silence from the Field of the Binding, when the last remnants of the Rose had faced the king's armies. None of the soulless soldiers had spoken or shouted or loosed a cry of pain.

For all he knew, the ships were empty of anything but sorcery. But in his heart he knew otherwise. There were living bodies on those ships, bodies stripped of souls, whose only will was the will of the one who ruled them. And on one of those ships was the king of Lys.

"What does he do with the souls he takes?" Gereint asked Peredur.

The queen's mage looked faintly startled. People usually did when Gereint asked one of his questions.

Unlike most of them, Peredur actually thought about it, then offered an answer. "The spell in its origin was meant to feed the Serpent."

"I know," said Gereint, "but what of it now? What is there to feed?"

"Power," said Peredur slowly, as if the thought were taking shape as he spoke. "Sorcery too great for mortal mind to contain. But a well of souls would swallow it without a trace."

"A well? A shaft in the earth?"

"It could be. Or it could be a Mystery, like what your lady carries. It could be anything at all."

"It must be small enough to carry," Gereint said. "Otherwise it's not practical. What was it when the Serpent was awake?"

"Most often," said Peredur, "it was a cauldron. Sometimes it was a cup. But when the slavemasters went to war, it was a vial. Whatever shape it wore, it was always made of stone."

"Serpentine?" Gereint asked.

Peredur's lips twitched. "Indeed. Or chalcedony."

"My lord," Gereint said to Mauritius who was, with the politeness of courts, pretending not to hear—but of course he heard every word: "do you think you could find such a thing? There's no time, there's nothing to work the spell but the web and such power as you can gather out of all that's rising, and altogether it's probably impossible, but could you try?"

"In the time we have?" Mauritius asked, but he did not wait for an answer. "We can try."

"Will you, sir?"

"You have a plan, messire?"

Gereint hoped he was not meant to be brought up short by his Knight Commander's careful courtesy. "I think I may, sir. But I need time—more than we have, maybe, but maybe not."

"The Rose is at your disposal, messire," said Mauritius.

Gereint did his best not to squirm. He was still not used to having any rank at all, let alone either respect or obedience from a Knight Commander.

But Mauritius was not laughing at him, and not rebuking him, either. Gereint decided to take it in the spirit in which it seemed to be meant. "Please, sir, if you will, find this thing— cup or vial, whatever it is. The sooner you can do it, the better. We're nearly out of time."

"I understand," said Mauritius. He was already turning toward Riquier. "Messire. If you please."

Riquier did indeed please: he was poised on his toes, ready to leap in whichever direction his commander bade him. Gereint hesitated, sorely tempted to join them in their search, but he had other prey to hunt.

The black fleet had drawn no closer. The wind had died, but the cold if anything was deeper. The sea's surge grew steadily stronger.

Mauritius and Riquier had gone below. Light began to shine through the hatch, steadier than any lamp or candle. Gereint felt the hunt along the edges of his awareness, a brief distraction.

He went to stand beside Averil at the prow. The last of the light was fading from the sky; the black fleet was lost in shadow. Their own fleet was still visible, marked by a lantern on each mast—dangerous in that it would draw the enemy, but the queen's commanders had reckoned to overwhelm them with confusion. Some ships therefore had two lamps or three, hung from prow and stern, and the occasional ship had none.

The queen's guards and her soldiers had taken their places along the sides of her flagship, each behind a shield. Eiluned moved among them in a soft glow of light, speaking to this one and that, while her mages met in a circle amidships. The hum of their working made Gereint's back itch.

Averil was remote from it all. Her awareness was far beneath the sea, in darkness beyond all knowledge, where the cold-drake rose blindly toward the sorcery that summoned it.

It had intelligence. That shocked Gereint almost out of the working. There was nothing human or mortal or comprehensible about it, but it was aware; it knew it was bound, and it knew that binding was magic.

What it felt was not exactly resentment and not exactly anger, but something both deeper and colder than either. Out of that roil of sensation, it drew power. Earth crumbled before it. Stone buckled and cracked.

The weight of the sea was nothing to it. It rose to destroy the ants, the motes, the specks of dust that dared lay this compulsion upon it.

The ship bucked and rolled. Down in the depths, a deep rumbling had begun.

The waves now were taller than the mast. When the ship rose to the summit of one, Gereint could see the lights of the queen's fleet scattered like flotsam. Of the land he saw nothing at all.

He clung to the prow, suddenly dizzy. Between the wilderness of water and the tangled web of magic all around him, he had to fight to keep his bearings. It was a long way down to the earth that nourished him.

He pressed his face to the dragon's icy neck, taking comfort in that penetrating but mortal cold. By the Paladins, he needed every scrap of strength he had—and for that he needed earth. And that was gone.

It was still there below all that water. If he remembered the feel of mud through his toes or grass underfoot or even naked rock stabbing his body with pain as he lay on it, the rest came to him, and he could hold on to it. His awareness ran like an anchor's chain down through the turbulent water to the root of his magic.

Averil's arms slipped around him. Her magic wove through his until every part of it was full.

She drew away, but he felt no cold of separation. Heat washed over him: elation tightly contained. Riquier stood behind them, and his grin told Gereint all he needed to know.

MAURITIUS HAD WORKED fast and hard, and his face showed the effects of it: deep hollows in his cheeks and shadows under his eyes. But he was smiling. In his hands he cupped a sphere of glass.

Shapes moved in it, images that came clear as Gereint looked closer at them. Mauritius was a master of this art: whatever Gereint saw, he recognized, and knowledge flowed in.

It was a vial of green-grey stone with a subtle hint of mottling like scales, serpentine indeed, and it lay in wrappings of silk within a box carved of chalcedony. The box lay on a table in a cabin much like the one in which Gereint was standing, below the deck of a black ship. That ship at first seemed like every other in the fleet, but there was no mistaking the flavor of the magic that rode in it.

Here was Clodovec, and here was his counselor Gamelin. The king sat and the priest stood under a canopy on the deck. Despite the tumult of wind and water, they rested in warmth and quiet. All the strands of magic in the fleet ran through Gamelin's hands; now and then the king reached to pluck one, either for amusement or to see for himself what his servant was doing.

"Messire," Gereint said without turning, "I don't suppose you know of a way to remove that box from the ship."

"What," said Peredur, "the most carefully guarded treasure in the most heavily guarded place on the king's own flagship?"

"Yes," Gereint said.

"There is no way," said Peredur.

"There must be," said Gereint, turning to face him. They both had to stoop in the low cabin; Gereint found himself eye to eye with Peredur. The gleam in Peredur's was not exactly human.

It did not dismay Gereint. "If we can find it, we can take it. They're fully occupied between the fleet and the thing below. There are no guards in the cabin, and no wards on the box."

"That you are aware of," Mauritius said.

"There would be no wards," said Peredur. "The spell that takes souls will swallow such protections."

"There are no wards on our Mystery, either," Gereint said. "As far as anyone can tell unless he knows what it is, it has no magic in it at all."

Peredur nodded. "Such things are often hidden in plain sight. But there is still the matter of where it is. The vial may not be warded, but the ship is—many times over. Even our bit of spying may have roused an alarm, though we're not aware of it."

"I don't think it did," said Gereint. "I think it's a weakness in the enemy's walls, and there is a way to get hold of it."

"There's not much time," Mauritius said.

Gereint scowled. He did not mean to be rude; he was thinking hard. A thought was trying to take shape, but it kept dissipating just short of comprehension. It had to do with the thing below, the spell that bound it, and the way magic was woven through the black fleet.

It did not help that the queen's mages were trying to quell the cold-drake before it broke through the earth into the sea. Their working overarched the queen's fleet, holding it together and drawing from the magic of everyone on it. It tried to draw from Gereint's, but he would not let it.

It was not doing what it was meant to do—and those who wrought the working were not even aware of it. Even these mages of Prydain, who would share the world with wild magic, were still constrained within the bounds of their orders. That constraint blinded them when they most needed to see.

The orders had to change. But there was no time now, and no time to be polite, either. The cold-drake was close to breaking through.

The ship rocked and heaved. Gereint braced himself against the hull just before he was thrown into it. Averil staggered against him. As the ship lurched again, he closed his arms around her and held on.

The cold-drake was not happy with the new spell that tried to bind it, at all. Gereint was beginning to understand how vast it was and how much power was in it. It could have coiled around the whole extent of both fleets and had room to spare.

The thought that had been trying to form was almost clear now, almost within reach. The cold-drake was slipping free of the spells that bound it—and it was not minded to sink back into the deeps. It was in a right rage, and it was hungry.

"Messire," Gereint asked Peredur over the roaring of the sea, "did any but the Serpent ever feed on souls?"

"Not in mages' knowledge," Peredur answered. "For the rest, living flesh was enough."

Gereint drew a breath and held it for a moment before he let it go. He had it, the thought. It depended on a thing that might be impossible, but none of it was possible otherwise.

He had to believe it could be. He also had to ask these dearest friends to trust him blindly, and that would not be easy. "Messires," he said. "Lady. I have a favor to ask of you."

They waited, expectant—even Averil, of whose mood Gereint was not at all certain. "Will you watch over me while I perform a deep working?"

Of them all, only Peredur did not stare at him as if he had gone daft. "A deep working?" said Riquier. "You can do—"

"I can," said Gereint, "because my lady knows."

Riquier opened his mouth as if to speak, then closed it again.

"He has the strength," said Averil. "I have the art. Though this may be more than I can do."

"I can help," Peredur said, "if you will allow me."

Averil frowned, clearly unhappy, but she was no fool. She said, "I will allow it. I'll even welcome it."

Peredur bowed to what they all knew was a great concession. "Then let's begin."

32

EVEN IN THE brief time that Gereint had been speaking with Mauritius and Peredur, the sea had gone mad. The ship hung on to the wave it rode, sustained by the magic in its timbers and the crew who were not entirely human, but it groaned with the strain.

The cabin was stifling with so many of them in it. The rocking and heaving, the sounds of the ship struggling not to break apart, the roar of water and the cries of the men who fought against it, overwhelmed Gereint.

Averil was his anchor. He focused on her face and presence and deliberately shut out everything else. It was hard: his head was pounding, and their bodies were flung against the wall again and again.

Peredur set himself beside Gereint, bracing him with strength that rooted deeper in earth than Gereint's own. For a moment Gereint rested in it and simply breathed.

There was not much time left. If the cold-drake did not break through into the sea, the ship would break apart in the storm of its coming.

Averil's magic was altogether a part of him. Peredur's own power slid into it like a sword into a scabbard, new and splendid and strong. The depth and breadth and height of it made Gereint dizzy.

He steadied himself quickly, before Peredur did it for him.

The others waited with tight-drawn patience. He was the hand on the sword, the power that moved the rest.

For an instant he lost himself again, tumbling down into an abyss of confusion. Once more Averil caught him and Peredur held him fast. He was sliding downward still, but now he saw ocean all around him, the cold black depths of the sea. Far below was the terrible thing, the power that would break this part of the world.

He spoke to it as if it had been a comprehensible creature, a particularly strange but sufficiently intelligent power among wildfolk. "Wait," he said.

The cold-drake barely paused. It was not deaf as snakes were said to be, but he was a gnat buzzing in its ear.

He drew from the two powers that bolstered him and raised his voice. "Wait. Hold."

That, the cold-drake heard. Words alone might not sway it, but Gereint laid no compulsion on it. He worked no spell. He simply asked.

No gnat had ever asked. That was so new a thing that the cold-drake stopped within mere ells of breaking through.

Gereint had no fine speeches to give it then, only a promise: great stores of fresh meat to feed on, if it waited on his word.

He held his breath. Mages of both sides had tried to bind the cold-drake with magic and earned its lasting ire. He gambled on a faint hope, that like any other beast including the human, this one would prefer choice to force.

He could not afford to doubt himself. He had no strength with which to overwhelm that creature of the earth's heart. He only had the simplest of lures: food for its belly and peace for the torpor thereafter, freedom to return to its deep realm and its long night.

It lay motionless beneath the sea's bottom. The spells that warred over it were stinging flies. Its vast hide twitched them off.

Gereint was ready for that. Through Averil he shaped a shadow of the great beast, to fill the enemy's working before he knew the cold-drake had escaped.

He could not both hold the shadow and seduce the cold-drake. Even as he lost his grip, Averil was there, with Peredur beside her.

The cold-drake sighed and stretched. The ship lurched and nearly foundered.

The great beast went still. It was awake, aware, but quiescent—waiting.

Its own promise was clear. It would give him what he asked for—and if he failed to keep his promise, it would feed; indeed. He and all his kind would sate its hunger.

It was a fair enough bargain. Gereint dared to rouse a little, to open his eyes and extend his awareness into the world his body lived in.

The sea was subsiding. The spell of calm spread across it once more, until the waves were again a gentle swell.

Gereint extricated himself from the cabin and ascended into frosty starlight. The wind was as gentle as the sea. Lights scattered across it; as he took in the sight of them, they began to move, coming together.

They were battered and some were limping and all were covered with ice and salt, but all hands were on the decks and the fighting men had returned to their stations. Shields were up, both mortal and magical. Every man who had a weapon had it drawn or strung and at the ready.

Gereint was no sailor and never would be, but he had climbed many a tree when he was younger. The mast was not so different. There were hand- and footholds built into it; he was not small or light enough to climb to the top where the lookout perched, but halfway up was high enough.

The black fleet was shrouded in shadow. Through that he found it.

It was not the fleet that he had seen in daylight. The king knew the uses of glamour, too. What had seemed to be a fleet of round-bellied, single- or double-masted, mortal and ordinary ships such as plied the seas out of any mortal nation, revealed itself in starlight to be something far more deadly.

It beat across the newly placid sea, each ship driven by bank after bank of oars. Each prow was sharpened steel. Each hull was strengthened by fire and sorcery. Armies of the soulless swarmed the decks.

There were half a thousand of these monstrous galleys, riding a tide of shadow against their unsuspecting enemy. The queen's men were looking for attack, but they were blind to this.

Gereint squeezed his eyes shut. He could still see the black fleet coming on. His magic was taxed to the limit already, and there was worse to come.

If the queen's ships were overrun and everyone on them taken and stripped of his soul, nothing else that he did would matter. He breathed as deep as his lungs could bear, then let it all go in a rush of wind.

The glamour shredded and tore. Up above Gereint, he heard a gasp and a boyish yelp, and then a long wailing cry.

Feet thundered on the decks below. Light blazed across the sea. The queen's mages had roused to finish what Gereint began.

For a few moments longer he clung to the mast, scraping together what strength he had left. When the fire arrows began to fly, he began the long climb down—but he had hardly gone a yard before he paused.

Every black ship was exactly like every other. Every one had the same shape, the same prow, the same triple bank of oars. There were half a thousand of them. And only one held the king and the counselor and the box of souls.

Even for what Gereint had in mind, they were too many. How in God's name was he to tell which ship was the king's?

Panic rose and crested. He rode it out. When he was as calm again as he was going to be, he made himself look out across the expanse of the fleet.

There.

They advanced in four long columns, one behind the other. Behind those, three black ships floated together. They were still as the rest had seemed: shorter, broader, twin-masted and black-sailed.

Clodovec was there. It was too far to see any one figure on any ship, but Gereint was sure. As soon as his eyes fell on the rearmost ship, he knew.

He all but fell the rest of the way, struck the deck with force that jarred his teeth, and called out to the queen. "Don't let them engage! Sound the retreat."

Eiluned looked up at the sound of his voice. He had not made any effort to soften it; everyone's head must be ringing.

He pushed through the crowd on the deck. "Majesty, you can't fight them. Open ranks and let them through, or beat a retreat, it doesn't matter—just don't get pulled into a battle."

The queen's captains and generals took in his youth, size, and Squire's cotte and failed to be impressed. Eiluned was less easily influenced by appearances, but she was not convinced, either. "Why, messire? What have you seen?"

It was not what Gereint had seen; it was what he knew. But

he did not want to explain that to her in front of a hundred strangers. "Half a thousand ships," he said, "each with half a thousand men, and all but the commanders with empty eyes."

"That may be," she said, "but we can't let them land."

"If we scatter," one of her admirals said, "they may divide to follow. Ships of that size aren't made to come up on shore. They're sea vessels; they have to stay at sea."

"Sea vessels carry smaller boats for landing," said another weathered sea-lord. "We can't risk—"

"My lords," Gereint said, pitching his voice to carry over the others, "there is no time to argue. Please, majesty, for the love of your people, get out of this place. If you have any power to spread wings, you should call upon it."

"Why?" she demanded. "What—"

"Do it, lady," Peredur said. He had come up from below, with Averil and the others behind him.

His face said everything Gereint was trying so desperately to say. Eiluned raised her voice for all to hear. "Beat the retreat."

Drums rolled, echoing across the water. Ships slowed and backed or began to turn. The black fleet closed in, driving relentlessly.

Out of their darkness, flames went up. They had loosed flights of fire arrows.

Nothing with mortal ships was swift. It took forever to turn; short of a wreck, nothing could stop a ship under way with any speed at all. When the rain of fire fell, the queen's ships were still well within range.

Around the flagship, most of the arrows hissed harmlessly into the sea, but a handful struck the deck. One caught in the sail and began to smolder.

Men leaped to quench the flames. They were stubborn: there was naphtha on those arrows, or some spell even more persistent. Even mages were hard put to put them out.

The queen's fleet had divided into a dozen smaller fleets and scattered. But the black fleet did not turn from its course. It was aiming straight for land—for Prydain.

Gereint was not a praying man. The good God either knew Gereint needed help or not; He would do as He would, no matter what Gereint had to say about it.

And yet he caught himself praying. The queen's ships had to be well away from the black fleet before he could set the rest of his plan in motion, but they were too slow and the black ships too fast. And now they were starting to burn.

The foremost of the black ships overtook the rearmost of Prydain's fleet and ran them down: plowed them under like weeds in a furrow. Bodies tumbled into the sea.

Ships were burning. Ships were sinking. They could not escape fast enough.

"Messire," Gereint said to Peredur, "help."

Averil was already in motion. With the first words she spoke, Eiluned started in recognition. Their voices began apart but then mingled, chanting in a language as old as the Serpent.

Gereint knew only enough to recognize it. He could feel the drawing of power from his own center as Averil shaped the working.

The wind freshened. It meant nothing to the black ships: their sails were furled as they relied on their many oars. For the queen's fleet it was a godsend.

It felt like a brisk breeze: strong enough to fill the sails but not so strong it overwhelmed the ships. It fed the fires, too, and one ship went up like a torch; but the rest began, painfully slowly, to gain on the enemy.

Far down below, the cold-drake stirred. It was growing restless. The sea swelled with its impatience.

"Just a little longer," Gereint said to it. "Wait."

It would wait—but not too long. Its hunger was rising. Soon it would feed; what it fed on mattered little to it.

"Peace," said Gereint as if it had been an impatient horse. "Be still."

The sea subsided. The wind grew stronger. Little by little the fleet began to pull away from the enemy.

Gereint waited with little more patience than the cold-drake. Three times he almost said the word, but his heart told him it was too soon.

The queen's ship was out of arrow range at last. The fires on the deck were out. The sail still smoldered, but as he looked up, a mage in a weather-worker's smock gathered what looked like a tiny cloud bleeding rain and cast it upward.

The cloud broke and washed away the flames. All that was left was a gap in the sail, rimmed with scorched canvas.

"Now," said Gereint. Peredur's voice deepened his, and Averil's raised it higher and stronger and purer. The word echoed threefold between earth and heaven.

33

FOR A LONG while nothing happened. The cold-drake seemed to have gone deaf, or else it no longer cared for any hope or promise that a gnat might offer. Maybe, now it was freed of its bonds, it would sink back down into its deep caverns, far away from the torment of light.

The wind faltered. The queen's fleet struggled. Black ships rode up over one after another of her slower and more crippled ships. And the fire kept falling.

The earth drew a vast breath. For a long moment everything was still: air, sea, even the clash of ships.

The great worm rose. Gereint's cry was more a yelp than the battlefield bellow he had intended. The queen's mages raised the power they had been keeping in reserve, filling every sail and driving every hull away from the black ships.

The sea yawned. From the queen's ship Gereint could see nothing with the eyes of his body, but his conjoined magic rode high above it all. The three of them together looked down from the height of heaven into the gulf of hell.

The depths of it were immeasurable, rimmed with teeth like spines of jagged rock. There was a shape around it, a vast blind head with buds of ears and hollows where eyes should be. It was pitted and scarred with eons of battles in the deep realms; its scales glistened darkly, as sharp as glass forged in the earth's own fire.

Even now the king's armies made no sound. The worm swallowed them, flesh and timber and steel, even the fire that fed the arrows it had rained upon the ships of Prydain.

It was larger than Gereint had thought. Much, much larger. It swallowed half a thousand ships and then more, the remnants of the queen's fleet that had been too broken to escape.

Gereint quailed at the thought of speaking again to so enormous a creature, but it had listened to him before. It had to listen to him now.

"Enough," he said. It took all the strength he had, with Peredur and Averil at his back, to say that single word—as always, not to compel, only to ask.

The cold-drake gulped seawater and ships and morsels of living flesh. Mages flung spells at it even from the depths of its gullet; it shook them off.

"There," said Gereint, opening his mind until it could see the three round-bellied ships that still clung to the open sea. He felt Averil inside him, coldly implacable; the words were hers, though his voice spoke them. "Those are your prey. Take them."

The worm lashed sidewise. The sea roared into the emptiness it had left. It lunged toward the three ships.

Bolts of power smote it again and again. It never slowed. It surged upward, an unimaginable bulk, streaming water and fragments of ships and bits of weed and flotsam and broken bodies. It hung in air above the tossing masts.

Still suspended like an eye in heaven, Gereint saw tiny figures swarming mindlessly beneath the jaws of their destruction.

The cold-drake dropped with all the weight of earth, full upon the king's ships.

GEREINT REELED TO the deck of the queen's ship. It pitched drunkenly in a sea gone mad. Water and air, air and water mingled in the howling dark.

The light Gereint had seen by, the light of his magic, had winked out. He was as blind as the cold-drake.

It had other senses than sight. So, as his body was tossed helplessly in the maelstrom, did he. He felt the great worm rise one last time to the darkened sky, jaws gaping as if to devour the stars.

The cold-drake bellowed, a sound so deep and broad and high that it filled the whole world and everything in it. It carried the beast down and down, out of air into water and out of water into earth, back to the darkness from which it had come.

34

A S THE COLD-DRAKE descended, it left part of itself behind. It was not a gift exactly; what it felt bore only a faint resemblance to gratitude. It gave Gereint understanding: of himself, of the magic he shared, and of the world that he could make if he chose.

He could be a god. Lesser powers than he had claimed that eminence, and won worshipers, too. Or he could be a king: had he not destroyed the king of Lys?

He fell back laughing on the icy deck, clinging to something cold and solid while the ship pitched and rolled. The pitching grew a little less, maybe, and the rolling eased little by little. The stars reeled overhead.

And he laughed, with an edge of hysteria but mostly with the utter hilarity of the cold-drake's parting thought. Gereint might dream of being a Knight, but a king? Not in any world he wanted to live in. Even a god was less preposterous somehow than that.

The stars were paler than he remembered. The sun was coming. The wind had died to a brisk breeze; it had turned back toward the shore, if there was any such thing left.

He sat up stiffly. He was cold and sore; he ached everywhere. Even the inside of his skull hurt.

People moved around him: sailors going about their inscrutable business, soldiers limping toward their posts, and the queen's mages rising as painfully as Gereint. One or two did not rise at all.

Queen Eiluned emerged from behind a wall of battered and salt-stained guards. Her hair was tousled and there was a bruise on her cheek, but she was otherwise unharmed.

Gereint could not see Averil anywhere. Any giddiness that was left in him vanished. She was alive; he could feel her down below what was left of his magic. But he could not tell if she was well or ill, still less where she was.

Dear God, had she fallen into the sea?

He stumbled forward. He was aiming for the queen, or maybe the hatch from which he dimly remembered emerging, eons ago. It opened as if the thought had laid a wishing on it.

Riquier climbed shakily out, with Mauritius behind him. In the pause as the Knight found his feet on the deck, the voice Gereint knew as well as any in the world echoed up from below. "Gallantry be damned! Get up there before you fall on your face."

Gereint nearly did the same. Peredur staggered up and out, his face even paler than the wan light of dawn would account for, where it was not streaked with blood. A linen bandage bound his brow.

Averil ascended behind him, blessedly and mercifully whole. Her eyes leaped to Gereint; the relief there melted his own knees, even as she glared at Peredur. "One would think," she said, "that a mage of your accomplishments would know better than to try to walk across a pitching deck in the dark while performing a great working. What did you think you were doing?"

"Going to earth," said Peredur, "and getting you off the deck before you were swept into the sea."

"That you did manage," she admitted. "But—"

"I'll mend," he said.

That was a remarkably subtle and skillful dismissal. She had turned away from him completely before she stopped, stiffened, and began to spin on her heel.

Gereint stopped her before she was well begun. He could not do any of the things he was thinking of, not in front of all these people, but he could say, "Thank God you're safe— however you managed it."

"Promise," she said. "If we ever do this again, we do it together—in body as well as magic. I've had enough of being kept safe."

"Lady, I can't—"

"*Promise*," she said fiercely.

"If I can," he said.

Her breath hissed, but she gave up the fight. She looked so forlorn then, so worn and frayed and yet so beautiful, that he gave up dignity and honor and took her in his arms.

She went stiff. He would have let her go, but as his grip loosened, she flung her arms around him and held him so tightly his ribs creaked.

No one said anything. The queen and her mages were taking stock of the fleet, reckoning dead and wounded men and ships alike. The crew had enough to do with keeping the ship afloat and on its course. The Knights and the rest of the fighting men had turned away deliberately to the task of guarding against an enemy who had vanished from the earth.

"He's dead," said Averil. "I can't find him anywhere."

"The king?" Gereint asked. He did not need to, really, but he wanted to be sure.

She nodded against his breast. "The king is dead. That means—"

Her voice faded. They both knew what it meant. So must everyone else on this ship who knew or cared about the succession in Lys.

Gereint cared very little. He wished he had never known what Averil was in the world.

Duchess, queen, what did it matter? Whatever she was, she was not for him.

In the bitterly cold morning, as the sun came up over the sea, Gereint understood how a human thing could be both fiercely elated and acutely miserable. Clodovec was dead. His serpent mages had gone down with him, all of them, into the belly of the beast. His soulless soldiery, the vessel of their souls—all gone. There was nothing left to find.

The sea was clean. The queen's dead had gone the way of Jennet's body, far down into the sea-folk's realm. Of the cold-drake there was no sign, except in memory.

High up on the mast, the lookout sang the sweetest song in the world: "Land ho!"

Gereint buried his face briefly in the sweetness of Averil's hair. When he looked up, his cheeks were unexpectedly cold. He had shed tears without knowing that he did it.

Averil turned in his arms. When once more he would have let her go, she held fast, leaning against him. They both could see it now, rising like a cloud out of the sea: the isle of Prydain.

They had come far from the sandy shores and the low marshes. Sheer white cliffs dropped into the water. Green hills crowned them. On one stood a walled city, whole and unscathed.

Prydain, like Averil, was safe. The tide of joy surged through the fleet, leaping from ship to ship. Somewhere among them, a clear strong voice rose up in a hymn of thanksgiving. Others joined it, weaving into it until it was all one shimmering wall of sound.

35

T HEY CAME TO shore on the morning of the Lady
Madeleine's feast day, bringing hope out of darkness, much as she had done. An army met them: the
levies of this coast under the command of the prince who
ruled on the headland.

He brought the queen and her companions to his fortress
of Dubris, where the people danced and sang and crowned
the victors with garlands of ivy and bay. It was a new song,
that of the kingdom's salvation, but the words and music
were very old. Their ancestors had sung that same song when
Romagna's armies suffered their great defeat.

None of them needed to know the truth: that the powers
of Prydain had had little to do with the victory, and a pair of
foreigners and a half-inhuman creature from across the sea
had won the battle for them all. Gereint seemed content to
be Averil's shadow as she settled uneasily into this new thing
that she was. She had neither wanted nor planned for it.

It was a terribly precarious eminence. She was not even in
Lys; God knew what was happening there, or whether anyone knew that Clodovec was gone. She had no strength left
to discover the truth. Tomorrow—she would do that tomorrow.

Mages in Lys must know their lord and master had been
swallowed in the sea. He had not brought all of his followers

to this war. He had allies, factions, rivals: a veritable snake's nest of alliances and enmities.

Averil had the same—already; even here in a kingdom that was not her own. People's deference had changed. When she was a duchess in exile, she had been noble enough. Now that she was the last remaining heir to the kings of Lys, she was royal; and that struck the wits clean out of some folk's heads.

She was still Averil. To the Knights she was no different. To Gereint she was the same as she had been from the first: the other half of himself.

Through all that day's celebration of victory, she moved as in a dream. When night fell, the wine flowed even more freely; the songs and dancing looked fair to last the winter through.

Wine never had taken her mind off anything, nor did it to-night. After the third cup she rose and excused herself. People begged and pleaded, but she hardened her heart against them.

She was out on her feet; she made sure they saw it. Then they were solicitous, vying to be the first to carry her to her bed.

Gereint put a swift stop to that. Between his bulk and his glowering face, he looked remarkably dangerous. All but the boldest fell back; those few found themselves face to face with Peredur.

He was smiling, but no man in Prydain would cross the Myrddin of Gwent. The last few fools dropped away; so, with a bow and a quite different smile, did Peredur. Averil found herself riding high in Gereint's arms.

She struggled, but he ignored her. She contemplated a blast of magic, but her head ached at the thought. Her body, craven thing, was glad to be carried off to bed like a child.

She was exhausted beyond sense. She could swear she only blinked, but one moment she was glaring and gathering sharp-edged words; the next, she lay in a billowing feather-bed, dressed in a clean linen gown, and hunting vainly in her memory for any connection between that moment and this.

The room was narrow and high and full of cold white light. It had a window, no more than an archer's slit. When she leaned into the embrasure, she looked out across a wilderness of white.

Snow covered the downs that rolled away beneath the window. The clouds were full of it; flakes danced in the air. She breathed in clarity and cold; then she shivered.

There was a hearth in the room, with a fire burning in it, but its warmth did not reach as far as the wall. She dived back under the coverlets.

"Lady," a stranger said: a woman, not young, dressed all in brown. It was not exactly servant's garb, and she was not exactly a servant. "Your sister queen asks your indulgence, and will you break your fast with her?"

That was not an invitation that Averil could refuse, not without giving offense. She was weary still, but her mind was wide awake. She let herself be dressed and combed and made presentable.

The brown woman tugged at Averil's gown, smoothing it with fussy precision. Averil waved her away. She was tidy enough. She had a clean chemise to replace the one whose hem she had sacrificed for Peredur's bandage; the gown she wore over it was plain deep green that in the light showed subtle brocade. With her hair plaited down her back and a veil of plain white linen over it, she was fit to stand in the presence of a queen, if not perhaps to be one.

Averil had thought to find Gereint waiting outside the door, at the top of the steep winding stair. But he was not there, nor was he anywhere within sight.

Almost she refused to go down, not until he appeared from wherever he had got to, but that was foolish. She breathed deep and smoothed her skirts and began the long descent.

The hall to which the stair led was larger than she had expected, with smoke-darkened beams richly carved, from which hung faded banners and trophies of battles long since won. Tapestries in antique style warmed the walls; the floor, somewhat surprisingly, was bare and clean.

When she came down to it, she understood. Heat radiated up from the pattern of broad, flat, slate-grey stones. The Ladies had such a thing on the Isle, in the house of healing; Averil well remembered how in the dead of winter the acolytes would vie to be sent there on errands.

It was rather startling here, but wonderfully pleasant. Her guide led her through the crowd of basking sailors and knights and royal servants and men-at-arms. Most were prostrate with drink and revelry, but those who could sit up or speak offered bows and polite words. Averil acknowledged them with a dip of the head.

It was a shock to pass through the warmth of that hall into the sharp chill of a courtyard, and to find a pair of Squires—one of whom was Riquier, but the other was not Gereint—waiting with a fur-lined mantle. The brown woman curtsied and left Averil in their charge.

Averil arched a brow at Riquier, but he ignored her studiously. For once since she had known him, he was all guardsman, with barely a flicker of his usual humor when he glanced in her direction.

She began to wonder, though not with alarm quite yet, whether she had been called to judgment—for what? Regicide? Practicing wild magic? Certainly not for saving Prydain.

There were no horses waiting, nor was there a boat below the cliff. The path down which Riquier guided her was well cleared of snow, which was odd: it wound away from the town by a postern gate, and the whole of it as far as she could see was deserted.

As sharp as the cold was, the wind had died in the night. The snow fell lightly, dusting her head and shoulders and now and then kissing her cheeks within the hood. She found herself taking pleasure in the simple exertion, matching the men's long strides easily.

The path descended in long terraces along the cliffside. The sea was quiet, rolling in softly amid the fall of snow. At first Averil was not sure of what she heard, but as she passed below the level of the cliff, she recognized music of harp and pipe and the sound of voices singing.

It was coming from the earth beneath her feet. She checked her stride, slipped and nearly fell, but caught herself before either Squire could move.

For the first time she saw a hint of Riquier's wonted smile. "Yes, we're going under the hill," he said. "Does that alarm you?"

"Only if it troubles you," she answered.

His grin escaped, but he did not add any words to it. He led her down a shorter flight of stone steps and around a corner to what seemed a blank cliffside. The path ended there.

Averil looked for the lines of a door, but there was nothing, only the white chalk and a straggle of winter-killed brambles, whitened with snow. Riquier walked straight toward it. Averil opened her mouth to warn him, just before he vanished.

The music was clearer, as if it wafted through an open door. Averil shut her eyes and stepped blindly forward.

She passed through coolness like mist, into light and warmth and the skirling of pipes.

It was summer here. It always seemed to be summer in the Wildlands, wherever they happened to be. She stood on a greensward surrounded by the tall silver trunks of trees. All around her, wildfolk danced, swift and light and wild.

It was most peculiar to loosen the clasp of her mantle and find the snow still on it, just beginning to melt. Riquier strode ahead; she bundled the cloak under her arm and hastened to follow.

The path he took wove through the dance, never touching the dancers. Most seemed oblivious to her presence, but a few caught her eye and bowed low.

On the far side of the circle, three tall chairs stood on a mound, side by side. That on the left was made of holly and bay; in it sat the Queen of Prydain. Beside her in the middle was a massive and ornate throne wrought all of wood: smooth grey trunk of ash, oakleaf and acorn, and flower of the thorn. He who sat in it was taller than a human man would rightly be, all smooth brown skin and kingly arrogance; his head and feet were a stag's, his crown of antlers spreading wider than Averil's arms could span.

The third throne, on the right, was empty. It was wrought of white lilies and a tumble of roses, red and white and gold.

Gereint stood in front of the thrones. The Knights Owein and Mauritius were at his back. So, Averil noted with interest, were Dylan Fawr and the young lord Fourchard—and, not at all to her surprise, Peredur.

It was a right royal and noble assembly. Gereint seemed in no way out of place. He held his head high and spoke clearly.

"Yes, I willed that the King of Lys be dead. If that is murder, then I confess it. I prefer to think of it as a just execution."

"You used no magic," the horned king said. His voice was as deep as stones shifting, yet there was a strong music in it. "You simply . . . asked."

"Yes," said Gereint. "Was that wrongly done?"

"No," the horned king answered. "Not wrong. Merely unexpected."

"Should we always do what's expected?"

The stag's face could not show expression as a man's might, but the dark eyes glinted. "Certainly not, young lord."

"No lord, I," said Gereint. "I have no lineage at all."

"No?" said the horned king. "Why did the great worm obey you?"

"Because I asked," Gereint said. "Everyone else was trying to command it. That only made it angry. All it needed was to be free to refuse."

"And if it had refused?"

"It didn't."

The horned king acknowledged the truth of that with a lift of the hand. Eiluned was smiling. It seemed she found Gereint refreshing—and interesting, too.

It was an odd sensation to watch another woman watch Gereint. Averil was not sure she liked it. Pretty, he was not, but he had a strong beauty, like a big gleaming warhorse.

He would have been incredulous if she had told him he was beautiful. *She* was that, he would have said.

At the moment he had no such thought in his head. His shyness in front of royalty was gone, swallowed by the worm maybe, or lost in the magic of this place. "My lord, my lady, if I'm on trial for my life, I can't plead innocence. I did cause a king's death. I'll pay whatever penalty that deserves, but I don't regret it. The world is better off without him."

"We have no doubt of that," Eiluned said. "You, with your allies, performed a great service. They gave you such knowledge as they had, but the strength and the choices were yours. We find those choices interesting, and perhaps disturbing. You are not like other mages."

"I am not," he said steadily. "I'm learning as fast as I can, but I'm still terribly ignorant."

"Not ignorant," said the horned king. "Pure. Your heart and your magic are unsullied. The Rose has done little to corrupt you."

The Knights bridled at that. The great head tilted. The liquid eyes seemed more amused than not. "You are wise," the horned king said to them, "for human creatures. Teach him what you have to teach, yes, but leave him free to follow his heart. That is the best part of him, and the clearest-sighted. It may even save you."

"It has saved us," Averil said, stepping forward boldly. "The threat is gone. Clodovec is dead."

"Clodovec is dead," Eiluned agreed. "That was well done—and no, this most unusual Squire is not on trial for his death. We are only trying to understand what he did and how he did it."

"He wasn't alone," said Averil. "I was part of it. So was your own mage, your hawk of the hilltop. It was the three of us. If there's any punishment to be exacted, we should all share it."

"No punishment," the horned king said, "but praise enough, and wonder, and perhaps a little awe. Your powers may be beyond us who are merely of earth or air. My heart tells me we will need all of them, to the last glimmer of a spell, before the long dance is over."

"It is over," she said stubbornly. "There's no fleet left. The king and his mages are dead. There may be a few still alive in Lys, and there's the matter of the other conspiracy, but the worst of it is destroyed. We're safe for this age of the world."

"That may be," said the horned king. "It is a great victory, certainly, and worthy of praise."

"Is that your judgment?" Mauritius asked. His voice was sharp, as if he had come to the end of his considerable patience.

"This is not a tribunal," said Eiluned. "We have questions only, and a fair share of wonder. And," she said, "a matter to settle."

"Which would be?" Mauritius inquired. He was bristling like a cat amid all this rampant wild magic.

"The matter of Lys," she answered without pause or prevarication. "Prydain is safe; the Isle stands untouched. And Lys is without a king."

"Prydain is mostly safe, majesty," Peredur said. "The land of Lyonesse is gone, sunk beneath the sea."

Eiluned's face went stiff—not with surprise, Averil took note, but with grief. "And its people?"

"Most escaped," he said.

Eiluned looked hard into his face. "And no one told us until now? How may that be?"

"Has there been time, Lady?" he answered: question for question. "These are terrible times, and terrible things have passed. Still more are coming, unless we take great measures against them."

"What is coming?" Averil broke in. "What can be worse than what we've just faced?"

"You know what is worse," said Peredur.

The Serpent's prison swayed under her chemise. It galled her suddenly, but not quite enough to rip it off and fling it in his face. "It won't happen now. All our enemies who knew of this are dead."

"So we can hope," Peredur said. "In the meantime, it's as my queen has said: Lys has no king."

"Are you kingmaking, then?" said Averil.

"Should I, lady? Is that what you need?"

"I need . . ." she said, then paused. God in heaven, there was so much that she needed, and more that she wanted—and peace and obscurity were the least of it. She began again. "I will not take this burden by Prydain's leave or under its command. With all respect, majesty, Lys is not and will never be a province of your kingdom."

Eiluned might have taken dire offense, but it seemed Averil had judged her rightly. She frowned, but not in anger. "Of course it will not. Prydain lays no claim to its sister kingdom. We remain allies, and if possible friends: equals. Never liege and vassal."

Averil stopped on the verge of asking her to swear to that. Then she would be offended, and rightly. "Equals will please me well," Averil said, "and friends even more so."

"Then you will take the burden?" asked Peredur.

Averil wanted to ignore him. She liked him no better than ever, but she had to respect him. She would have been false to herself if she had not.

As for his words, she had to think about them. She had hoped foolishly for a little time—as if in a world ruled by magic, any victory so great could escape the notice of the lowliest hedge-wizard. The whole world by now knew that Clodovec was dead.

"If I take it," she said, "I can't stay. Winter seas or no, I must return to Lys. Is there a ship that can carry me?"

"For one of the three great saviors of Prydain, a hundred ships would vie for the honor," the horned king said.

Averil's hands were cold. She knotted them together, clutching the heavy woolen mantle to her breast. She kept running out of breath.

Gereint did not move, but she felt as if he had come to stand behind her, raising that familiar wall against the world. For an instant she sighed and let herself rest.

It was the briefest portion of a breath, but it worked its magic. She ran her gaze over them all, taking in each one. Behind her, the dance had fallen silent.

Fear shuddered through her once again. She was about to bind herself to a country more than half destroyed, an army of men without souls, conspiracies of serpent mages, mages of the orders and priests of the church corrupted or soultaken, and a royal court so thoroughly cut off from all of it that it lived as if in another world. She was a girl, a child, a sheltered flower from the Isle. Maybe she was fit to rule in Quitaine under the careful hand of her Lord Protector and her father's counselors, but even after all she had done since she left the Ladies' care, was she fit to rule in Lys?

Surely she was no less fit than Clodovec. She lifted her chin. "Tomorrow," she said, "when the snow stops, we go."

36

No one cried out against Averil's decision. Mauritius dropped to one knee and bowed as if she had been queen already. "The Rose is with you, lady," he said.

She raised him and kissed him on both cheeks. "Without you I could never do it," she said.

His smile barely reached his lips, but his eyes were warm enough to put her heart at ease. He bowed again and gestured toward the throne of lilies. "This is yours, lady and queen. Will you take it?"

She shook her head. "Not here. Not until we come to Lutèce."

That, unlike the rest, did not please them all. She knew a moment's doubt, a brief gust of regret. Should she have done it? Should she have taken that throne, to make it harder for anyone else to lay claim to it?

Maybe, but her heart was bidding her wait. There was a time for everything. If she sat on this throne here beneath the hill in Prydain, across the sea from the land and magic of Lys, she would unravel threads of time and fate that should be knit up tightly.

Eiluned understood. So did Mauritius. The rest mattered less.

"Tomorrow, then," the Knight said. He held out his hand. "Will you dance, my lady?"

"We should go," she said, "and prepare."

"There is time," said Mauritius.

None of this, gesture or words, was casual. It had significance. Like the throne she had declined to take because this was neither the time nor the place, what she said and did would shape all that came after.

She took the hand he offered and turned with him. The music began again, flutes and pipes and drums beating a familiar rhythm. As she stepped forward, the rest of the dancers opened a path, then closed around her.

They had made her their center—and that too was significant. She shut off the impulse to duck her head and flee. Mauritius' hand was warm and strong in hers; his smile encouraged her to let her own smile escape.

She could be glad, even exuberant. She had won a victory. She was young and strong, and she would be queen.

In this land of eternal summer, where every breath was full of magic, darkness and fear had no power. Her feet skimmed the undying grass. Blossoms sprang up where they passed, white lilies and blood-red roses.

The air was full of petals, white and red and gold. They clung to her hair and tangled in her skirts. When she crushed them underfoot, the scent was supernally sweet.

With each step and turn of the dance, the earth felt more solid. She was not at all surprised, as the music changed and her body spun to match it, to find that Mauritius had slipped away. Gereint stood in his place, tall as a standing stone and remarkably light on his feet.

This dance was swifter and wilder. It set her blood to

singing. She spurned the dull grey earth; she whirled away among the rivers of stars.

When she came to rest, all dancers but one had fallen away. Green grass still grew under her feet, and trees rose in a circle around her, casting a dappled shade.

Gereint's hands were locked in hers. He was flushed; his eyes were bright. She stretched as high as she could go, but it was not quite high enough. She had to pull him down to his knees to take the kiss.

They were all alone in this place between worlds. There was no honor here, no duty, not even time: only the two of them, body to body, and the memory of all that they had done and been to one another.

There would never be another man for her. She had known that from the first and acknowledged it long before this. But here and now, in the clarity of this moment, she stood in the balance.

He did not move or speak. It was not passivity; quite the opposite. Of the two of them, she had the most to lose. The choice should be hers.

His lips were like wine; they made her dizzy. Her knees were weak; her body was melting, with a shudder of pleasure that tipped her against him. He closed his arms around her.

He was holding himself rigidly in check. It cost him high, but she could feel his pride in it. Slowly, haltingly, he was learning Knight's discipline.

Damn discipline, she thought. The thought echoed through them both, startling laughter out of Gereint. She kissed him yet again, slowly, savoring every moment.

Then she slipped free and stood apart. He regarded her

ruefully but with clear understanding. Even beyond the world, she had obligations—as did he.

"I'll always be with you," he said, "wherever you go, whatever you do. We won't be parted again."

"Never again," she agreed. And if—when—she took a husband, what would he say to that?

Nothing. If a king could do as he pleased within the strictures of the law, so should a queen. She would do her duty, but she would do it in her own way and in her own time. And Gereint would be beside her.

She took his hands again, this time only to hold them—whatever the cost of that. The world took shape around them, filled with music and song and the scent of roses.

Tomorrow they would cross the sea. In the days and months thereafter, they would face a bitter winter and a troubled kingdom and all the destruction that Clodovec had left behind. Today, for just a little while longer, they could indulge in joy.

Still hand in hand with Gereint, Averil sprang back into the dance. Her laughter echoed his as it whirled them both away.

ENVOI

The night was bleak; the wind blew cold. Sleet rattled on the roof and hissed at the shutters.

Prince Esteban sat by the fire with a book in his lap. Every vision he summoned and every divination he ventured had yielded the same result. Clodovec had died of his arrogance.

Esteban did not mourn him, nor—yet—did the city of Lutèce. Tonight, only mages knew. The people of Lys lived in ignorance for yet a while. Whether that ignorance was bliss, Esteban could not have said.

His allies in Gotha and Moresca and in Lys itself had driven one another to hysterics. They were mad to seize the throne and set one of their own on it. Esteban had reined them in with difficulty, and would have more reining in to do before too long, but for tonight their clamor in the aether had subsided.

As he turned the page, he barely remembered the words over which his eyes had wandered. The last of them fled from his head as a drift of rose petals fell from the new page, brittle and dry. They were still faded gold, with a ghost of their old sweet fragrance.

Quitaine's golden rose was lost to him now beyond the sea. He dreamed of her more nights than not; often she was standing in the cavern beneath the royal lodge, staring down at the image of the sleeping Serpent. He knew every line of her face and every long sweet curve of her body.

He was half in the dream again, with the scent of roses wafting around him. He started awake.

His servants were all in bed. His doors were barred and his house secured against both mortal and magical invasion.

Or so they should have been. The door of his study fell open. Darkness seeped in, smelling of salt and fish and the depths of the sea.

Esteban sat very still. All his defenses were armed and ready, but he had no will or power to wield them.

The figure that stepped out of the darkness was wet to the skin. Beneath the pale circle of a tonsure, a fringe of lank white hair clung to a narrow skull. Dark eyes burned, sunk deep in hollow sockets.

Slowly and carefully Esteban rose. Equally carefully, he said, "Father Gamelin. To what do I owe the honor?"

King Clodovec's erstwhile counselor glided past him with hardly a glance and stood as close to the fire as a man could safely go. Steam rose from his black robe, with a strong reminiscence of docksides and tide pools.

"So," said Esteban. "Your king. Did he escape with you? Is he miraculously saved?"

"No." Gamelin turned to face Esteban—or perhaps simply to warm his back. Then Esteban saw that he clutched a bundle to his chest. He held it out.

Esteban hesitated. Any gift from that one must by its nature be deadly. But curiosity was his besetting sin.

The outer wrappings were soaked with seawater, but those within were oiled silk. They had kept their contents dry: an ancient and rusted spearhead and a packet of dingy linen.

Esteban nearly dropped them in shock. "*Dio!* How in the name of all that's unholy—"

Gamelin's cold stare silenced Esteban's babbling. Perhaps it was a trick of the light, but on those cheeks was a faint, dull gleam of scales. They were less hollow already, growing fuller as the fire's warmth restored him to himself. "We have found the third Mystery, and the one who keeps it."

Esteban sat down hard. The two lesser Mysteries tangled with their wrappings in his lap.

"In a day or two or three," said Gamelin, "the Mystery will come back to Lys. You and your allies will be waiting for it. And when it comes . . ."

Gamelin did not finish, but Esteban had no need to hear the rest. Of course the Rose would return to its ancient home with fire and sword. And . . . Averil?

The Serpent's priest nodded as if Esteban had spoken aloud. "She is coming. The crown is ready; the scepter waits for her hand."

"As do I," said Esteban.

Gamelin's smile was a frightening thing. "So you do. And so it begins."

"A beginning, even now? Not an ending?"

"That, too," said Gamelin.